29 Locks

Nicola Garrard

HopeRoad Publishing
PO Box 55544
Exhibition Road
London SW7 2DB

www.hoperoadpublishing.com
@hoperoadpublish

First published in Great Britain by HopeRoad 2021

A CIP catalogue record for this book is available from the British Library

Supported using public funding by
**ARTS COUNCIL
ENGLAND**

Print ISBN: 978-1-913109-84-4
E-book ISBN: 978-1-913109-18-9

Printed and bound by Clays Ltd Elcograf S.p.A

Dedicated to the memory of
Mahad Ali
1999 – 2017

A note on the text

Some of the words and expressions in this book are from multicultural London English. A Glossary at the back will help explain these to readers unfamiliar with them.

PART 1

London

Chapter 1

I ain't always been a boat boy.

First up, I lived with my mum on Mare Street, Hackney, in a room above a chicken shop. All night in my dreams, I heard people cussing and getting their food and cars pulling away.

Now, most babies sleep in a cot, but when I woke up mum was right next to me on our mattress. It was nice like that. And when it was cold, I'd get up close to her like we was some knot what nobody can't undo.

And the room was nice too. I mean, it got everything you need: microwave for making stuff hot, mini-fridge for making stuff cold, suitcase for moving, telly for watching, toys them Key Worker Ladies brung us, and this Snake and Ladder set we got from the charity shop in Dalston for 10p.

Later, at birthday parties, I seen how some kids sleep on their ones and they got carpets and more bedrooms round next corners. I'm talking about kids like Seb from my first primary school, in them big houses with the trees what go snap and dash their branches on cars, alarms going off in the night. I remember thinking, Seb gets scooters and

3

bikes since time, but the pavement outside his yard ain't no good for wheels. Roots vandal up the concrete, sticks trip you up. That ain't looking after kids. Council should do something.

Anyways, that room was all ours but there was plenty others what shared the house. The walls was MDF, like marine ply-board or Dutch barge partitions. Me and mum could hear everything; beefs going down, farts in the bathroom.

'You'll have to cross your legs, Don,' mum goes, this smile starting up on her, a little twinkle in her eyes. 'That fella from Number Three – he'll be a while. More like a Number Two, if you ask me.'

Them other peoples was always changing up. No hello. No goodbye. Sometimes in a little hour, a big family drag suitcases down and one man brings up his rucksack. Mum used to wait a week before checking the food they forget. She chucks milk and meats what's open, but pasta and tins was ours. And potatoes, if they wasn't manky.

'Finders keepers, innit, Don.'

One time, next door was left open. The mattress got yellow circles like someone pissed theirself every night. A window blind hangs sideways, shanking up the shadows in slices. This weird silver bug swims like a fish on the floor. It turns to dust under my finger; just like that, like it never was a thing.

Landlord Man comes up wearing rubber gloves, goes down a little time later with two bin bags. Now that room was some lady's life, all her stuff there, like she run down the corner shop and she's going to come back in a little minute. I get on the bed, of course, and jump like a donkey till mum whispers,

4

not vex but like she means it, 'Don, leave it out! You'll get us terminated, babes.'

I'll tell you something you won't believe, but deep under Hackney, under the ground, when it's late and them tube trains and pipes and street noises calm down, you can hear water. Real water. It goes under the building, maybe even through the building. One time I heard – maybe I dream it, it ain't easy to tell in London – this split sound, this *crack*. Like the whole building's broke free, like it's floating away.

When I turn four, I start up school. Teacher Lady say my clothes dirty, my skin ain't washed. I never tiefed though. I only ate what other kids didn't want. But I totally get it now, what they put down in my files. I seen it too; Black kids in my class dripping in Palmer's and I check myself. Like ash. What makes it worse is I get eczema on my fingers and inside my elbows and I scratch and blood comes and that's what they said mum was supposed to fix with the cream. But she ain't never forgot like they said. That cream bare stings and it was me what didn't let her. It was me.

But the once upon a time I don't show up at school, they call Children's Services and my Key Worker Lady makes one of her passing-by, just-popping-in kind of visits. She knocks on the door and I do my best to answer it. I try, I do. I stand on a chair, reach up to open it, but she don't like that.

'Move right back, Donny,' she yells. 'I'm going to push the door hard. Stand by the window, please.'

So I go to mum on the mattress and I look at the door. Key Worker Lady bangs it open like it's nothing, like it's made of balsa wood.

I show Key Worker Lady my Maccy D bag. Five chips left and I say, 'I make breakfast by myself.' And I tell her mum ain't hungry because I don't know shit about what's going down.

Lady goes to the mattress so quick I get frit.

'Donny, what's happened to mummy?' she says, like it's my fault, which it kind of is and kind of isn't.

I still don't get it, so I tell her, 'Shh. Mummy's sleeping,' and then I ask her if she's going to take me out, like to a café or the park, and I start up begging biscuits.

Key Worker Lady's foot knocks mum's spoon with the grey stuff on it and if you don't know what that is, I ain't going to be the one to say it. She shifts mum's spoon to the shelf so I can't reach it. She don't know I won't never do that.

'Mrs Samson? Jade? Can you hear me?' she says and takes mum's belt off. Mum's eyes is open but I know she's sleeping because I can hear her breathing, loose and stopping a bit just when you think it's coming. And I wait, thinking, When's she going to breathe in? But she always takes that one big fat one. Makes up for all them little lost ones.

Key Worker Lady pulls mum onto her side, raises her chin and gets on her phone.

After time, yellow and blue lights dance on the ceiling and over the walls. Big-up feet on the stairs. Two yellow-coat mans leg it to mum and I'm not having this, so I say, 'Don't wake my mummy,' and I'm frowning like some Younger.

They got blue gloves on and all kinds shit in a bag. They put a strap by her arm – Key Worker Lady might've saved them the bother because she only just took off mum's belt – and they feel up her arm, where the skin's

6

cut, where the scabs and scars is even more whiter than mum's good skin. When they don't find what they was looking for, they let go the strap and cut her jeans. Now they look down mum's leg.

I can't take this so I start playing. I make this line of blocks and packets and shoes and socks. I see two shiny black boots. One of them mans touches my chin with the back of his finger and says, 'I like your race track, mate.'

'It's not a race track,' I tell him. He don't get that it's a river and goes to mum and I'm making it because part of me knows what's going to happen next.

'You're a brave lad,' he goes. 'We're going to take your mummy to hospital now.'

I get that but I still don't think it's fair. So I tell him, 'You can't take mummy. She's mine.'

'Hey, I didn't mean take. I meant borrow,' he says and winks at his mate like I made some joke. 'She's going to be all right.'

This still ain't fair. 'Don't borrow mummy,' I say, hardest frown on my face, and I work faster, lying down them blocks and socks till they get to mum's feet. My Key Worker Lady kneels down by me. Training tells them, go down to the kid's level. She's got her phone stuck to her ear but she ain't talking to nobody. I watch them mans lift and stretcher mum downstairs.

I know she's gone when the flashing light calms down.

So my Key Worker Lady turns on her right-little-man voice and says, 'Let's get you to school,' like nothing happened. She finds my school top on the fridge and picks dry stew off the arms. My socks is wet on the cold heater

7

so I tell her we can put them in the microwave if she likes, because microwaves heat stuff up and heat dries stuff out. Key Worker Lady says something vex about living this way, everything damp, but it ain't that simple. It's like them clinker-built boats in dry dock. Owners think they got to dry out over winter, but wood hulls keep better shape in water. Except, I'm mixing this. I was only little then. I didn't know shit about boats when this goes down. I got to say though, I know nearly everything about boats now.

Anyways, my Key Worker Lady shakes her head and tells me about electrical safety and then I get it and I start crying.

'I want my mummy,' I say, because she's mine and they ain't got no right.

Key Worker Lady tries shutting the door but the lock's swinging on one screw. There's a big crack down the frame where she stuck her shoulder in and I'm thinking now, If we ever get back, which we never, there ain't no room for a new lock. Lady sticks one of my blocks down to keep the door shut and takes my hand. She does both them things without asking me and we go out to her car and she never asks me that neither.

At school, me and Kasim play like we do and I don't say nothing about mum. Most of the time I ain't even thinking about her. But Kasim can sort of read minds because at lunchtime he puts his arm round me and says, 'Maman says you can do a sleepover again if your maman says you can. She's doing couscous and baklava for afters and we can stay up late.'

So when the big peoples come to get their kids in the playground, I tell my Key Worker Lady thank you very much but it's all sorted because I got somewhere better to stay till mum comes home and I take Mrs Zidane's hand to prove it. Key Worker Lady gives me that look they do, that sorry face, like it's proper killing her but she got to say it anyway. Mrs Zidane don't speak too much English but she gives me the same look, gives my hand to my Key Worker Lady so I know it ain't going to happen the way Kasim says.

He grins and tells me, 'Laters,' and don't neither of us know how much time 'laters' is going to mean.

Chapter 2

First night away from mum I sleep in a warm room. There's a photo of a long boat with red flowers on the roof. These days, I know it's a widebeam. Now, people don't get that there's two types of boat on the network. With a narrowboat, you can go anywhere; they're six foot ten width, max. Widebeams though, and it's more like ten, twelve foot. You got bare more space in the cabin, but you can't go here and you can't go there, on account of the lock gauges. You're stuck on them canals like the Severn, Kennet & Avon, Trent, bits of the north.

That ain't freedom. Not really.

Trees bend over the boat in the photo. Yellow leaves tickle the water. My Short-term Placement Lady brings out toast and warm milk and asks me if I like the boat. I nod and I'm thinking, Does the river laugh when it gets tickled by the trees like that? Except it ain't a river. It's a canal, the greatest engineering feat of the eighteenth and nineteenth century. Andrew told me that and he ain't chatting because he runs the Hertford Union section.

But I don't know any of that then. I don't know nothing. I'm like six, maybe seven tops.

My Placement Lady shows me a plug light, says it'll stay on all night and sits with me till I'm asleep. I wake in the night, my sheets wet, and I yell out for mum. Lady gives me a bath and new PJs. When I get back to bed, them sheets all been changed up. Just like that.

Sounds good, don't it? But for me it's like dry dock and my hull's shrinking.

Don't feel down. It ain't all bad because I meet her little dog in the morning and it wags its tail at me like I'm the best kid in the world, which is what my mum says about me and all. I drop my hand under the table at breakfast and he's licking my fingers.

'He likes you,' Placement Lady says. She spreads bare jam on my toast, like she don't care if it runs out. 'And he's hungry. Would you like to give him his breakfast? Let's take him to the park. You can throw him a ball. Would you like that?'

I don't say yes like I want to. I feel like, if I move too much, Placement Lady going to change her mind. I can't tell you what she look like now or what she calls herself, but I don't never forget that dog. He was proper trained; sits when you say sit, comes when you say come.

Now when they let me back with mum, they give us this room in a B&B for ladies and kids. Straight up, I see mum looks different. Her skin's good and she ain't so thin. She gives me one of them hugs she gives where you almost can't breathe but you don't want to let go neither.

'Don, love, I'm so sorry,' she says. 'I'll make it up to you. Mummy's getting better now.'

I know I can get stuff when she's deep in the Sorry Zone so I ask for a dog.

'A dog?' mum says. 'Don, I can't even look after myself. I can't even look after you sometimes, let alone a freaking dog.'

'Then I'll look after you,' I say, and I'm totally serious about this. 'And me. And a dog. I'll feed it and give it water. I know how.'

'You seem to know a lot about dogs all of a sudden.'

'I'm not a baby,' I say.

In no time, I got a puppy with cloudy eyes making these little squeaks in my hands, a black and white Staffie, not quite seven weeks, mum says. I kneel on the bed and hold my puppy and I feel like I've scored. He wriggles and I do my best not to drop him or let him cry, but he starts up anyway. He cries and don't touch the milky bread mum puts on the floor.

'He wants his mummy, don't he?' I say.

'Nah, dogs forget. He'll get used to it,' mum goes and I ain't sure she's right. Crying gets bare loud and fills up the house.

Warden Lady knocks on the door. Dog Man takes my puppy.

Week after, mum brings me this bike because she's sad too. It's got stabilisers and I can probably ride it on my ones but mum kicks off her shoes all the same and runs with me round our park. She holds my hood and I tell her not to let go.

13

'I won't,' she says. 'I got you, babes.'

Now without them heels what make her walk funny, mum ain't slow. We race round and laugh our heads off till she begs a rest. We sit on the bench and watch someone dash balls for their dog. Mum lights a cigarette and lets the smoke out the side of her mouth, so it don't go on me, but smoke comes my way anyhow.

'Shift over, Don,' she goes, standing up. We swap seats but it don't stop the smoke, no matter what the wind doing or where I sit.

This toddler wobbles up on a balance bike and grabs my curls, fat hands full on. Kid's mum's there too, typing on her BlackBerry. I don't say nothing, though it hurts. Lady gets her kid's fingers out my curls and says to mum, 'What a darling little girl you have. Perfect curls! Stunning!'

Mum stonewalls the lady and takes a suck on her cigarette so hard it crackles and ash races up the stick.

'Those stabilisers will come off soon, Don,' is all she says. She's squinting, turning her face to the side when she lets out another stream of smoke.

And I don't know if you've ever been down City endz in London, but when the sun goes behind them new mirror blocks of flats, the air goes straight cold in a little second. Mum puts her feet back in her shoes and says we got to go home. There's some Youngers leaning on the fitness stations by the way out and they're smoking. Mum pulls her jacket over her front, stretches up her back so she looks more higher than the little size she is and switches up so she's between me and them boys. She got her hand on my shoulder.

'Crackwhore,' one of them Youngers goes. The others laugh. My stabiliser wheel scrapes sideways because she's dragging the bike with one hand. And I don't know shit, really I don't, so when we get out I ask, 'What's "crack or"?'

Mum stops and goes in her bag for a cigarette.

'*Cracks or,* Don,' she says. She looks up at the sky and takes a drag. 'Cracks or monsters. It's a game. Don't step on the cracks or the monsters'll get you.'

'Is it!' I say, a bit frit. 'Monsters?'

She gets down on my level, like she done the training too, but with mum, her nose touches my nose and I feel we're the only peoples in the world, full stop.

She swallows. 'Not real ones, Don. Only pretend.' She strokes my cheek and lifts a lock of mine. Her finger fits, like my curls was made for her. Like I'm her ring. '"Darling little girl", I ask you! Come on, babes. Ain't no monsters. Play the game.'

I skip home, left and right on the slabs.

Back at the B&B, mum drags my bike in. Chain oil gets on the stairs, tyres mark up the wall, pedal chips the banister paint.

Warden Lady knocks our door and takes my bike down to the yard. Mum says we'll get a lock in the morning; it'll be safe for one night, she says. But this is Hackney, you get me? In the morning, my bike's nowhere and mum goes spare. I wipe her eyes with my sleeve and I tell her it's okay, because I've been bare good – home, school, all year – so Santa's basically got no choice but to get me a new one. It'll be probably better than the one she got me, I say, because that one was Salvation Army and Santa makes stuff box-fresh.

And she looks at me and says, 'You're right, Don. You been good. You always been good. Santa ain't got no choice.'

Small time later, this man comes in and I don't like him at all because he lies on our bed like he owns it, rank feet sticking out the end. And he never asked me. Mum tells me to wait in the TV room and I do that because I can see she means it. Warden Lady chats to me and I think about my belly and ask for food. She gives me a biscuit and chats some more, all friendly. I'm still vex so I tell her about the man. Next thing, police come wearing everything they got. The rest you can guess. Man's taken. Mum's nowhere.

Chapter 3

I'm nearly ten when I seen the river first time. My Children's Services Lady goes on chatting rubbish like, 'Great. We'll be in Peckham in twenty minutes,' as if that makes leaving Hackney okay.

I ain't in the mood so I quit looking when we've gone past the endz I know, like the park with the towers and them walkways made of wood and slides you can climb on. Mum's little and that makes her good at chasing me down tunnels. The other grown-ups is too big to play. They stay on the benches, staring at their phones.

We drive past Ataturk's Newsagents. Sometimes mum sends me in on my ones going, 'Stick a chocolate in your pocket, Don. Erdan won't mind.'

Most of the time he don't, but you don't mess with a man with that much chest hair curling up out his shirt so I hold my breath. The times he does mind, mum just says to him, 'Erdan, baby, you know I'll see you right.'

Children's Services Lady takes us past the pound shop. Mum sometimes gives me the three quid she's put by that week and says, 'Pick three toys you want, Don. Any three you like,' and I go down the rows getting all happy seeing what I want and what I don't even knowed I want.

We drive by Iceland. Now they know mum in Iceland, but they don't exactly know me, so one time, when the restaurants and bars is kicking out all the white peoples on Chapel Street, mum waits behind on the pavement. Mr Security Man sees me and smiles. I look at him, this hench-built Black man. He could be my dad. Trust me, he's that good-looking. Except he's got two neat scars on his cheeks. I don't know if that makes him African, but my dad was St Lucian. I go in and take a thing of milk out the fridge. Outside, mum's waving for me to come. I walk past Mr Security Man, who ain't my dad but could be, and the automatic doors open. He sucks a deep breath through his nose, his big-man chest gets more bigger and he turns, like something going down in some next place he needs to be.

Mr Man lets me go, I'm sure of it.

No alarm, this time, but a fox comes out the back of a dustbin and for one second I'm shook. Fox looks at me like he feels nothing, like I'm nothing, and he jogs down the centre line, chicken-shop bone in his teeth. I think we're like the same, me and him; getting stuff so we can go home.

'That's my boy,' mum says, putting a finger in one of my fat curls. Her white skin goes see-through in the streetlights. Only her freckles stay orange. 'Let's have us a hot milk and a biscuit before bed, eh?'

So when these endz go by, and I don't know the names of them manors outside and when rain drums the car

18

roof so I can't think, I close my eyes. I seen enough water coming down shop gutters and metal drains. Them pipes can't take no more; top gutters need cleaning out, blocked up by plants and shit, so water dashes the pavement and it ain't safe for bikes. Council should do something about that and all.

'We're nearly at Tower Bridge, Donny.' Children's Services Lady's chatting like I'm some tourist. 'Look out for the River Thames. Look – the Tower of London's on our right.'

'Do I look like I care?' I say.

I'm so fresh I don't even know that's Limehouse downriver and I don't know the names of any of them boats I'm going to see from the bridge, like leisure cruisers, Ribtecs and all that. I don't even know they can go all the way to Hertford if they wanted, even Scotland if they like, or America.

Basically, I'm only thinking one thing. *I want my mum.*

Every red light, I go over my plan.

Open the door.

Jump out.

Run home.

I count the time it takes for the lights to change.

One elephant, two elephant, three elephant.

Next light, I press down my seatbelt button but I keep the strap over my front. My Lady knows nothing, I'm that quick. Light goes green. Car drives on.

Next one, I think.

'Honestly, it would be faster to walk at this rate,' Lady goes, smiling at me.

The river comes up quick and full. I ain't never been this far south, so I don't know it's tidal, that it ain't always that

19

high. It goes down; you just have to wait. All I know is, I've come too far and there's only one more traffic light before the bridge. It goes red. I dash the seatbelt off and pull the handle. I tug and tug but it don't open.

'Donny, stop ... You'll break it! It's child-locked.'

She pulls up on double reds. The engine cuts but the wiper blades go on screaming. A traffic camera flashes and I almost start up feeling sorry for her but then I remember what she's trying to do to me and I properly switch.

'Let me go!' I tell her so all London can hear. 'I want my mum!'

'Hold on, let's talk about this a minute,' she says. I keep tugging on the door till I give up and start crying. 'I know this is hard,' she says, like she knows how I feel. 'You'll see your mum in a few days. You'll get an hour with her every week. You can talk to her on the phone, write to each other. There's no limit on the number of letters. The new prison voicemail system ...'

I don't know why they think that's enough. That ain't even nearly enough.

'I want my mum!'

'Give this foster family a chance, Donny. They're nice. Just give them a chance.'

Traffic stops halfway on the bridge. I might've seen a Thames Clipper going under, maybe a pilot craft; police or customs, probably. The river's full and glassy; they call that slack tide, when water don't flow neither way. They got a name for everything, them boat people.

I smooth out the mash-up photo I was given and this time I see it. My new Foster Lady's smiling at me. Her arms is tight wrap-round her man and two boys like she ain't never going to let them go. Maybe she'll be like that with me.

'Delighted to meet you, Donald,' Photo Lady says when we get to Peckham. Her voice is soft and posh. African-posh. She gives me a towel. 'It looks like monsoon season out there,' she says, picking up a plate of cakes. 'Would you like something to eat after your long journey?'

I like her and I'm hungry but I say, 'No thank you, miss.'

Children's Services Lady tells me she's called Mrs Adeola and that she's going to take good care of me. Other side of the table's her two boys and they don't look at me. Photo Man's there and all. When I don't take a cake three times, Mrs Adeola nods to them and they clean up the dish. I start up wishing I took one, and now it's too late.

'Leave one for Donald, please,' Mrs Adeola says, like she can see in my brain.

The littlest boy smiles at me and puts back what's in his hand.

'I think he likes to be called Donny,' says Children's Services Lady.

'Sorry,' Mrs Adeola leans to me, gives my arm this little pinch, but not so as it hurts, and says, 'Donny.'

She tells her boys to introduce themselves.

'My name is Prince,' the littlest says. 'I am nearly nine years old. I am good at football. I play centre forward, like Adeode. We nearly got the same letters too. Nice to meet you.'

He talks like he's doing assembly and shakes my hand, but I like him.

21

'My name's Michael,' says the bigger boy. 'I'm thirteen. I'm way better at football than he is. He's capital-R Rubbish.' I hear feet under the table. Mrs Adeola frowns. Michael stands so he can reach me to take my hand. 'Nice to meet you.'

Big man goes last. 'My name's Olu. I'm fifteen,' he says and I know that means he ain't their dad. 'And I am out of here. Got places to go, people to see, business to do.' He stands up, tall like a grown-up, and winks like we know each other. 'Nice to meet you, Donny. Laters.'

He kisses his mum's cheek and goes.

'Do not be long, please, Olufemi,' Mrs Adeola says at the shutting front door. She got colour where he kissed her. When the latch already gone click, she says, 'We're having a special meal to welcome Donny tonight.'

Metal door on the ground floor goes slam. Mrs Adeola gets up and looks out the kitchen window to the courtyard.

Children's Services Lady gives me my *Family Ties* book.

'You can write in it and share what you've been doing with your mum,' she says. She goes to the window and for a small time them two ladies stare out.

'One never stops worrying about one's children, no?' Mrs Adeola says. 'Corners on tables. Fingers in doors. Holding one's breath when they learn to run. Climbing. Oh, Lord, climbing! And this.' She waves over the flats in front of her. 'This!'

'You have a fine son there. All your boys are so polite, so accommodating.' Children's Services Lady looks at me. 'I'm going to go now, Donny. One of the team will be back Monday and they'll take you to visit your mum. Okay?'

When she's gone I got a question.

'Mrs Adeola?'

'Call me Mama Folu, child.'

She faces me and I start to think I can do this.

'When's Monday?'

'Three sleeps, sweet boy,' she says. 'Three sleeps.'

Chapter 4

The Adeolas got six whole rooms in their flat and it's all for them, nobody else; three bedrooms, a kitchen, a TV room and their own toilet. Prince shows me his Star Wars Lego and his truck with the batteries what still work and the bottom bunk what's now mine. Michael takes his poster down to make space for my stuff.

Keys rattle in the door; Olu's back.

'Still listening to dad's nineties shit?' Olu says when he clocks the poster. 'Skee-Lo versus Skepta, bruv. Skepta would mash him. Shut down! So you wish you was a little bit taller, short-arse?'

Prince smiles through his fingers. Mama Folu chucks them all out.

'Go play, children,' she says.

When it's just me and her in the kitchen, she dials a number from *Family Ties* and goes on speakerphone.

The front door goes bang. Twenty beats later, the ground-floor door goes slam. The noise kicks round the courtyard so you hear it again before it stops.

'We're in a queue,' Mama Folu says. 'We must have patience.'

She don't hang up though. She gives me a tub of playdough and stands at the sink where she can see out. There's a feeder, what's stuck to the glass there, and birds eating and fighting. Music on the speakerphone cuts out and starts up again. I slide off the chair and go to Mama Folu. She lifts me up and I'm kneeling, my face at her level.

Her boys is playing in the playground, three floors below, dashing this baby swing over its frame. The chain gets shorter and shorter till the seat wobbles over their heads and ain't no baby can get to it now, not even if they got a lift up. Mama Folu sounds vex, like she's going to beat them, only the words coming out ain't like that. She's chatting like they're the best; stuff like, 'How strong!' and, 'My boys!'

She turns a big yam in the sink, peels and slices it and she never looks at the knife. It's like she don't know that blade's there. She washes meat and pats them chunks dry with tissue, and all the time she's looking out.

She opens the window and yells, 'Put it back!' and them birds on the feeder bounce. 'Put it back or I will come down and chase you!'

They look up, grinning, and I smile too because she won't never catch them if they was running. They wave up at us and dash the swing back till it's right again.

'There's three calls ahead of you,' Prison Lady goes, along with donkey other stuff; call volume greater than usual, thanks for your patience, your call is important, et cetera.

Next second, click. The line goes dead.

Me and Mama Folu look at each other for time.

26

'But I only want my mum,' I say in a little voice. I squeeze a lump of playdough in my fist so it comes out through my fingers like toothpaste and it feels like my heart is being squeezed out like that and all.

'I know,' Mama Folu says. 'We will try again.' She takes my chin and zones in on my eyes. 'In God's queue, the last will be first and the meek – like you, Donny – the meek will inherit.' She makes inherit sound longer than the three beats it's really got. She looks at the ceiling. Her lips move but sound don't come out. She's quiet for time and I wait for her to go on. 'Little children suffer, but Jesus will love you forever and always. Matthew, nineteen.'

And she smiles, like she ain't never was sad before.

'Is it!' I say. 'What's inherit?'

'It means you will get all the riches of heaven and sit with sweet baby Jesus.'

She shows me a beardy white man in a photo frame over their gas fire. Now, I sort of know what she means. Sometimes mum talks about Jesus and all, but never like a baby, more like, 'Jesus Christ, Don! Meter's run out!' But I don't mind Mama Folu banging on about it because she says her husband sits by Jesus' side and I know that means he's gone. As well, she says I'm a beautiful child of Jesus like her sons, and one day I'm going to be an important man just like them. I don't know how she knows that or even if it's true, but it's nice to hear it said.

Four o'clock and there's feet on the balcony. Their front door feels cold because it's made of metal, frame and all, and I think, This manor's bare safe. Prince and Michael come in, punch my arm, one bump each, and go in, but Olu – he's getting his creps off on the outside mat – he pulls them back by their hoods.

27

'Michael, Prince. Don't bring that street shit inside,' he says in this voice like it's coming from the bottom of the sea or some deep volcano place.

'They're clean, bruv,' Prince says.

'No, they ain't. Streets made of shit. Off, bruv. Undo your laces properly, Prince man. You'll break them creps.'

When they done doing what they're told, Olu says, 'Okay, pocket-money time.'

He shows us his roll of five spots, gives one to Prince and one to me. I'm all smiles because this is now the second time ever I got a five spot for no reason. The first time was when I seen one once, flapping in the street. Some old lady dropped it so I get it before a bus comes along and mashes it up, and I say to her, 'Lady, you dropped this,' and she goes, 'Keep it, honey,' like maybe it weren't never hers in the first place, or maybe she got enough money already and don't need no more. There are peoples like that.

Anyways, Prince goes, 'Thank you very much, bro,' and runs in with the cash. But I don't understand because Michael shakes his head. He ain't taking no free dollars, not even from Olu who ain't no stranger neither.

'Like that, is it?' Olu says, frowning at Michael. Michael looks at the floor. 'Get in,' says Olu. Then he looks at me, like he's seeing me for the first time.

'You like it?' he goes. I nod and he smiles. 'There's bare more for you, then, my new little bro.'

After eats, Michael says, 'Donny, man, it's your story tonight,' and he pulls me on the sofa. 'It's you. Look, man!'

28

The big-up Black man on TV's nothing like me. For a start, he's wearing sandals, a dress and armour and I'm more of a sport-casual kind of youth. Thick dreads flow down his back and his arms is hench and Mama Folu translates because he's chatting Yoruba. But the thing is, Michael's sort of right. It is my story. The man's got my name, Samson, and I don't forget that. He's got my name, dad's name, and he kills a lion with his bare hands and smashes up an army on his ones. I don't never forget that, even though it don't go too good for this particular Samson, because when the music goes soft, this lady – blacker than black and even prettier than pretty – she brings Samson a plate of fruit.

Sounds good, don't it?

But watch!

'Look away, Donny,' Michael goes when them actors kiss. He dashes a cushion at Prince's face. 'You're too young.'

'Enough! Watch the programme,' Mama Folu says. 'It is his wife.'

She turns up the sound.

Wife Lady tells the servant to cut Samson's locks while he's sleeping.

'That's low, blood!' Olu says, sucking his teeth. Mama Folu hits the mute button.

'Where did you get this teeth thing, Olufemi? And this "blood"? Do you think you are American now? Mmm? Yes? Speak properly!'

TV Man wakes; no locks equals no power. The soldiers get him and he asks them to allow him to go pray.

29

'Stupid,' Olu says. 'They're mugs. You don't let a prisoner go like that. No mercy!'

Samson leans against this pillar and prays for strength. Big drums pound. *Bam!* Prayer comes true straight away; he pulls down the pillar thing holding up the whole entire set, and it's all mashed up, killing them soldiers one time. I know them blocks is budget, but I don't care. This man, Samson, who's probably my great-great-great-great-et cetera-grandad, he could waste.

'Better get you a shape-up, blood,' Olu says, tugging my braids. 'Before you bring down this manor like Samson himself.'

I feel shame; I know they're grown-out.

'Back home,' Mama Folu says, 'people would say you British boys wear your hair like little girls.' She looks at me like she needs to explain. 'Where I come from, boys have nice, tidy hair. Short hair. Not these London styles. I have seen boys here with bunches, even Alice bands. It is so American!'

'Would you like me with a fro-hawk, mama?' Michael says, giggling. She frowns at him. He acts like her stare sends him into a backflip onto the sofa.

'Oh, my goodness,' she goes, but I know she's laughing underneath. 'Olufemi, would you take Donny with you to the barber, please? Now, Prince and Donny, hands, teeth and bed!'

Mama Folu turns off the light when we're ready, tucks Prince in and touches my shoulder. 'Can I call mum now?' I ask.

'Tomorrow,' she says. 'Right now, you need sleep to grow tall and learn.'

Room goes dark. I roll on my side, close my eyes and listen for tube trains and water. Someone's shouting outside, footsteps on the stairwell. I still got Samson in my head. Man's hench but he don't try to escape. Not properly. I twist a braid and slide off the elastic band mum put in time ago. My hair is all broke in the knot.

The room goes more lighter. Mama Folu fixes Prince's cover on the top bunk, then gets down close to me.

'Come, wakeful child,' she whispers. 'Come leave your mum a voicemail. She will hear it in the morning and feel joy.'

Later, I still can't sleep. I unwind a braid and think about Monday. Me – Donald Leroy Samson – smashing shit up, holding mum's hand, showing her the way out the mash-up prison.

It's like a plan, but it don't go to plan. I forget it by morning.

There's a letter for me in the post-box. I start at the top.

'*In replying to this letter,*' I read out loud, '*write on the envelope Number: AC–650–CJ. Wing: B.*' I frown. 'That ain't mum.'

'You can ignore that part,' Mama Folu says. 'It is for when you write back. Would you like me to read it for you?'

I shake my head and go on. '*Hi Don. I hope you are okay. I am fine. I got your letter. I don't know about cars. Can you draw it for me? I'm glad I have you. I don't know what I would do without you. You're the only thing I have. I hope I will never lose you.*'

I get my pencil case and empty out my colours.

'Go on,' I say. I give Mama Folu the letter and start to draw. 'You read.'

31

'*Can you get me Mrs A's number for the okay list and more credit? It will be cheaper for her if I call you.* We can certainly do that, Donny,' Mama Folu says, 'but do use the telephone here.' She carries on reading: '*I hope she takes you to a park to run about. Your key worker said you're settling in good at school. You always surprise me with the stuff you can do at school.*'

'Wait,' I say and dash to the bathroom. I don't need to piss. I need to sort out my brain.

I want to tell mum about my first day at school in Peckham, how Mama Folu held my hand nice and waited for me for time, even though I was on a go-slow because I didn't want none of it, and even though Prince and Michael was already on the ground floor in their iron-flat shirts, polish-up shoes, shouts bouncing off the brick walls. I want to say how it's okay because Mama Folu's done the training and I ain't going to disappoint.

As well, I want to tell mum about the time when we was walking to school and Mama Folu gripses up Olu's wrist and pulls him down like he's made of jelly, locks in on his eyes and says, 'Jesus keep you safe, Olufemi.' I know that bit would make mum laugh. And Olu starts sweating because his mum, right there on the street in front of all his crew, says, 'Use the pedestrian crossing,' and Olu goes, looking at the ground, 'Yes, mama. I will. I promise I will.'

And I want to tell mum how Olu opens up like a penknife and how his head and shoulders is so much more higher than Mama Folu and his voice is low like earthquakes or the 345 bus rolling by, because I think that's how it's going to be with us one day when I'm grown. And I want to say how, when Olu goes down the street and them other Year Elevens step to him and shake his hand, he looks bare important from the primary gates, just like Mama Folu says he's going to be. And that's how I'm going to be when I'm full grown.

But I ain't telling mum how Prince runs off when we get in the playground and Mama Folu calls him back and holds his face up close till their foreheads touch and my heart starts up hurting.

'I will collect you at three, Prince,' she says. 'Work hard. Remember that your father was –'

'I know, mama. Dad was an engineer,' he goes, pulling away, and she puts up her eyebrows at me and tells me, 'I will cook your favourite tonight,' and she squeezes my arm. And just like that, my heart's okay again.

And I ain't saying how when this boy Jermaine goes, 'That your mummy?' I go, 'Yes,' till Prince looks at me side-on and I say, 'Sort of.'

'Are you all right?' Mama Folu says now, on the other side of the bathroom door.

I dry my face and go back to my car picture.

'Go on. What's mum saying next?'

'She has written about the adult education opportunities. Listen: *I'm learning too, done numeracy and a parenting class! Now I know all them things I got to say no to, so watch out! Hope to see you soon. Don't forget me, babes. I love you so, so, so much, Mummy. P.S. You're my boy. My one, plus only, plus best* – look, Donny, she has written it as a sum – *equals you.*'

'I'm going to make her a number sentence back,' I say because Maths is my thing. 'What do you think? Column addition or something with division?'

Most times after school kids dump their book bags and jumpers on the ground by their people. I watch Jermaine's dad. He gets Jermaine every day but he goes down low and hugs him up like he ain't seen him in weeks when it's only been six hours. I wait with my Teacher Lady in the playground because Prince is home on account of his cold and Olu turns up for me, finally, on the pavement outside.

I tug her sleeve and point. 'My foster brother,' I say.

'I know Olufemi,' she goes. She waves. 'I taught him a few years ago.'

Olu gives her air and takes my hand. I don't think he likes white people very much so I ain't going to say nothing about mum in case he don't like me neither.

On the way home, Olu takes me to his barber shop. The window photos is all shape-ups and relaxed hair and I start getting angst. Barber Man's clippers buzz like a road drill. Mum always uses scissors so I'm thinking up a way to say no.

London Evening News is on the TV; a stabbing on Peckham Rye and the shank looks big-up on widescreen. I don't know what it is; maybe a meat knife or one of them cutlasses for chopping down bush. Barber Man lays down his clippers and touches the gold cross on his neck. He looks at a customer, who looks at Olu, who looks at me. Politician Man comes on TV saying, 'Crisis in the family, single mothers,' and they switch it off. No one says nothing. One minute later the old man looks at his watch and turns the TV back on. Clippers start up buzzing and he goes, 'Who's next?'

Olu swings into the chair.

'Shape-up please, boss,' he goes, winking at me in the mirror. Barber Man picks up his clippers and puts them down again.

'Olufemi?' he says. Olu looks at Barber Man in the mirror.

'Yes, boss?'

'How are your grades?'

Olu shifts, grips the chair, lifts and lowers back down, muscles flexing. 'I'm working now. I don't got time,' he says.

'This is not good.'

Olu says, 'But boss, uncle. It's DC Sport.'

He tells the man he's going to make manager. 'I get free creps. Look,' he says and holds up his knees to show them off more better.

Barber Man shakes his head. 'Go to school,' he says.

'Uncle, I –'

'Go to school.'

When they're done, I say I'd rather grow out my locks now, if it's all the same to them. Like Samson. Barber Man laughs. He pumps up the chair and I get wrapped in a Batman cloak he got specially for little kids so they don't get frit over them clippers. But it ain't about Samson or them clippers that make bare noise like they're going to take the skin off you if you move. It's more like, I don't know what mum's going to feel if she sees me with some nice ten-quid shape-up. It ain't like she don't want me to get no nice ten-quid cut. I just don't want her to go thinking I got better than

35

what she gives me, so I reckon my locks is better left the way they want to go.

It don't matter though. I get cropped anyways.

I get to mum before my Maths letter does. Maybe I even overtake it on the train back to North London to see her.

We're in line at the Prison Visitor Centre and I ask my Social Worker Man if we can go see my best friend Kasim after, because he lives by these endz, not far from the canal. I can show him how to get there, I say, and he wouldn't even need his Oyster. Man says it ain't appropriate, the way they do in Children's Services, so I don't see Kasim for time.

Prison dog gives me air when I say hi.

'Don't touch,' Dog Lady snaps, like I done a big thing wrong. 'He's working.'

She opens a pack of nappies what a lady with a baby's got in her bag. The dog gets bare happy, wagging its tail and, tell the truth, I'm merked he likes them rank nappies more than me. Maybe they put dog food in them. Lady with the baby and the nappies kicks off and them officers take her away.

Now I don't know if you've ever done Visiting before, but you might think it's all walls and bars. It ain't like that but they ain't mugs neither. They put the windows by the ceiling, so you need a ladder to get up there. They should open up them windows though, because it stinks of sick and sweat and cleaning stuff.

Not saying they don't try to make it nice though. Youth area got a bookcase and real fishes in a tank. Kids can pull picture books out and dash them on the carpet and no one says clean it up like at school. The top shelf's like the windows;

you need a ladder to get down them encyclopaedias and fact books they got up there, so no one bothers.

Some mums sit on playmats with sticky toys and animals what got the stuffing coming out, and even though they try to make it okay, babies still don't like to visit. Not really. They twist round, little fat fingers reaching out to the people what brung them here.

There's rules on the noticeboard, but I make up my own.

One: don't say nothing about Mama Folu and the Science Museum.

Two: don't say nothing about how Peckham ain't got no electricity problems. I don't even think they got meters in South London, like they nearly don't got no tube and no canals neither. Search it up on Google if you think I'm chatting shit.

Three: don't say nothing about hot baths and warm towels on the radiator.

Four: when mum asks what the food's like, don't say I ain't never hungry. That one's hard, because even now my mouth still starts up thinking about Mama Folu's cooking and all them eggs and cornmeal porridge for breakfast, hot meat pasties at lunch, evening time filling up the flat with tasty smells.

So when mum asks, I say, 'Okay. A bit African, innit.'

We play football in the courtyard after school. The goalpost's from the corner of Andover House to the old wooden sign fixed up on the bricks what says *NO BALL GAMES*. They don't mean it. That notice comes from when their manor was first built when kids weren't probably allowed to play. There was

37

no swings or slides in the courtyard then and my Teacher Lady says we'd be up sweeping chimneys.

Olu's got bare skills. He nutmegs me and Prince all the time but he don't do contact when he tackles. With Michael though, he goes in hard. One time he drops him on the concrete. Michael picks bits of rock out his elbow where it's bleeding and looks up at their window. Mama Folu sees it all and knocks on the glass so Olu picks Michael up and brushes him down, like he cares so much, but all the time he's running his hands down them grazes and that's got to sting.

'You messed up big time,' Olu says. 'You were supposed to watch out for them OKR soldiers, man, not play with your little girlfriends. I told you a million times: if you ain't concentrating we going to get jacked. Somebody's going to get hurt. This ain't no game, blood. We lost ten ounces because of you. You got to watch, blood, defend our endz.'

Michael hides his hands round his back, trying not to cry. Olu gripses him up hard.

'You know you're lucky you're fam, blood?' he says through his teeth like he thinks Mama Folu's got laser hearing. He folds Michael in close so he can't move, pats the back of his neck, and goes, 'Bossman wants to know what I'm going to do about you. Says he's going to allow it for now but you owe him ten back. You got one more chance. Then I can't protect you no more.' A tear on Michael's face starts running down on its ones. 'Quit weeping, battyman. Go wash yourself up. Dinnertime.'

Olu looks at me and Prince, and he's smiling again. Just like that.

'Come here.' He goes down low. 'Want to help your brother out? Earn yourselves some dollars?' I ain't sure so I look to Prince. 'One rule. You say nothing to mama. Okay?'

Olu brings out his fists, one each. 'Promise me now, little mandem.' Our fists bump. 'Ow, man!' Olu goes, springing a backward roll like we got superpowers in our fists and back up to his feet in one move.

Me and Prince do a belly laugh. We can't help it.

Michael's standing by the entrance, staring at us. Three floors up, the window opens. Birds bounce to the trees and Mama Folu waves. Olu brings us close to his side. He keeps his hand on my shoulder, all the way to the door and swipes his fob. Me and Prince try to open it but it's too heavy. When Olu takes over, the door smashes that brickwork like it's nothing at all. On the stairs, two older boys nod at Olu and shake his hand. One of them big boys gives Olu a little packet and goes on down. No one says nothing.

Mama Folu's kitchen smells lovely the way it always do, always something nice in the pot.

'Watch,' Olu goes, winking at me. He stands behind his mum and puts his arms round her middle, kisses her cheek while she's trying to work the food. He tucks a roll of ten spots in her apron pocket.

'That's for church, mama, from my Saturday pay.' He sticks his chin on her shoulder and his hand in the pot, tiefing a bit of meat. 'Mama, that's so good!' he says, chewing.

She elbows him away, humming, but he carries on, kissing her and reaching into the pot over her shoulder.

'Get out of my way, Olufemi,' she says and pushes him into a chair. Olu lets her shift him like he's surrendering to the Feds, hands in the air.

'You think you are a big man now? You think you are the man of the house, because you have a job? Sit down.'

'But mama!'

'You are not too old to feel my hand,' she goes, laughing.

We hold hands and say the food prayer. When she's done all her thanking, she opens her eyes and says to me, 'My Olufemi, my first-born son, grew taller than me when he was just nine years of age.' Olu smiles, perfect teeth showing.

'And his eyes were the most perfect eyes!' Prince says, giggling.

'And his skin was burnished gold!' Michael says, doing that posh voice she got.

'And his hair was …'

'Hush, children,' Mama Folu says, swiping the air like she's trying to catch some fly. 'Eat.' She dishes up big spoons of stew pork and rice on our plates. 'Tell me, what have you learned at school today?'

'Sir said …' goes Michael.

'No! Do not tell me now. Eat!'

Chapter 5

'Does your mum think you're still five?' Prince says.

I don't think he's taking the piss so I don't get vex, and to tell the truth, we done *Going on a Bear Hunt* back in Reception.

'I find it most appropriate,' Mama Folu says, showing us the book they sent with the recording mum made. 'It is about courage and home. What do you think the bear is feeling?'

I know the answer to this one. 'He feels like he's on his ones,' I say. 'He's not what they think he is. He ain't scary, just on his ones and he don't want to be like that no more.'

'It's stupid,' Prince says. 'No one in Year Five has bedtime stories no more.'

'Any more!'

'For real, mama, it's only us and maybe two more kids who get stories read them.' He giggles through his fingers. 'Ones with rich parents.' Mama Folu says she don't believe it for one minute. 'It's true,' Prince says. 'They play Fifa on their phones till their eyes drop. Can I get a phone, please, mama?'

She tuts. 'Nothing is free, except Jesus' love. Mobile phones are expensive, and you are not old enough for such responsibility.'

Prince looks to me for back-up.

'My mum got me books sometimes, for nothing,' I say, like that's going to help.

'For free?' Prince says.

I nod. 'Totally free. And the library lady let us off even, when we had to move rooms and we left a book at the old room, and we couldn't take it back because some next man started living there, and the lock didn't work no more.'

Mama Folu swallows the way she does sometimes. She and Prince don't say nothing, so I go on. 'I read them books to her. Mum don't always get tricky words, and she goes on about me and school and helping her out.'

I press play again to hear mum reading. Her words go stop-stop-go-stop and I know how hard she's trying.

'You are a good son, Donny.' Mama Folu does her death glare at Prince. 'I wish my sons would help *me* when I find something hard.'

'But you don't find anything hard,' Prince says.

She looks at the photo she got of her old man. 'There is always something one finds hard.'

I play the CD again but I don't listen to the story this time. I'm listening to the sounds around her when they pressed record.

'What kind of room do you think she's in?' I say.

42

'Like what, kitchen or bedroom?' goes Prince.

'Like, was it empty or was there carpet down?' I look at Mama Folu because she'll know. 'Was the door open or was it shut?'

'You will have to ask her on Monday. She will explain how it was.'

'I mean, was there other mums there, maybe nans and all, waiting for a go? Was there some man helping her with the buttons, or was she on her ones?'

Prince shrugs. 'I don't know. It's just a story.'

I play it again to hear if she's getting any better. I try so hard to listen if that was only her, on her ones, and nothing else inside her.

'She sounds nice though,' Prince says. 'Let's go play.'

We go to the youth area where they got a pitch for football and basketball. It looks more like it's for cage fighting but they don't let nobody fight in there and I'm glad of that. Metal fence makes it safe from nutters and needles. As well, it's got anti-climb paint and CCTV and they scrub out graffiti same day but you can still read tag shadows.

Olu's come to see us, making dumb faces through the bars. We go to him and he holds our hands and says, 'Come, we'll go the long way home.'

Me and Prince skip to keep up, because he walks bare fast.

'Let's play Cracks or Monsters,' I say. I drop Olu's hand and jog backwards. 'It's a game.'

'Is it the one, like, if you don't touch a crack your mum won't die?' Prince says.

'No. Okay, maybe, sort of.'

43

We use Olu's arms for lifts. It's only a game but Prince put that nasty idea in my head and I start up worrying what might happen if I go on the cracks because I don't know what lives underneath. Mum said they was pretend but them South London monsters might be for real. The pavement splits like spider webs. Soon it's no use trying no more. Olu's Nike Js land on every crack.

'Only chat, ain't it?' I say to Prince. 'About your mum dying?'

We get to the big junction by Aldi. Road's empty in both directions: no cars, no buses, no bikes. Prince goes to cross but Olu catches his hood.

'Wait,' Olu says. He pushes me to the traffic light. 'Press the button, little man.'

I know why; he promised his mum and you don't never break a promise to your mum.

Green man starts and Olu walks us to the other side of the estate where there's a play area for babies. He takes out a phone and gives it to Prince.

'Stay here till I come back,' he says. 'But watch. Don't play nothing. See mandem at that door? Press send. Here.' I look over Prince's shoulder at the screen; a blank text message. 'Don't go nowhere. Don't play. Don't touch nothing. I swear down.' Olu gives us his fists. 'Safe.'

Olu jumps the playground fence with one hand, and goes to the flats. Our legs swing off the bench where grown-ups watch their kids and their phones. A little plant is growing in the gap between the bench leg and the plastic ground and it's even started a white flower.

'Where's Olu now?' I say, shoving Prince.

'Don't know,' Prince says. He kicks my shoe. 'Where's your actual mum?'

I point to the main road. 'North London. That way, but the other side of the river. She's getting better,' I say, looking at the flower. 'She's at some safe place.'

'Olu says she's at Pentonville and that's prison for serious mandem.' Prince grins. I can't get vex though, even when he chats dumb shit like he says next: 'That make your mum a man?'

I land a punch. 'No. My mum's female.' My ears go hot. 'It's like hospital, innit. Holloway. She's getting better and doing bare education courses and everything. Workshops.' I count them on my fingers. 'There's Literacy, same phonics like us, Parenting ...'

'What's that?'

'Saying no and stuff to your kids. Learning how to look after them. Employability. That's getting money for doing jobs other people don't want to do.'

Prince nods. 'Your mum is in hospital, yeah. With a bit of school. That's what mama said.'

I slide off the bench and flick fag ends and bits of Rizla around with my toe. The little white flower looks nice and I want to take it on Monday when I visit mum. I ask Prince to help get some more of them flowers. We can put them in water. They keep fresh in water. They keep for time in water. Forever even.

'Do dogs mind flowers?' I say. 'Like, police ones?'

'Police flowers? What are you chatting? Don't touch it,' Prince says. 'Some dog peed on it, for real. Some crackhead spat right there. It's infectious, probably.'

I drop it and check my fingers. Ain't no crackhead spit there but I wipe them in case.

Bus goes by. Asian lady goes by with a supermarket trolley what don't work. Youngers go by on pay bikes, legs spinning fast, wheels going slow.

'Mandem?' I shove Prince.

Bike crew look our way. We get two fingers and one goes, 'Bang!' but they don't stop.

'Not their endz,' Prince says. 'Sit down. Olu soon come.'

Two floaty-dress white ladies come in the park with a dog. One flips a bag into the dog-shit bin and that starts us up giggling. I know we're supposed to be working, but we can't help it.

'Must have been difficult to choose,' one lady goes. 'But did you really have to go for that breed?'

'I'm afraid Battersea don't do Spaniels and Cockapoos. There are literally hundreds of Staffordshire Bulls, just dumped on the street by ASBO-wielding psychos.'

'She went cock,' I say to Prince.

'And poo.'

'And balls!'

'She never.' Prince digs my ribs and puts me to rights. 'Bull is a kind of dog.'

'My bad,' I say. I knowed that.

Dog trots to the baby park fence. I put my hand through them metal bars and wonder what my puppy's doing right now. If it got more bigger and stopped crying. If it got a home now and maybe a nice lady like this one.

'Miss, can I?' I say.

'Certainly,' The woman gets a biscuit out her bag. 'Give her this.'

'No, Donny.' Prince kicks me. 'Olu soon come.'

The ladies go away, dog too.

'When mum's better, we're going to get a dog,' I say. 'Probably.' Prince asks what we're going to call it but you can't tell these things straight up so I say, 'I don't know. You got to see a dog first, then think up a name.'

'I know, I know! You're going to call it Cock Poo!'

'I'll tell Mama Folu.'

Prince laughs. 'Tell her what? Hey, Donny's dog's called Ball Face!'

'I dare you!' I go. 'Say that to Mama Folu.'

'What? Arse Poo?'

'Nah. I ain't speaking to you no more, Prince man. Grow up.'

We don't say nothing. Leaves and empty crisp packets dance in a bit of wind in the corner. No one else comes, no one else goes and that door don't open but soon, it's done. Olu opens the gate and we sprint over. He throws a punch at my arm, zone-boxing like it's going to mad hurt but his fist stops short, even when you're sure it's going to land.

'Keep up, keep standing!' Olu says. He holds the top of Prince's head, pushing him down. Prince laughs and tries to get back to his feet but his knees buckle out and he drops.

'Brotherman's hench. I give up,' Prince goes, and just when Olu takes his eye off the ball, Prince headbutts his belly hard. I don't think Olu feels it though; he got abs like Batman.

Olu lays out his hand for the phone, all serious, and scans the estate like there's snipers watching us. His eyes is red. I worry he's been crying or got hay-fever, but he flashes his smile so I know it's okay.

'Good,' he says.

Prince runs to the climbing frame. 'Can we play now, bruv?'

'No, blood. You don't want to do that little kid shit,' Olu says. 'You Youngers hungry?' 'Always' is always our answer. 'Hungry little mandem, eh? Now, let's see ...'

And that's it; job done.

Olu gives us a pound. Prince hangs on the chicken-shop counter from his elbows and slides down so I start up the same. Olu tells us we got to quit that stupidness and behave, and makes us stand up straight and proper. He says he ain't going to say nothing because we ain't little no more; we got to order and pay with our own coin. Me and Prince, we both get the thigh and chip box, because that's our thing, and take our penny change.

'Don't forget them less fortunate, you get me?' Olu says and shakes the charity tub. We drop our left-over pennies in the slot. 'Say thank you.'

'Thank you, boss,' we say, noses on the counter. Chicken-shop boss nods, pushes two lollipops our way and goes back to his chicken.

I want the window table because they got the best seats and you can watch everything: the bus stop, the Nisa shop, the pound shop. Next-on shop is empty, only this tramp sleeping in the door so he don't get wet when it rains.

48

As well, we get the high stools. I don't like it though, because my one wobbles. I look at Olu. He sucks his teeth the way Mama Folu hates and fetches me a different one. But that one wobbles and all, so Olu sucks his teeth some more and folds up the menu four times and puts it under my stool leg. When I know my seat ain't going to tip me, I get my carton out the bag and eat my chicken first, fat dripping down my arm. Olu's stool scrapes back on the floor and he goes to the counter. He comes back with a stack of paper tissues, the kind what don't never work but they're better than nothing.

'Wipe your fingers,' he goes, mouth full of chicken.

'Olu,' Prince says. 'What's an engineer do?'

'Man what build stuff.' Olu waves over the street. 'Blocks of flats and shit.'

'Was dad an engineer, for real? That's what mama says,' Prince goes on. 'So why don't we live in some nice house if dad was a big-up engineer?'

'Blood, don't tell mama I said this,' Olu goes. 'I seen my birth certificate and it say *student* for dad's occupation. And student mean he didn't have no job. Whatever he was or wasn't back home in Nigeria, he couldn't be the same here. He drove a cab nights and he study days. No matter what, they don't let us get on. You get me?'

Prince looks at his food like he don't want it no more. Chicken fat soon goes cold so you got to eat it fast. Olu takes out his wallet to shows his paper, sticks it under Prince's nose.

'Smell that, little man. That's the smell of luck. You make your own luck. Money is where it's at. You ain't free if you ain't got green.'

49

'Bruv, they're brown, man.'

'Don't be cheeky.'

My ears is burning. 'Olu? Can money make my mum come home?'

Olu clears up the cartons and tissues into the bag and ties the handles so the bones don't come out and kill pigeons. He turns my cap backwards and says, 'For sure, little man. Money buy law, innit.'

He stands up and his fingers brush them ceiling tiles. I think we're leaving, but he goes to the counter and buys a wing and Coke deal.

'Now, don't tell mama about this,' Olu says, closing the chicken-shop door. 'Be sure you eat all your dinner. She cooking all day, you get me?' He scans the road, left-right, and waits for a bus to go by. 'Wait here. Thirty second max.' A crew we don't know comes up on bikes. 'Count it down. I'm coming back.'

He jogs across the street, puts the wing and Coke deal by the tramp man, but he don't wake him. And that's the long way home.

Chapter 6

Mama Folu says she washed my new jeans on account of factory dust. I didn't ask for them new threads and it weren't like going down the high street with mum. Shop ladies smile at Mama Folu. She puts a card in a machine and types her numbers, says thank you and walks out. No hurry. No angst. No legging it for the bus after. I don't take the bag because it don't feel right but she says it's okay, it ain't her money she's spending. My allowance is my money and all them after-school clubs is covered too.

I colour the next square on my calendar. When mum gets better, when she comes out and Mama Folu's only a name on my file, I know some good things is going to end. Hot food. Hot baths. Dry towels. New stuff. But for now it's like I'm disrespecting mum, so I turn out my drawer looking for the threads I was wearing my first day in Peckham. I want to wear them when we go Visiting, not new ones. But I can't. The old jeans stop way above my ankles and the middle's too tight to do up. This is what time look like in threads.

Mum only takes one little second to clock.

'Nice jeans,' she goes. 'New shirt? Mrs Adeola get you those? Cost a bit, I bet.'

'Mama Folu …' I start, but Mum's face twists so I stop. Her lips go thin and she's trying not to cry. I got to make it better but I can't. 'Mrs Adeola, she took me to –'

'Mama now, is it?' Mum makes like she's smiling and it comes out wrong.

'Mrs Adeola.'

'It's okay, all right? Look at you. Anyone can see she's doing a good job. You've grown since last week even. I can see that.'

I pick up her hand to stop it shaking. Her veins criss-cross like the tube map or blue rivers. I follow one to the scars on her forearm and stop at the bend in her elbow. A bit of bruised skin there makes me think of a traffic light. I let go.

'Are you getting better, mum?' I say, frowning.

Mum folds her arms and sits up. 'What you done at the weekend then, Don?'

'Don't remember.'

Her head goes to one side and she smiles. 'You look older. Very grown up. Very handsome. Nice haircut. Going every week, now, are you?'

I ain't doing this. I ask my question again.

'Are you getting better?'

She looks at the clock on the wall and up at the window like they stuck the answer there. I know the answer though. It's in her eyes. I'm nearly ten and I know enough things about things now, even if I look little.

'We don't have much time,' mum says, gripsing up my hand. 'Tell me what you done, Don. Tell me about it, what you done. Did you get to a park?'

'There's a convenient park right there, mum.' I can hear my words go like Mama Folu's. 'Down the stairs. You don't have to go to it. It's already there.'

'Convenient.' She sighs. 'You ain't going to want to leave, are you?'

'Mum, do you know Jesus?'

A smile goes round the side of her mouth. 'What?' She starts up laughing. Stops herself. 'Go on.'

'Mrs Adeola says Jesus can make people go free. For real.'

She strokes my head. 'There's some what says that in here and all.'

Officer Lady calls time. Mum's face drops a mile and she gripses my shoulders hard.

'Don, listen to me. You're my baby boy, ain't you? I love you. Maybe I'm not the greatest mum you could ask for, but I'm the one who loves you most.'

'I know, mum,' I say. I shut my eyes.

She holds my face and says, 'I'm working on it, the free bit. Look at me, Don. Ain't Jesus can do it. It's got to be me. Look at me. I'm working on it.'

They call time again. Mum looks at the clock and I want to rip it off the wall. I can see it, smashed on the floor, my feet stamping on the pieces.

'Goodbye, Don, love,' she says. 'Be patient. Won't be long now.'

'I know,' I say, instead of goodbye.

Prison Ladies go out. Doors close. Kids hanging round the fish tank bang on the glass and no grown-up tells them to stop.

'Come,' Mama Folu says. 'Help me fill this. *Look at the birds of the air*,' she says, *'for they neither sow nor reap; yet your heavenly Father feeds them.'* She winks. 'But our Father appreciates a little help.'

I tip seeds through a paper funnel into the feeder. We stand back and the birds go mental for it.

'Donny. See this one? He thinks he is the king of this estate. See how he tells the other birds what to do? He has no concept of how small he is.'

The bird's belly is red like he's been shanked. He flies at other birds when they try to eat, proper switching. Ain't enough food to go round so he got to defend his endz.

'If he learned to share, he would eat. No?'

'Yes,' I say. Now I know she can read what's going on in my brain. 'What is he?'

'He is a robin.'

'And that one, on the balcony?'

'He is a starling. Now, see how he looks black, but wait, watch! His feathers change in the sun: green, metallic, purple. He is alone now but he has thousands of friends. In the evening, he finds them and they fly together and make shapes in the sky.' She waves a big circle in the air. 'Like a great sky monster.'

Cracks or monsters, I think, and I wonder if they got bird feeders where mum is.

'And that one?'

'He is a jay. See his pink belly? And when he rests, look at his wing. Can you see the blue stripe?'

She tells me about all them birds she seen in Nigeria, back in the day: ostriches what run faster than cars; vultures what smell a dead thing from ten miles away; the national bird of Nigeria, the black crane, what's got a fluffy crown and struts round like he's the Emperor of all Africa. She says about them birds she seen growing up and never thought she'd see again, how they fly on their little wings from outside her town in Nigeria, up Africa, over the Mediterranean and the whole long of Europe, all the way to Peckham.

'Why?' I say, because I don't get leaving home at all.

'To enjoy a cool, wet summer, Donny. English weather.'

I don't get this neither. I know it's bare hot in Africa and peoples there don't have no problem getting their threads dried out. They probably don't even got laundrettes in Africa, so they don't have to say the dryer's too much coins. They probably just dash it on some wall in their yard and *ka-boom*, it's dry.

Mama Folu gets out a fact book about birds and reads it in her most posh voice, but I can see the words tell a different story. It says them birds is proper British, and they only go fly to West Africa for some winter sun. They come back home to England in summer. I don't say nothing though. She reads out names and stuff about them, like the nightjar bird what sounds like an engine; house martins what sit on electricity wires, liming in thousands; them mean cuckoos and shy wagtails, et cetera.

'These birds,' she says, closing the book and going freestyle, 'are shared birds. They fly over the heads of politicians and

55

soldiers, customs officers and checkpoints. Their tiny hearts beat a hundred times a minute,' she tells me. 'Can you see how strong the small can be? Almighty God gave us these wonders for our joy and as a lesson to His children.'

'Get up, sleepy heads!' Mama Folu tugs my arm and strokes Prince's head. 'We are going to the beach today. Get up, my beautiful boys. Get up, all of you. Arise, my children!'

Now Saturdays is mostly for carrying bags rammed full of fruit and weird food back from market and playing football in the park. But this day's special and it's nearly my birthday. Mama Folu's been planning it for time: one bare-long train ride to a holiday place on the seaside called Bognor, and pack-up pasties and cut fruits on the way, though we only just ate breakfast.

An hour out of London and we're the only Black peoples in the train and not a lot of other peoples there neither. Old white man gets on and walks past all them empty seats to the next carriage. But this is my first time out of London, so I don't know what I know now. I don't know these people are for real but you got to learn it someday. London ain't the whole world you think it is.

Train Inspector Man comes, reads our tickets slow like he's still learning to read, turning each one round. He stares at Olu for time, thinking, thinking and I'm thinking, What is that man thinking? Mama Folu shifts like she's sitting on some rock, clears her throat like she's sick.

'I'll need to see an item of photo identification, please,' man goes. 'I see you have a Kids for Two Quid ticket here.'

'He is fifteen, sir,' Mama Folu says. 'And he is my son.' Her smile ain't real.

Olu kisses his teeth and goes low in his seat. He looks out the window like nobody ain't said nothing to him. Mama Folu says in this high voice I ain't heard before, 'Olufemi, please show the good gentleman your London Oyster photocard,' but Olu don't move. 'Olufemi,' she goes again.

'Allow it, man,' Olu goes.

Inspector Man's white lips go so thin they disappear.

'I'm going to have to charge you a penalty fare. If you choose to continue on this train after paying the penalty fare, you may be charged the full single fare to your destination station.' He acts like we smell bad. 'You're clearly not a child, now are you, son?' Olu looks out the window; he ain't saying nothing. 'If you choose not to pay, I'm going to have to call the Transport Police.'

Man gets his phone out one of them special pockets in his uniform. I can tell he likes this bit of the train job.

'Olufemi,' Mama Folu says in a whisper. 'Do not spoil our day. Donny has never been to the beach before. Please?'

Olu looks at me; he screws up his face and lets out a long breath, takes time to find his Oyster and slams it on the table, wrong way up. Inspector Man flips it and looks at Olu, the photo, Olu, the photo.

'Don't believe me?' Olu spits. 'I don't care, man. Go on, give me a penalty fare. I don't care.' He gets out three twenty spots from his wallet and dashes the paper down the table. 'Take the penalty fare, man. Take it.'

'Your identification looks in order.' Inspector Man ignores the notes, puts the Oyster down like he's touching dog shit. 'Thank you. Son.'

Train door shuts on Inspector Man like it's breathing out a big-up sigh.

'Why don't he like us?' I say.

'Because that man's racist,' Olu says.

'No,' Mama Folu goes. She blinks, trying not to cry. 'Because my sons are too loud. Lower your voices. Your father never raised his voice. Never.' She brings her big handbag close up to her. 'What must people think? What must they think? Behave yourselves!'

Now I don't know about no racists, but to me Olu looks like a big-up man; got big-up veins on his big-up hands. His jaw ain't soft like Michael's. It's more like it's been cut out of rock. He's more taller than most grown-up mans and better-looking too. He even got hairs growing on his top lip. Soon now, he's going to have to shave.

We get out at the last stop before the ocean starts up and there ain't no more land for a train to go on. Straight away I hear seagulls and the sky smells like we're the first ones to ever breathe it. The holiday park's right next to the beach but there's inside pools and water rides so you don't have to go outside if you don't want to. Them inside pools is how I think of St Lucia: steaming air, palm trees and flowers. It all looks for real, but the flowers is made out of cloth and them trees is hollow if you tap them. Fibreglass or moulded plastic, probably, like what they use to make sailing dinghy hulls, because it's light and moulds the way you want it.

Olu, Michael and Prince get changed before I even open my bag. They run through the shower and out to the pools and they don't look back. Mama Folu waits outside my cubicle.

She lets me know she's there. 'Take your time, child,' she says. 'Take your time.'

She don't change but she shows me a shallow-water bit, a play area for kids what can't swim. She sits down on a deckchair and starts up a book. I lie down on my belly and watch Olu tip the others into the waves the pool machine's throwing at them. Michael dives under, grabs Olu's ankle and brings him down. Olu pushes Michael's head under the water, Prince gripses his back, but he don't stay on long. Olu grabs behind him, lifts Prince over his head and dashes him in a wave. Them muscles in Olu's back and arms move and I think, He is a grown-up. Inspector Man only doing the job he's paid to do.

Lifeguard blows his whistle. They stand in height order like they're getting their photo taken, and I swear down, under them yellow lights, their skin is made of gold. Lifeguard tells them to cut it out or he'll get the manager.

'He's chatting shit,' Olu says. He points to the white boys next to them. 'Ain't only us. Come, let's bounce.'

Lifeguard knows it too, but he ain't going to step to that.

Right there, I start wishing my skin was black like Olu's, not cafe au creme like mum says. I start wishing I can swim so I can get told off for fighting in them deep, rolling waves. Most of all I start wishing Olu was my brother for real because it feels like he is already when he pulls me out the baby pool and takes me to the waterslide.

'It's okay, Donny,' Olu says, 'You don't have to swim to do them tubes.'

We run up a spiral staircase dripping water to three slides; blue, red and black.

'I heard people stick razor blades in them slides,' Prince goes.

'Relax, fam,' Olu says. 'That's rubbish, innit.' He gets on his knees. 'Now why would mandem even do that, little bro? Nah. And how could they even stop for long enough to do that shit. Nah.' He holds Prince's shoulders and nods to the first tube. 'You take the blue. Michael, the red. Safe.'

Red-hair Lifeguard says, 'On you go,' when the green light come on. They dash into them tubes and they're gone. Olu's gone, they're all gone and the water goes down after them. No sound even, nothing to say they ever been.

The window up there is plastic, scratched and wet both sides, but you can see the beach a bit. I'm shivering but I want to see so I stand on tiptoe.

'Go,' says Lifeguard.

The sea's high up the land, dashing its waves on the stones. I look at the fence for a gap, to see if there's some way down to the shore. Fence metal's cut at the tops and peeled down in leaves, sharp like knives to protect the holiday park from, I don't know, whatever it needs protecting from. The beach is empty, except for a few seagulls and this lady walking on the stones carrying her shoes. She puts a hand down to stop herself going over and her dog runs circles round her, light on the stones.

'You can go now,' Lifeguard says.

But I can't do this. I go back down the steps.

Mama Folu buys us chicken and chips for lunch, with cola in glasses packed to the top with ice. She don't eat the same. She takes little bites from a pasty she made yesterday and watches us stuff our faces. Olu makes big eyes at the waitresses, smiles when they're looking. They blush and go back to the kitchens or see to another table, but some smile back. Michael and Prince clock that and all. They laugh.

It stops raining so Michael dares us to do the fairground. Olu hangs back. He looks at his phone and frowns. 'No, thank you,' he says. 'I'm busy. Got stuff to do.' He points at the rides. 'Anyways, I'm not into this kid thing.'

'Big man! Big man!' Prince goes.

We line up for the ferris wheel. Mama Folu sits on a bench where she can watch us, worry in her eyes. We get in, Prince with me, Michael on his ones, waiting for the next pod, and the safety bar comes down. That window at the top of the waterslide tower stopped this wind but on the wheel my ears sting. Michael's below with his hood pulled in.

At the top it's like I'm crying except I'm not.

Bare seagulls is jacking a fishing boat and more out where the sea goes black, and this boat – must've been some racing-class yacht – hammers the waves sideways. I don't know nothing about weighted bulb keels and wide beams for buoyancy, nothing about centreboards and daggerboards neither, so I wait for them sails to touch the water and go down. I don't even know the word 'capsize', but I'm thinking it without the word. I mean, how could it not?

'You frit?' Prince says.

'Bit. What if them peoples can't swim?'

'What are you chatting for?' Prince says and I get he ain't seen the boat so I say, 'Nah. This is nothing. My mum could do this.'

61

'Not this one, she couldn't,' he goes. 'Adults aren't allowed. Too old. Their hearts would stop, innit.'

'Not my mum,' I say. 'She's little. She goes on all the rides at London Fields.'

'Is it!' Then Prince clocks something across the park. 'Look,' he goes. 'Olu!'

Olu's talking to this white man. They shake and he walks our way, typing on his phone.

'Hey! Olu! Olu!' shouts Prince.

At ground level, the bar releases and Mama Folu's up in our faces like we been gone for time. Like we crossed the Atlantic Ocean. She's still hugging us up when Michael's pod comes down. She puts her arms out for him too, but he legs it straight past her, pointing at the pink sky. Birds fly over the holiday park to the beach, and I know what it is.

'He found his friends! Billions of them,' I say. 'Sky monsters!'

Mama Folu's mouth drops. She stares at the sky and says, 'I believe the correct term is murmuration and it occurs,' she looks at her old-man's wristwatch, 'at dusk.'

'UFO! No, a heart,' Prince says. 'No, an S – look, a W! They're writing to us. The birds are writing to us!'

'Mama!' Olu calls. The starlings carry on behind him and I don't think he's even clocked they're there. He only gone and got us five massive ice creams, three scoops each. 'Yo, people! Mama!' he goes.

Mama Folu frowns. 'Olufemi, you should keep your money for yourself.'

'But I work, mama,' he says with a big-up smile, 'so I can buy my beautiful mama all she wants.' We try to get our cone but Olu balances on one leg, holding them ice creams out of reach. He taps my knee, like kicking a football in slow motion. 'And these wastemans.'

I act like he dropped me and hold my knees to my belly like it hurts. I don't know why pro-footballers drop so much like that. It's embarrassing. Kasim never drops. When you learn to play on the streets and on concrete courtyards and tarmac playgrounds, he says, you get superior balance. So when you're up against a county team what's got wrap-round grass at their school, none of them can stay on their feet. 'It's like taking candy from a baby,' Kasim says. 'They can't help it. Some peoples is just born with disadvantage.'

Now Prince and Michael pile on Olu, trying to pin him down.

'Penalty, ref!' Michael says, tugging at Mama Folu's sleeve.

'Yes, quite so. Orange card for you, Olufemi,' she says.

'Should be red, mama, red,' Prince says. 'Or yellow, because you're soft.'

Olu gets me up and winks. We eat our ice creams and look back at the sky. Them starlings is gone.

Mama Folu sighs. 'The colours of sunset. Come, my boys. It is time we go home.'

On the way to the station, Michael leapfrogs Prince but I ain't playing. My head's somewhere else. Mama Folu holds my hand and I don't shake her off.

'Bet I can lift you,' Prince says to Michael.

Next second, they fall over and Mama Folu tuts. 'Walk nicely,' she says.

Olu's balancing on a high wall and wants us to see because he goes, 'Pssst!'

63

'He's a cat,' Michael says. 'He walks up walls and jumps fences.' His voice goes low. 'She don't know it, but he goes AWOL at night.'

'It's parkour, blood,' Olu says, frowning, but Mama Folu don't care what it is because she goes to him, all vex-up, 'Get down from there!'

Olu stretches out his arms like one of them Olympic high-board divers and leans forward, except ain't no water under him. He lets himself fall and does this last-second somersault to his feet, like gravity is some choice he makes when he feel like it.

'Someone will call the police!' Mama Folu's on him now. 'You must behave better than white boys. Do you understand me? Better! You must be better and do better in every way.'

On the train back I realise the day's done and we ain't got to the beach. Now there's nothing but county outside; bare trees and cows chewing grass. Soon there's more bricks than fields. Houses thicken up. I see lines of planes waiting on a runway and I think, You don't need to go flying no plane to some tropical place when you've got tropical right there in Bognor.

And I'm still wondering what sea tastes like, but that don't matter. This day's the best and I make a big-up promise: when I'm a grown man, I'm going to bring mum to that holiday place. I'm going to buy the train tickets, the fry chicken, the cola, the rides, the ice creams, everything. She's going to blush and say, 'Don, you keep your money for yourself.'

Now, by that time I'm going to be more taller than her so I'll look down when I say, 'But I work so I can buy my beautiful mum what she wants.'

And after the pools, I'll find a gate they forgot to lock, or some other way through the fence, and show her the beach. I'll take off my creps and roll up my jeans. She's going to laugh her head off and say, 'No, Don,' but she'll do the same in the end and we'll go barefoot on them stones and I'll keep hold of her hand, no matter what.

It's almost like mum was coming back to Peckham at the same time and all, because when we get to the flat there's a letter waiting for me.

'She has enrolled on a new workshop,' Mama Folu says, 'called Look After Yourself. She is learning resilience and self-esteem. Good!'

I don't know what resilience means but it's okay because Mama Folu reads minds.

'It is about keeping oneself upright,' she says. 'She is learning to suffer the slings and arrows of fortune, as the Bard once said, and rise up against a sea of troubles.' Mama Folu gives me a postcard of the holiday park and a number one stamp. 'But you must tell her about the seaside, yes?'

I think for a bit and start up writing. *Dear mum, We went where this picture is. I saw a boat nearly go over but it didn't. Love, Donny.*

Mama Folu asks me if there's anything more I want to say, like about what I did, the meal, swimming, ice cream, et cetera. I shake my head.

'Let us pray now,' she says when I stick down the stamp. 'To send it on its way. We thank You, Jesus, for Donny's dear mother and pray she finds strength and courage. We thank You for our children ...'

I don't move when she's praying, keep my eyes shut. Praying don't scare me now. Them prayers is like she's collecting an Oscar. Jesus gets thanked for her sons, and sometimes her dead old man what worked so hard. She thanks God for them boys and lists what exactly she's thanking for: first up, their growing and strength; their handsome black skin and hair; plenty food at market; them boys' big appetites and the fact they don't never go hungry. It's all in her thank-you list.

I think them prayers is just a loud kind of love.

I feel like some next-level celebrity in the Sunday suit Mama Folu gives me. She says it's silk, hand-made in Abuja.

'It belonged to Olufemi,' she goes every time we get ready for church. She brushes the shoulder pads. 'He looked so handsome in it when he was your age.'

We drive to the Church of the Blessed. It ain't a proper pointy church like you think. It's this warehouse on the industrial estate, next to the Polish sausage factory what smells so good. You don't even know it's a church except when you see the sign of the pastor with his hands out and it says in big letters HE THAT BELIEVETH ON THE SON HATH ETERNAL LIFE. It takes fifteen minutes to get there because South London traffic on a Sunday morning is a lot like North London traffic on a Friday night when I wait for Kasim to come out their madrassa so his big brothers can get me some eats.

We wait by the car for time so Mama Folu can hook up with all them ladies she knows. She always clocks stuff, like fresh weaves and new wheels, pregnant bellies and babies in white blankets. She says nice things to everyone. Church

66

uncles chat business in their business suits, except it ain't like the City, because City businessmans don't keep their babies close or let their kids swing off their arms, now do they?

'We pray, mighty God!' the pastor says and it goes quiet. His voice comes out speakers on every wall and it takes a bit of time for the back ones to catch up. 'For the forgiveness of those who stray. We pray, mighty Father, for those enslaved in mind and incarcerated in body. Know today! Only Jesus and He alone can set you free!'

Mama Folu squeezes my hand and I'm proper up for this; I'm going to tell mum some more about Jesus. And when the service is done, Prince and Michael hold Mama Folu's hands to the car and she's all smiles. I want it to be like this for mum and all.

Olu's walking next to them. He turns for no reason.

'Bruv,' he says, and nods for me to catch up. His hand feels bare heavy on my shoulder.

Most times Mama Folu's cook-ups is better than chicken shop. Sometimes it's better than Jerkz as well, but I wouldn't never say that aloud. Prince and Michael hold my hands for the food prayer and I look through my lashes at the meat stew, wondering how long praying is going to take and if I can get more meat and leave out the yam. It ain't like I don't like yam. It's only that her meat is the most tasty thing I ever ate. Don't get me wrong. When mum cooks something like her cornflake sandwiches for dinner, I know it's random but it's also okay if it's what we got. Still, Mama Folu's meat is something else.

'Mama, why do bare people have more money than us?' says Michael when the praying is done.

67

Mama Folu's eyes roll all the way up to the ceiling. 'Bare? Rephrase!'

'I mean, like, most people got more money –'

'That is not true, Michael,' she says. 'We are the richest people in the world.'

Olu snorts. He turns the snort into a cough quick when he clocks she's looking.

'Okay,' she says. 'I could send you home to your grandmother to see how orphans live on Abuja's streets.'

'What's orphan?' I ask.

Prince laughs. He gets his leg kicked under the table but I can't tell who done it.

'It's a child without parents,' Mama Folu says.

'So who looks after them?' I say, pushing a bit of yam round the plate.

'Jesus. This family. Our church. We send money. Maybe we should send you – Olufemi, Michael – to help too?'

They all frit now. Olu sits up in his chair. 'Delicious rice, mama,' he says. 'Your jollof is the best.'

She shuts her eyes. It's like she knows if she only don't see his good-looking face, he ain't getting nowhere.

'I will tell you a story my grandmother told me, from the old country, about a farmer whose son was getting married. The farmer picked out a young rooster from her flock of chickens a few weeks before the wedding ...'

'I know this one,' Prince says, sticking his elbow in me. 'This one's good.'

'She wanted him fat, so she knotted a piece of string around his foot. Whenever there were scraps in the kitchen, she took them straight to the rooster with the string. The rooster said

68

to his sisters, "See how rich I am? I have jewellery around my foot and better food than you!" His sisters warned him, "Do not trust the people! People are dangerous!" But he laughed at them and said, "With that attitude, you will always be poor and live in the mud and dust".'

Mama Folu does this chicken walk round the kitchen, nose in the air, and they all laugh.

'So the rooster grew fat,' she goes. 'So fat, the farmer could hardly lift him! On the morning of the wedding, when the farmer came out, he ran to her gladly. He let her pick him up, tuck him under her arm and carry him back to her thatched hut. He shouted to his sisters, "See how I have been chosen? I am better than you. I am going to live with the people now. I am rich!" The flock fussed and tried to warn him, saying, "You will never be rich! You will be killed and eaten!" He was so pleased with himself, he did not hear their clucks.'

'Leg it, chicken!' says Michael.

'In the hut, the rooster felt the fire and thought, Tonight I will be dry. He saw a clean cloth spread over the floor, covered in dishes, and said, "I will eat with the people tonight." He saw the people dressed in their Sunday clothes and began crowing, "I am so much richer than my sisters!"'

'Run, chicken, run,' says Prince. 'Get out that hut!'

'So, the farmer took her sharpest knife and lay the rooster down.' Mama Folu acts the knife in her hands, like she's cutting yam, and though there ain't nothing in her hands, you can see it there. '"I will have my nails trimmed now," the rooster said happily, "ready for the wedding." Now, the farmer was a humane woman and she killed the rooster quickly with her knife.'

Mama Folu spreads her fingers on the table, looking at her sons. They go silent. I wait till I can't wait no more and I have to ask, 'So, what happens next?'

Michael and Prince look at each other. 'They ate him with ofada rice and he was tasty!' they say, laughing their heads off.

'That chicken was stupid, man. Why didn't he listen?' I say, but I can't help it, they start me off laughing like mum starts me off.

Mama Folu sighs. 'He could not listen because he thought he would be – what? My boys, who will tell Donny the moral of the story?'

Olu lows down his head and brings up his long arm.

'Olufemi?'

'If something seems too good to be true, it most likely is,' he says in flat words. He whispers in my ear, 'So don't go running after no white-arsed teacher when they promise you shit.'

'But is it a true story?' I want to know.

'Yes,' Mama Folu says. 'So true, it happens every day.'

They carry their plates to the sink and I do the same. They wash up, dry down, splash each other with water when Mama Folu ain't looking and I think, This is what it's supposed to be like.

Chapter 7

'Double numbers! One-zero!' mum says like she's high. I look round the Visiting Room to see if peoples is staring at us. 'Birthday boy! Countdown!' She waves at the lady on the next table. 'Hey, Sandra, ain't he handsome? My baby boy, ten years old on Wednesday! I ask you, how did that happen?'

'Give over, mum.'

'Give over nothing! It's my day and all. I done it, babes. It was me what done it.'

I want to go. I lean in close and say, 'You don't have to chat about it though.'

'Chat about it? I'm going to shout about it!' she says.

But I can't just go. I can't leave her so I fold my arms and put my head down.

'My baby boy's growing up.'

Officer Lady comes to the table and mum makes her face all serious. Lady whispers something into her ear and mum bites her lip, still smiling, eyes still sparkling.

'When you was first born you had blue eyes.' I look up. 'Yes. Blue, they was. They went brown after a bit, like your

71

dad's, but they started out blue, like mine. And you could move, I swear it. You was just born and you could shift yourself and you lifted your head and looked right at me and said something I won't never forget as long as I live.'

'What?'

'"Nando's!"'

I smile. 'Give over, mum. It weren't like that. I know it weren't.'

Mum frowns and takes my hand. 'You're right. Come here. I got to tell you something, Don. I've been doing this twelve-step thing and part of it's to say sorry to people we hurt – and I hurt you, babes.'

I shake my head. 'You never.'

'I didn't mean to, but I did.' She starts up whispering. 'I didn't take care of you when you was growing inside me and that made you poorly and I'm sorry. That's it. That's all. I'm sorry. But you're okay now, ain't you, babes? You're okay?' I nod. 'So what you going to do on the big day? I wanted to get you something, but …'

'It don't matter.'

'It do. I want to. I'll make it up to you, Don. I promise. When I get out, I'm going to treat you, big time. I'm talking cinema, babes, Nando's, bowling. You can bring a mate and all.'

Wednesday comes and there's a DC Sport carrier bag on my bed. In it is a red tracksuit and matching creps, legitimate Adidas with the silver medal I ain't never taking off. At my new primary, you don't have to wear no uniform if it's your birthday so these was my threads for school all day.

Prince sits on Mama Folu's lap at the kitchen table, in his pyjamas and dressing gown, head on her shoulder and her hand on his head.

'Come here, my baby,' Mama Folu says. Prince wraps his legs round her waist and she carries him into her bedroom. 'I will call the school.'

'You know he's lying,' Michael says to me while she's out. 'He just wants to bunk off.'

'I heard that!'

Michael lowers his eyes when she comes back.

'Michael.' She pulls him onto her knee, kisses the back of his neck, and a smile creeps up on his lips. 'Have a little compassion for your brother. He has a temperature.'

'It's true though. He wants a day off school.' Michael catches my eye. 'He probably put hot water on the thermometer so he can stay with you. And you buy it because he's your favourite.'

'Hush.' She brushes his blazer sleeve and picks at hairs what ain't there. 'I don't have a favourite. I love you all more than life itself.' She strokes the badge on his chest: a bird, wings out, fire trying to drag it down. *New South Academy* in gold letters. 'You see this bird? Like Jesus, the phoenix is stronger than death. He rises out of the fire.' She winks at me. 'It was an African bird originally. It flew to Europe for the summer.'

'It's not, mama.' Michael squints through his glasses and wrinkles up his nose. 'We had an assembly about it. Sir says it's Greek. That makes it European.'

'No, Michael. It is Egyptian, like Moses. African, like Jesus. We rise up, too. Come.' She gently pushes Michael to

73

his feet and stands. 'This is not a day for envy or argument. It is Donny's birthday and we must make him happy.' She opens her purse. 'Michael and Olu, please collect Donny from school today and take him for his special birthday treat.'

'Chicken shop?' Michael asks.

'No. This is a special occasion. Donny may choose. Perhaps Nando's?'

The boys look at each other and grin.

'I got this, mama,' Olu says, snapping her purse shut. He kisses her head.

'Mama?' Prince goes from the bedroom. 'I think I'm okay for school now.' But it's too late.

Before we go, Olu and Michael stick their heads round Mama Folu's door. Michael gives a big-up grin and calls out to Prince, 'I'll save you a bone, bruv.'

There ain't a minute I don't think about that treat. I tell everyone what we going to do. Lunchtime, I lay tissues down so I don't get food on my birthday threads. I'm Stair Monitor so at three o'clock I stand on the halfway-up landing. Bell goes and Teacher Man takes the classes down and I make sure they all walking right at the back, especially them Year Ones because sometimes they don't know how to behave. Year Five boy says to me, 'Neat creps, Donny.'

Olu and Michael's sitting on their bikes at the primary gate and they're holding the handlebars of another bike. I don't know how they got it here; would've been some mission riding three bikes.

'Happy birthday, little man,' Olu says. 'Them trackies look fresh.'

Other side of the playground, one of the teachers flaps her arms. She calls out to Michael and Olu and walks over because she's clocked the bike between them.

'How are you? Olufemi, isn't it? Michael! How are you getting on in secondary school?'

When Olu don't answer, Michael says, 'Fine thanks, Mrs H.' I can tell he likes her. She must've been his favourite teacher back in the day.

'You must come see us sometime. Actually, we could use your help here. We've had to lose quite a few assistants this year. When's Work Experience week?' she says, smiling. 'You could come in and help me with Year Four.'

Olu strokes his chin and looks at the gate. Michael waits for him to say something. When he don't, Michael says, 'Thanks, Mrs H, but they don't do Year Ten Work Experience no more.'

'Year Eleven?'

He shakes his head.

Except, in the now times I know they do. Not everywhere and not every school, but they do and I know because I done it in Hertfordshire when I was older. And Andrew said I was the best Work Experience boy he ever had on the canal and I won the prize for it. You don't know what other people got until you go there and see it with your own eyes. So I take it as a heap of the biggest bollocks that Michael ain't never got to do it. How comes county kids get everything like that? Michael would've done as good as me, no lie.

Teacher Lady frowns.

'For real, miss. They got no money to run Work Experience no more.'

'Well, come anyway, next Inset day or when you've finished your exams. We'd love to see you.'

I don't know why Olu blanks her but she gets the message. When she's gone, Michael goes to Olu, 'How comes primary teachers bare nice?'

'True that. Primary don't lie. Secondary lie, blood. Time and time. It's like – I don't know.'

I'm staring at the third bike. Last time I was on a bike, it had stabiliser wheels and mum was with me. There was no cars, no junctions, no crossings, no traffic lights in the park going red, yellow, green. Just her hand on my shoulder and them paths doing circles round the flowers.

'What are you waiting for, birthday boy?' Olu puts his big hand on my shoulder and smiles. 'You're ten now. Listen up: we make our own Work Experience. Time we got you a job. Time to meet Bossman.'

I get on. The seat's too high to sit on and Olu don't have no tool to change it but I can handle a grown-up bike. Michael wants to ask the caretaker to help but Olu stripses. I'm going to have to stand on the pedals the whole way but I don't care. I roll my trackie legs up to my knee, like Olu and Michael done. Kids is laughing at me but I don't care.

'I'm not sure that's such a good idea!' one of them teachers yells. 'He needs a helmet!'

Olu and Michael overtake me. I try following, shooting red lights where dumb cars got to wait. We ride the pavement and down the alley. Olu pulls a wheelie for the longest time, Michael jumps off kerbs and I can't do no stunts yet, but I don't care. Ain't no car can match me, no light can stop me.

I wish mum could see me riding on a proper road. As well, I'm glad she can't.

I ain't never been to Ashmore House on the other side of the estate. It's a twin; same alleys and stairs round a courtyard, trees, playground in the middle with swings and a climbing frame. Grown-ups got to use a car park round the back, so kids can basically run, cycle and skateboard anywhere they like and ain't nobody going to get killed by no car. I remember them lorries rolling down Mare Street in Hackney, when you can taste black stuff in your mouth, and I think the man what built this place must've really liked kids.

Olu lays his bike on the ground so the wheel don't spin and smooths out the rolls in his trackie leg. He don't lock his bike and runs up them concrete steps four at a time and I try the same but I can only do threes. On the first floor, I look back. I only just got that bike and it's new. I tug Olu's sleeve.

'Brother Olu, what if somebody jacks them?' I go. I remember when the bike mum bought me got nicked.

Olu laughs and grips my chin in his big fingers.

'Then they is on a suicide mission, innit. This is our manor, so chill,' he says smiling. 'Got respect here.'

On the top floor, Olu knocks and we wait. Bossman's window is brand new like Mama Folu's, same like all the windows the council changed up for plastic ones in them manors, but it's covered in wet and mould on the inside. They got a sheet hanging in the window for a curtain so you can't see in. Olu knocks again, harder this time. He lifts the letter-box flap to see in and sends a text.

Next door opens and this old Chinese lady steps to the balcony. She goes down on her knees and starts up sweeping round her door. She got pots of growing things and flowers on her windowsill. I say hi. She looks through me like I ain't there, chews her lip and leaves her dustpan by the pile of Rizla papers, bits of cardboard, Red Bull cans and wrappers she brushed up. She goes back in, locks her outside bars and locks her inside metal door. Every flat on this estate's got extra security on their windows and doors and no man can squeeze through or break them down. It's nice and safe. Next Visiting, I'm going say to mum about getting a flat by Mama Folu. We can be neighbours and Prince and me can play in the park forever, and if I don't fancy cereal again I can go round Mama Folu's for eats.

Olu knocks again and sucks his teeth. Michael leans on the railing and kicks a can through. It clatters on the courtyard; sound goes round the manor like them walls can sing.

Olu slaps Michael's head. 'What you playing at, blood?' Michael punches Olu in his chest, but he don't care. 'Think there's a little fly out here,' Olu goes, brushing down his T-shirt, looking around for the imaginary fly what's really Michael. 'Some insect landed on me. Going to get squashed if it try it again.'

Michael moves down the balcony a bit and kicks them railings till they hum. Olu sucks his teeth again. 'Quit that, blood.'

'So we going Nando's or what?' Michael says. 'Because I ain't wasting my time. It's Donny's birthday, remember. Are you dumb?'

Olu don't look happy. Michael's lucky his brother's phone goes ding because he would've got himself mashed. Three locks slide and click on Bossman's door: top, middle, bottom. It opens and I hear machine guns and bombs exploding.

'Behave yourself now,' Olu goes.

A boy sticks his head out and scans the balcony. He opens the door so little we got to squeeze up and go in sideways. It's bare dark. All them windows is covered up and light bulbs ain't working neither or else they ain't been put in right. As well, smoke's so thick it's like someone's burnt toast but it ain't bread what's burning. Bread don't burn sweet like that.

I trip my foot on a weight-lifting disk lying about and I straight away want a go on that big-up gym frame they got. I want to lie on that bench and see them chains and wires going up and down. I want to see if I can pull them weights like a big man. I bet my pound Olu can. That flat is like being in a real gym what people pay money for, except it's for free. If you lime with Bossman and his crew.

Olu dashes his fist into a punchbag they got hanging up. It's bare heavy so it don't swing or nothing. I try and all but it hurts my hand bad. Olu shows me the way, 'Like this, little man.' He takes my fist, pulls my thumb out and lays it on the outside of my fingers. 'Breaks your thumb if you keep it in,' he says. 'Go again.'

I hit the bag again and it don't hurt.

Olu nods because I done good. 'Safe,' he goes. 'When time comes to fight, you're going to remember this move. Right?'

They got everything here. Three mattresses down for sleeping on and a widescreen and six surround-sound speakers. If you lime with Bossman, you get all that for free and all, and it ain't only for boys. This girl's sleeping on the first mattress, probably in Michael's year, thick arms hugging up her knees and her leggings is see-through, stretched by her bigness. Her pants make a letter T over her back and down her arse and that don't look comfy. Number two mattress is sheets and blankets.

Two boys I know from my school is on number three mattress hammering wireless controllers, top-range Bluetooth PlayStation ones like nearly nobody got. I don't know their names, they're in Year Four or Five, but I tell them boys, 'What's good?' They don't hear me. They got to concentrate. Any second they're going to get killed, but they still think they can make it out alive. It's one of them point-of-view shooters what looks real, like you're watching a film. Blood splatters up the screen when a soldier gets shot up and they move their mans house-to-house over bombed-out burn-up rubble. Most all of their soldiers is screaming or dead in the mud and this tank rolls up, barrel stepping in their faces. It's sad. I would say that level is way too tricky for Year Fives. They can keep firing all they like but they already lost. They ain't got no chance.

Olu takes me to Bossman in the kitchen. It's like he just moved in, boxes everywhere. Fridge got all kinds of shit stuck to it though, so he must've been here time: Most Improved Attendance certificate from my primary, two of them red bills what mum puts in the bin, Florida fridge magnet and a photo of an old lady. I don't think she lives here no more because she don't look like the kind of lady who'd let her kitchen go like the back of Victoria station, crew tags sprayed up the walls.

Bossman's mixing up a jar with a teaspoon too little for his fingers. He nods to Olu and lifts his elbow for a dap instead of shaking hands, on account of his hands being all dirtied up with cooking. His apron says *I Love Mom* and the strings nearly don't reach round his middle.

There ain't nowhere clear to sit so Olu shifts some takeaway boxes and dried-up food to a black bin bag in the sink. He puts a big-up yard cutlass what was on another chair in a drawer. I'm glad of that because all these kids is here, little ones and older like me, and they might get cut up. I sit next to him, leaning a bit on his shoulder, thinking about what Bossman's cooking and if he's going to hand some out because it's gone three o'clock and I get bare hungry after school. As well, it is my birthday.

Two boys come in the kitchen. One's looking at his phone. He got a nice set of no-wire headphones round his neck and nearly got a moustache on his top lip. He looks like them pharaoh boy-kings we learned about at school, eyes the shape of almonds. His great-great-great-grandaddy must've been some king back in the day. I can't see the other boy's eyes because he's practising a rap, screwing them shut like Mama Folu does when she's praying, and his hand is keeping the beat solid, the way they do in church.

'Safe, Olu,' Bossman says. 'What you brung me?'

'Introducing Donny. He's top-of-the-class Maths smart.' I like it that Olu's proud of me, that he read my school report. 'Put him on counting. He'll account good for you.'

'Tag him Dr-D,' says Bossman. He goes back to cooking. Them big boys look up.

'Boss?' they say.

'What?'

'Dr-D's taken,' one goes. 'Manor's already got a Dr-D.'

81

Bossman quits stirring. He looks down the long of me and sucks his teeth. Deep lines in his forehead go more deeper. I look at my creps and the holes in the floor and try not to move.

'D-Man, then,' he says and goes back to his jar, working faster.

'But there's a D-Man on the OKR crew,' the other boy says. 'They're going to think we're copying them. We're going to look like mugs.'

The jar snaps. Bossman cusses, scrapes paste off the bits of glass. He picks more off and stirs the rest back in, only he's left splinters in the paste and I want to tell him it's still there because glass ain't safe. It could hurt someone.

'He's little, innit,' Bossman says, looking at me, red eyes watering. 'D-Boy, then.' He points a pastey finger at me. 'You count, D-Boy?'

'Yes, boss,' I say, big smile on my face.

'D-Boy,' Bossman says with a little laugh. He nods like he's done with balancing a big-up equation. 'D-Boy!'

Them boys say my new name, 'D-Boy, D-Boy,' and look to Bossman for what's next.

'Go on then, Jay, Lazer. Spit it,' Bossman goes and they smile at me. Lazer does beatbox. Jay makes his fist into a microphone, spitting freestyle.

'Don't misunderstand me/D-Boy look like candy/He ain't no plan D/Sharp like a Stanley/Modus operandi?/Take care of his family!'

Jay knots his arms. Lazer carries on: 'Yeah. See him get handy/Put his enemy in agony/D-boy look like a boy/But the boy bare manly/Allow it! D-Boy!'

Bossman and Olu and them laugh their heads off, knees to chest, gripsing up the table so they don't fall. I don't think they're laughing at me but I ain't sure.

Michael's in the doorway. Two sheets hanging on the window let in a little line of yellow light, ceiling to floor, and it cuts between me and Michael. Dust and smoke swim about, like looking in water.

I check Bossman when he's busy laughing. He got tattoos on his chest, but he ain't really a grown-up. He's the Older round here but he ain't got much on Olu.

Bossman's face drops like he's vex.

'Get him a phone,' he says, voice deep like a V8 engine.

Jay comes back and throws a box-fresh phone at me like it ain't nothing at all. Olu winks. His eyes say, Go on, take it, it's yours.

Bossman goes back to playing with the paste like it's playdough time at nursery, making it into shapes and wrapping it in plastic. He tells Olu it's going Caterham, by train, delivery only. After the holiday park, trains is my thing, so I pull my hoodie round my face like a proper Younger. I want to be on that train and I hope I ain't too little to deliver. Besides, I got more height now I'm ten and I bet my pound most grown-ups will clock me for twelve. I take a step forward.

'Not D-Boy,' Bossman says, frowning at me. He looks at Michael. 'Get me Harry there.'

'He?' Olu goes. Michael shifts to the door.

'That's right. The full Hogwarts, you get me? Feds all over county line, blood. Come, Michael. We need uniform. And you got debts to pay, innit.'

Olu gripses Michael so he don't bounce.

'Do the Math, blood,' Olu goes, pushing him to Bossman. 'You owe us for them ten ounces. How you going to pay that, blood? Going to be a zero-hour bikeman? One dollar a delivery? Going to deliver flyers? One cent every letterbox? Click, clack, woof. Nah! Roadman, for real; one fat hundred and you're free.'

Michael screw-faces Olu and says, like Mama Folu did when she told us the chicken story, 'We will always be poor and live in the dust ...'

Olu slaps Michael's head hard. 'Believe it,' he goes. 'You only getting this chance because of me. Think about it. Don't let me down, bruv.'

Michael takes the wraps and comes back from the toilet like he got ants biting him up his arse.

'Don't cry. We all done it, blood. Now tuck that shirt in,' Bossman says to him. He wipes his fingers on his apron and gets a wide-toothed comb. 'Now, my mum would've said you look like a ragamuffin. You need fixing up. Tie, blood.'

He fixes Michael so he looks like it's morning and he's late for school, not going Nando's for chicken or home to Mama Folu for cake like I know he wants.

'Good.' Bossman counts out five brown notes from a fat roll and tucks them into Michael's blazer. 'Get an off-peak return. The rest is yours to keep. Five more tens when you get back. Even after you pay what's owed, you can still make some Gs. Deal?'

The sun goes behind the next manor. That yellow line's gone and the dust and smoke is gone and all. And so's Michael.

'We got to sort business,' Bossman says to Olu. 'It ain't good. We got to make a move.'

Olu nods like the general he is. 'But get D-Boy counting next door first.'

Jay takes me to the bedroom and I sit on the floor with big-up piles of paper money. He shuts the door. Now I ain't never seen so much dollars, but straight away I got a plan. I sort them notes into stacks of fives, tens and twenties. I get my pencil case out my bag, the new one Mama Folu got me when it weren't even my birthday. I make a grid in my rough book, like Teacher Man showed me, making the lines with a ruler. I count each pile and fill in the grid in my most neat handwriting.

Now's the hard bit; one fat column of multiplication. I bite my lip. I'm about to multiply the totals when there's a crash. Three dead thuds, like they're hitting the punchbag. It sounds like somebody switched, dashing chairs on the walls.

'Wasteman!'

I drop the dollars and go see who's vex. Bossman dashes his fist into the wall and it goes right through. Most of them flats made of plasterboard, so it ain't that hard to mash, but to me, he's the real Hulk.

'Call I batty?' Bossman yells at Olu. 'I will break you! Watch!'

Olu's got his sleeve on his nose. Blood runs through his fingers, dripping off his elbows. Bossman's fist got blood on it and I don't get it because they're supposed to be bredren. Olu told me Bossman's got our backs so we don't have to fear nothing or nobody.

'Come on, Donny – D-Boy,' Olu says. 'This is whack. Man needs to chill.'

Olu don't look at Bossman and Bossman don't look at him. Olu opens the front door. I don't want to feel like that wall so I'm out of there quick-sticks, except I left my new phone in the kitchen and I ain't leaving without my phone. Olu waits for me outside. He keeps his head back to stop the blood coming out his nose.

Bossman's bench-pressing a stack of weight disks. The tank is moving on the widescreen, explosions hurt my ears. I don't think them boys still got their lives. They restarted the game for sure. I go past them like a ninja to get my phone from the kitchen. Coming back, the girl's still sleeping, but she's turned over and her pants is more down. I see a triangle of black hair. I want to look some more but it don't feel right so I get a blanket to cover her up except the blanket moves and this little arm comes out.

The light from the door's enough to see it's a baby, dressed up all nice in Sunday clothes, wrapped up in a white blanket, most littlest gloves on its hands. I got to smile a bit because them Nike baby creps look better than my Adidas.

Baby looks at me for time. Brown skin, same tone like me. Black curls, same like me, only that girl must use olive oil. Its eyes are grey-blue and I remember mum saying my eyes was blue and I thought she was chatting but now I know she don't lie. Baby thinks I'm funny and starts up laughing so its dummy comes out. Now it's looking at me like that was my fault, asking me a question it needs to know and it don't like waiting for no answer.

Some next bomb goes off on the PlayStation and the boys reload their AK-47s behind a wall. They run out into the street; bullets, ammo, mud, blood and inside-body stuff going all over the shop. Man gets out his knife and shanks some soldier in the neck and I want to turn the sound down because it ain't nice for no baby. That mattress is nasty so I wipe the dummy on my threads – it's okay, they're clean – and put it back in the baby's mouth. I tuck in them blankets and say, 'Bye, bye, baby. I hope you're okay.'

Outside's got too much light. I take down my hood and screw up my eyes till they can see again. We're on the top floor, right where the birds is singing and making their nests, and a bit of me feels like singing and all because I got tagged. I got christened. I'm glad they like me and I like my new name and them lyrics was all for me.

D-Boy. D-Boy. That's me.

I give Olu my new phone so it's safe. I see our bikes is where we left them. Olu was right about respect. They could've walked, but they ain't going nowhere on account of Bossman.

'Who was that girl?' I ask. A car goes by, sound-system on full so I wait till it's gone to finish my question. 'Is she okay? I mean, her pants was out.'

'Chill,' Olu says. He don't look at me. 'She's LaShawna. She had bare trouble with her uncle. She came to us and now she got no trouble.' He frowns. 'She ain't no crackwhore, if that's what you're thinking.'

I think about cracks and monsters and the girl. I tug his sleeve.

'What's a crackwhore?' I say.

Olu snorts. 'For real?' he says, biting his lip. I nod. I want to know. He takes a big breath. 'It's like a girl who, like, gives out, for crack, you get me?'

'Gives out what?'

'Gives out, like – Nah, man,' Olu shakes his head, laughing. 'If you don't know, I ain't going to be the one to say it.'

'Is my mum a crackwhore? I heard people say that.'

Olu shakes his head again. 'No, blood. No! I ain't having that. No one said that. Never.'

'They do though.' I pick up my bike.

'Next time, you come straight to me. Tell me and I'll sort it so they don't never say them things again.'

'And that baby?'

'Safe, man! Got milk. Got bed. Allow it with the questions!'

Olu's blood's gone dark. He picks at it and crust flakes off. I ask if Bossman is our deadly enemy now and if we better start locking up our bikes. Olu laughs but his eyes ain't finding it funny. But after time and we're riding, he goes, 'Relax, fam. He don't mean it. Trust me, Bossman switched for no reason. He gets stressed out sometimes, is all. Man got bare responsibilities. Plenty pressure. We're down ten ounces and he don't like it. Makes him look like a mug. Makes him look weak. But Michael's going to make it right again.'

'What's batty mean?'

'Big Ears, you hear me? Too much questions,' Olu says. 'I don't want to hear them words no more, bruv.' He stops and points his finger in my face. 'Don't go bringing them bad words home, I swear down. Say them words by mama's ears and I swear down!'

Back at our manor, Olu pushes me on the swing till Mama Folu clocks us.

'You are early! Have you eaten already?' she yells out the window. 'And where is Michael?'

She's baked chocolate biscuits and Prince put ten candles on my birthday cake. He ain't even changed out his pyjamas. Olu don't take no biscuits and he don't say nothing to Prince so Mama Folu knows something ain't right. She takes his chin.

'Olufemi, your nose!' she says. 'It has been bleeding.'

Olu chats some next story about an accident, how he'd tripped up teaching me to ride.

'Liar,' she says, winking at me. 'I can tell when you are lying, Olufemi. A mother knows her children. Prince and Donny: do not follow the example of this child. Wear your helmets and look where you are going, not at pretty girls across the street.'

It gets dark and Michael still ain't home. Mama Folu asks Olu what he knows.

'Am I my brother's keeper? I don't know where Michael is,' he says. 'He could be anywhere.'

Mama Folu sends Olu out on his bike to look. He comes back, no Michael, and she closes up her eyes and starts praying.

She calls Michael's phone again. No answer. She tries his friends again. No answer. At eleven o'clock, she calls the police. The door buzzer goes and my belly goes tight. I know them shiny black boots. Me and Prince is supposed to go sleep, but Mama Folu's crying in the kitchen, Police Lady holding her hand. Olu sits in the corridor, head between his knees, shoulders shaking.

'Michael was never involved in that kind of thing. He is just a little boy,' Mama Folu says. 'He is a good boy.'

I can hear some words, other times it's whispers. Police Lady talks slow like she's trying so hard to be nice. She says Michael's at the East Surrey now and the South London coroner's going to see him. There's going to be something called a *post mortem* and an *inquest* which means Mama Folu's got to make an appointment if she wants to see Michael and be sure she brings ID.

I hope he's okay and comes home soon because he's missing out on bare cake. We ain't been Nando's yet and I know he was getting happy about that. As well, I been ten for time and they ain't even sang the birthday song.

Police Lady gets up and we leg it to our beds. The front door's locked, unlocked, locked again then left open like Mama Folu thinks maybe Michael forgot his key again.

Mama Folu comes in, fixes Prince's cover and kisses his head. I squeeze my eyes shut. She lifts my cover over my feet and pulls the door to so the room goes dark except for a thin line of light from the corridor. I wait a long minute and creep out.

Olu is washing mugs, one hand holding the sink like he'd fall if it weren't there. Mama Folu tells him to stop and look at her. I ain't never heard her talk like this. Her words is slow, her whole body trembling, and for a bit all she says is, 'Michael, Michael, Michael, Michael ...'

Olu tries to put his arm round her and she switches.

'You were loved, sweet Jesus,' she says. 'You were loved! Why? Why this?'

'Mama, I'm ...'

'Your father!'

Olu makes himself go high and looks down on her. 'Get real, mama. You think I don't know about dad? That he worked a cab? Not even licensed?'

Mama Folu steps to him, chest going like she's trying hard to breathe.

'How dare you!'

'What about you, mama? You never said no to the money. You took it, time. Don't tell me you didn't know. You knew and you told yourself you didn't know. It put food on our table when the benefit messed up and we had to wait weeks. It got us fifty quid a pop shoes for school. Got take-out. Got widescreen TV. Made the pastor all "thank-you-sister" to you at church.'

'Olufemi, you were not raised to disrespect your elders.' Mama Folu's voice sounds weak.

Olu scowls. 'Well, ain't you mum of the year,' he says, lips close in on her face. She sits herself back down, lows her head and twists her gold ring round her finger.

'You told me you were promoted to assistant manager,' she goes in a whisper. 'Sweet Jesus! You lied to me.'

Prince wakes. He tiptoes out and joins me in the hall.

'Get real, mama,' Olu says again, louder this time. 'You still believe in fairies. You always believe there's a thing like a career ahead of me, even when my grades was crap and I got excluded. I seen what's ahead of me: zero, man. Zero hours, working like a mug – like dad. I'm not a mug. Yeah, you believe in fairies, mama. Jesus and freaking fairies.'

Olu walks the kitchen up and back. His voice goes even louder. Prince takes my hand and I don't let it go. Olu digs at his wet eyes which makes it worse. Man needs a tissue.

91

'And you still believe,' he goes on, 'even after dad passed, that a poor man, a Black man, can make it in this country if he only work hard and trust in Jesus. Wake up, Mama! I was born here but this ain't my home. Yeah, they like it when we sing and dance and stick a ball in the back of a net. But can't you see, Mama? They don't want us here, not really. They're cool with us when we're little, and then, when we get grown, they hold tight their bags, and switch seats on the bus, and they cross the street like they going to get jacked. They take one look at our name – "Oh my gosh, Adeola. Sounds foreign!" – and put the application in the trash. They hide all the career ladders they ever got given and say to us, "Black man! You tripping? We ain't never had no ladders! You know whites is just good at jumping!" And time and time and time after again they tell us what we missing – the car, the creps, the clothes, the tech – and then they tell us, "No! You ain't never going to get it 'cause you ain't good enough." No way! We got to make our own business.'

'What about the addicts? Donny's mother?'

'Mama.' Olu sounds like he's trying to get through to a small child who won't heed him. 'They choose it. They get what they ask for. It's like a service. Come on now. Plenty things kill and people get rich. Cigarette company get rich selling people cancer; government cool with that. Tell me, what's the difference? *Tell me!* Liquor kill. Diesel kill. Sugar kill. Plenty kill. I never hurt no one what don't want hurting.'

'But this? But Michael? My Michael? *Michael?*' She's screaming now.

'Yeah, this. Yeah, Michael.' Olu turns his back on her.

They so vex up about Michael, I'm frit he's going to get licks when he comes home, even though Mama Folu ain't like that.

Prince whispers to me, 'Brother's going to get grounded for this.' And I think he's right, on account of doing so much stupidness he got to sleep round East Surrey all night. 'And maybe she ain't even going to let him come with us when we do get to go Nando's,' Prince goes. 'Maybe he's going to have to wait by home.'

'No, man,' I say. 'Your mum's bare soft. She won't stay vex at him. Not for long.'

'But if she do, me and you can fix it so we bring him a bit of chicken anyways, wrap it in paper or something, and bring it him?'

'We can try, but it'll be greasy. Need some tissue ready. You carry it, Prince man. I ain't putting it in my Adidas.'

Tears run down Olu's chin. Mama Folu's got fat tears and all. She makes like she's going to touch Olu but her hands go back on her knees. She takes a deep breath in and tries again and this time she strokes his cheek.

'They're taking Donny tomorrow,' she says.

Prince looks big eyes at me. He squeezes my hand.

'There will be no more boys,' she says. 'Not now.'

'Good. I don't know why you do it for,' goes Olu.

'*Be not forgetful to entertain strangers, for thereby some have entertained angels unawares.*'

Olu snorts. 'Angels? Ain't no angels here. We're living in hell.'

She strokes Olu's face like she's stroking a real-alive angel. Her hand drops.

'You must go in the morning, early. Go before I rise.'

'No,' he says. 'You need me. I want to see Michael. I'm coming with you to see him. I want to say goodbye.'

'No, Olufemi, I will not allow it. You must go in the morning. Do you understand me? Pack your things now. You go before I rise.'

'But, mama –'

'I have only one son now and his name is Prince. You will not see him. You will not touch him. He is mine and I will not let him go.'

It's still dark out. Olu touches my shoulder.

'Little man, D-Boy,' he says. I sit up. Olu puts a phone under my pillow. 'Santa come early. Don't tell no one you got it.'

In it, he says, is all the numbers I'll ever need. I don't know what he means but he says it's all done now. Over. Finished. This shit has gone too far, he says, and it's time for grown-ups to step up. He looks at Prince, sleeping on the top bunk, and leaves.

At breakfast, the pastor's praying, and there's more of them church ladies what can even fit in one kitchen. Ain't no food cooking neither. Children's Services Man turns up and, tell the truth, I ain't sad to go; devil and sin talk is starting to frit me. Man helps me pack, sticks mum's letters on top of my threads and zips up my bag.

'Precious boy,' Mama Folu says when it's time to bounce. 'Little angel.' She ain't creamed her face; grey lines show which way her tears went. 'Go be a good boy now. Jesus keep you safe and love you, always.'

Her smile's fake. She smooths my hair and does up my coat.

Police people on the balcony and stairs look the other way when we pass. I get my bike.

'We can't take it,' Children's Services Man says. 'Leave it for now.'

'Where's Michael?' I ask.

'I'll explain everything,' he goes. Only, he don't explain nothing. No one don't explain nothing. No one ever does.

We go round the back of the estate to the car park. Police vans is double-parked, lights still flashing, so we sit in his car, waiting on them to shift. I remember my homework on the side.

'Don't fret about your homework,' he goes. 'None of this is your fault. You won't be in any trouble. They'll give you a new book when you start your next school.'

'So I can go live with mum now? We're going to go get mum, right? You know she can look after me now.'

He takes a deep breath and I know that look. I seen it time.

'Donny,' he goes, 'it's not that simple. We'll talk it through with your key worker. Don't worry about anything. I'll explain everything,' he says again, explaining jack.

I take out Olu's phone and open the contacts. It's only got one entry, his name: Adeola.

Chapter 8

I lived for time in a children's home in Islington, waiting and waiting for two fat years before they say mum's ready to look after me again. Then we're back together, in Hackney where we belong. Our new flat's by the canal, near the locks where they move bare water up and down. But it don't last. It don't never last.

It's not like we're in them new flats what look over the water, but we're only one block away. You can smell the canal from here: oil, ice cream, beer. One last street and the cobble track goes down where buses and cars ain't allowed and the boats line up – red, blue, green – and you can hear the water birds getting hyped up on their own beefs.

'Let me do it,' I say because my Children's Services Lady thinks I'm weak and starts carrying my bags out her car. I look up at the lines of balconies. 'So which one?'

'25C.'

Mum's waiting for me. She looks old. Her face is lined. Peoples is going to say she's my nan at parents' evening. She mashes her cigarette in a cup and kneels down, arms out and I run.

Except this feeling starts up and before I get to her, I stop. I look back at my Lady. I don't want to go back to the residential, but …

'Don,' mum goes. 'Don.'

I been waiting and wishing on this for time, wanting it, crying for it but I got this drag in me, like a sea anchor.

'Don,' mum says again.

I lean in and she puts her arms round my head. She smells of fags and feels like chicken bones wrapped in a bit of the *Metro* newspaper. It don't feel right and I hate missing Mama Folu after all this time, but when she hugged me up it weren't like this. It was more like softness and cocoa butter.

'Don,' mum says. 'Don. I won't leave you.'

Her voice cracks. She's crying. I try wriggling free but she ain't going to let me.

'Why don't we go inside, Mrs Samson?' says my Lady.

'We'll be all right now, thanks,' says mum. She pushes me in by the back of my head, squeezes herself through the door and says, 'Thanks very much, miss. Thank you.'

'I need to come in too,' the Lady says through the letterbox. A whine comes from the kitchen. I know mum's trying to keep her voice light, but it comes out funny.

'Been checked a million times,' mum says through the letterbox. 'We're all right. Don's bed came this morning and the cooker's working. Ten quid's on the meter. I expect you'll be ever so busy, won't you? What with all them austerity cuts they done. Go on and help some people what really need you.'

'Mrs Samson?'

'Thank you, miss.'

Kitchen door opens and a Staffie pup skids to my feet. I drop to fuss him. He flips over, kicking my knees, and starts going mental in circles.

'We're going to have to put mats down, Don,' mum says, laughing. 'Torvill here can't cope.'

'Torvill?'

'Like Torvill and Dean? They was famous ice skaters, back in the day.'

'Come, Torvill!' I say, trying it out on him. 'We could call him Leroy. That's my middle name and dad's name, innit.'

'Yeah,' she says. Her shoulders go stiff. But dogs can lick vexation clean off of people and she starts up laughing.

'I like the name Torvill,' I say. Long time later, I find out mum got it wrong. It was Jayne Torvill and Christopher Dean what did the ice skating, but Torvill don't care if he's got a girl's name.

Torvill jacks my left crep and shows me round the flat with it in his mouth and I don't even care it's got dog spit on it because this is the most bestest place me and mum ever had. She shows me a sofa what turns into a little bed and says that's where she's going to kip.

'This'll be your bed, then,' she says, kicking a massive cardboard box in the bedroom. She puts her hands on her hips. 'Ain't going to make itself, is it? You're a big boy. Help your old mum.'

We lay out poles and bolts and instructions on the floor and put Torvill in the kitchen because he ain't no help at all. When the bed's made we lie on it, Torvill and all, and mum says we don't need nobody else but us. She starts up asking questions she knows the answers to and some she don't.

'Got a girlfriend?'

'Mum!'

'You're blushing.'

'No, I ain't.'

'You are.'

'No, I ain't.'

'Course you ain't. You're twelve. Girls don't look at twelve-year-olds anyways.'

'Might do.'

'Might.' She looks more young when she laughs.

'Mum,' I ask. 'Are you better?'

'Yes, Don.' She strokes my hair. It's grown out since Peckham. Feels weird at first, someone touching me for no reason. I ain't sick. I ain't dropped. I ain't scored no goal neither. I put my head under her arm and I can't help it, I start up crying and all the time mum strokes my head.

'Will you remember me in a year, Don?'

Now that is some dumbarse question. It twists a knot in my belly. I ain't forgotten her in the two years she's been inside, have I?

'Answer it. Go on, Don.'

'I ain't never going to forget you. You know that.'

'Thank you. Will you remember me in a month? Just answer it, Don.'

'Okay. Yes.'

'Will you remember me in a week?'

'Yes.' I'm starting to get vex now.

'Will you remember me in an hour?'

'Yes. What is this?'

'Will you remember me in a minute?'

'Yes.'

'Will you remember me in a second?'

'All right!'

'Knock, knock.'

'What?'

'It's a joke, Don. You got to say, who's there? Try again. Knock, knock.'

'Who's there?'

'You forgot me already? Jesus Christ! What are you like?'

I know it's funny but I ain't laughing. Mum wipes up my crying and rubs my back and says, 'You know I love you more than anything.'

'Not more than dope, you don't,' I say because I ain't a mug no more.

Mum holds my shoulders and shakes me when she says, 'Yes, more than anything. I'm clean.' She holds my face like I might smash to bits if she drops me. 'I've beaten it. We got to celebrate!' She gets out her purse. 'Chicken shop or Maccy D's?' she says and I tell Torvill to give me my crep back, quick-sticks. I want to go back to our chicken shop on Mare Street, where we used to live. But mum says we ain't going back there, never again, because it's always going to be better than that now. We got big plans and we can't know what's round the corner.

We wait at the number 30 bus stop because Maccy D's too long by feet, but mum clocks something and goes pale. A skinny little white man is looking at us and I know what's angsting her now. Marcus. She says we got to walk to the next stop now, which makes no sense at all because by the time you get to the next stop you might as well walk it all anyway. I get vex-up because this is going to take long and I'm hungry. I walk slow to piss her off. Mum gripses my arm to make me go more faster. She looks over her shoulder. Marcus skips our stop and all, following us in a little jog and waving like we should be glad to see him.

I ain't glad. My fists ball, thumbs on the outside, and I think, Now I'm big, can I defend her if it comes to it?

'What's he want?' I say.

'I got this,' mum goes, hand on my back. She pushes me across the street and a van driver winds down his window and calls her a cow because we walk out and don't look first and he has to put his foot on the brake. Mum sticks her middle finger up at him and van man goes, 'Dirty slag!'

I want to kill him for saying that but his engine goes loud and he's gone in a cloud of diesel blackness.

When the smoke clears, Marcus is crossing the road.

'Want to go flying, Jadie?' he goes. 'First rock's free.' He smiles at me with hardly no teeth in his mouth. 'Donny, my man, you've grown. Why the frown, boy?'

'Don,' mum warns me. 'Don't say nothing.'

'Don't be like that, Jadie. You know what?' goes Marcus. 'It's your lucky day. You got no idea how pure this is and for you, my darling, it's buy one, get one free, all year.'

'You can BOGOF and all,' mum goes. 'Go on, bugger off.'

But he don't listen. He touches her hand.

'Get out my face,' mum says. 'Leave us alone. You come near me or my son and I swear I'll do time for you.'

102

'She'll come back, Donny,' he says, grinning at me. 'And she'll do more time, sooner or later. You know she will.'

We run to the next bus stop and this time he don't follow. I tap my Oyster. Mum ain't brung hers so she gets in the middle doors and sits at the back. She wipes her eyes and tries to smile.

'Mum, I swear down I want to kill him. We should've brung Torvill. Torvill would bite his balls off.'

'Mind your language, Don. Anyway, Torvill's a pup. He would only lick him. Listen, calm down. I can handle Marcus. You and me got plans and they don't involve him. We got plans. Real plans.'

She puts her arm round me. 'Ain't this nice?' she goes. She tries to hide it but her body is shaking. 'I been waiting on this for so long. Just me and you, so don't you let him spoil it, Don.'

She holds my hand, cuts of white on her wrists so everyone can see because she don't bother wearing long sleeves. Her teeth don't look good neither because some ain't there, though not so bad as Marcus. Back at the flat, making the bed, it weren't nothing. She looks how she looks. But two streets from the academy I got the uniform for but ain't even been in yet, I look in case anyone I knowed from primary's about. I feel a pulse start up in my neck.

We get a table in McDonald's. Mum gets me a Happy Meal and I play with the toy even though I'm too big for it. Mum says she ain't hungry and watches me eat, drumming the table with her fingers. I remember what she said about my birthday, about the cinema and popcorn and Nando's.

'Can we go see this film, mum?' I say, holding up the toy. I ain't even serious. It's only some stupid kid film. But mum's face twists. She's starting to hurt again and I want to stop her hurting. I say, 'Forget it, mum. I was only joking.'

It's too late.

'Think I'm made of money?' she goes. 'Think we got a pound tree growing in the toilet? Make up your mind, Don. You telling me you want Marcus back in our lives? I don't know what you think I am.'

Two girls on the next table stare. They might be twelve like me or they might be sixteen. You can't never tell with girls when they got make-up on. 'What you looking at?' mum says to them, on her feet.

'Mum, don't,' I say because they might go to the academy. They might be in my year. 'Leave it, mum.'

'What you laughing at?' mum goes, stepping in them girls' faces. One of them looks mum up and down and sucks her teeth.

'Crackhead,' she says, and the manager lady comes.

I close my eyes and see LaShawna and her little baby wrapped up in blankets. I see deep cracks right down to the earth's core, and all them monsters is licking their lips, hungry for us.

Take a walk down Regent's Canal to Vickie Park and you got London for what it is; people mixed in with bricks and trees and boats and water. They got mutant lobsters and turtles and even birds of prey. I swear down, ospreys stop off on the canal for a fat carp or perch on their way up to Scotland and bird people get bare happy looking in their binoculars. Walk them endz to London Fields and you'll see white people drinking coffee and eating food from all kind of countries, but mostly donkey kind of wraps: fajita wraps, burrito wraps, kebab wraps, pulled pork wraps, falafel wraps, jerk wraps. City mans pull up their Porsches and get white wraps from Youngers on bikes and don't nobody know because they keep it so smart, grass cut short and lock gates painted black and white.

Next left's the Hertford Union Canal.

Back in the day, me and mum ain't never gone that way because it goes to Tottenham, and like anyone from Hackney or Islington knows, don't nobody want to go there.

Keep walking on the Regent's to Limehouse, and if you ain't paying attention and go left, you get to Limehouse Cut and that don't go no place, except the Lea. You know you're in Limehouse Cut because they start playing Bhangra from the flats and the curry smell starts up your belly rumbling. Canal water's rank that way; I seen a dead rat floating in the oily ballast them boat hippies dash in the water, there's piles of crap on the offside bank and most barges don't have no one looking out for them. When a coot makes her nest in a tyre fender, that shows how much that boat don't move. It's the same with flats. Fat pigeon makes his nest on a new balcony means ain't nobody living there. Them flats is for people what don't live in London but still want a bit of it.

When me and mum lived near the canal it weren't nothing at all seeing that and other stuff, like the island we go to when it's nice out. It ain't a real island but a lock with some grass and water nearly all the way round. Today we sit there and watch the fishing mans trying their luck with a fly and make out like we're on a boat. Flat black water on one side, the other's white and racing and if the water's locked out upstream on the King's Cross side, the drop's more than from a first-floor window. I don't know how that lock gate keeps it in. It's only made of wood. And I think, What if it broke?

When we're done, we walk up the cobbles to that off-licence by the Fields.

'Come on, Don,' mum goes. 'Let's go in the offie and get us an ice cream.'

London Fields ice cream cost two quid plus and I want dinner later, so I say thank you but I don't fancy it no more. Mum goes in anyway, thinking shop man's going to be like Erdan but he ain't. I wait outside so I don't see what happens.

She comes out rubbing her wrists. 'All right! I'm sorry,' she goes. 'Keep your bloody hair on.'

Shop man shouts at her and puts the Sunny D she took back in the fridge. I don't care about ice cream but something bothers me. 'Thought you was getting Mint Cornetto?' I say. 'You know I hate Sunny D. What was you doing?'

'You're my baby boy,' she goes, little smile on her face. 'I know what you like.'

We go back to the towpath and sit on a bench looking at them barges float by and mum brings out two Mint Cornettos the shop man ain't seen. They gone soft in her pockets and drip down our fingers.

Mum says the next boat's a City boy party because they're all white banker mans dressed up like Michael Jackson, sweating in afro wigs. I ask her how she knows and she goes, 'I know them types. I worked in places they go.'

I feel sorry for them because my 'fro is mighty and real and they ain't got no ice cream neither. None of them is having a time like us.

'Don?'

'What?'

'You happy, babes?'

I know what she's getting at but I want it from her so I ask, 'What do you mean?'

She laughs like I just made some joke. 'I don't know. Like, you okay? Like, now?'

I nearly say, 'Maybe, I don't know,' but when I think about it some more I change up my mind. 'Yes, mum,' I say. 'This is happy.'

Because we got bare reasons for happy now, more than we got fingers to count it. We got nice sun on our faces and them coots is hooting like they do and the Regent's Canal on a hot day is just about the most nicest place you can be. The water acts like some big-up fridge, cooling up the air so you don't sweat like you do on the street. Or maybe it's the vibe and all the peoples liming slow because it's their day off or their lunchtime and they don't need to hurry no place quick. Or maybe it's the smell of them canal boats and all. It's different. Nothing like buses and cars and lorries. It ain't a smell you forget. It's like all them boats know they're going somewhere far away and all them cars is stuck on the street waiting for the lights to change. And also, I'm happy because mum's proper smiling and she peels my Cornetto for me like back in the day and makes sure all my chocolate bits get off the lid and on my ice cream before she gives it me. And maybe it's because she done all that and her hands don't shake at all, not once.

That last bit's not a maybe. It's mostly all because of that.

'You know what, Don? I think I'm happy, right now.' She looks at her fingers like she just got her nails done. 'This is what happy is. Get this: I ain't in no pain. Nothing hurts. Know what that means?'

'You're better?'

'Yes. But no as well. It's more than that. I feel … like me before. Happy.'

'That what you call happy? Not hurting?'

'I suppose. I don't know no words for what it's like. I don't want you to ever even know. You ain't a little kid no more so I can tell you a bit. What I was taking, it brings total pain when you stop. It's everything, like the whole world is paining you and there's nowhere to go, and – I don't want you to ever know what that's like. I promise you, I ain't going back there. I got big plans for us, babes, and I ain't letting nothing stop us. I know I said this before and again more times, and every time I mean it just the same. But this time, I know this is it.'

'I'm proud of you, mum.' And I hold her hand which messes up the day because now I've gone and made her cry. 'It's okay, mum,' I go and I mean it because it is.

Boats cut their engines for the day and the canal goes quiet. Skinny bird brings up a fish and I remember Mama Folu saying, even though them birds don't reap nor sow – saying like they ain't got no dollars – they do okay.

And that's how me and mum is. Torvill runs like some mad donkey because he don't care, mum gets what we need and that's how we roll.

Only, I get this feeling I need to step up. It don't do trying to decide between ice cream and dinner. Or dinner and the lekkie. I got to start bringing in some dollars.

First day at my academy, mum gets my new blazer and holds it out like I'm starting primary. It's got the same phoenix as Peckham because them academies is like Subway or Sainsbury's; there's loads more than one of them. My one's called North Academy and that's what's written in gold letters. It crackles with static when I try it on.

I think of Michael and Bossman, telling him to wear school uniform. *Get me Harry. The full Hogwarts.*

'You don't have to take me to school no more, mum,' I say. 'I'm thirteen.'

'Think I don't know how old you are? I gave birth to you.'

'Nearly thirteen, then,' I say.

Mum walks me to the 30 bus stop. She should turn round and go home because she's wearing a vest and pyjama bottoms, but she gets on the bus and goes on about the interviews she's got lined up. She says she going to have a job by the end of today and by Christmas I'm going to be sitting in a cinema with a new phone in my hand and fresh creps on my feet.

The bus stops across the road from the student entrance. She gets off, goes to kiss me and I turn away. There's bare kids coming in, even though it's after registration time.

'Work hard, Don,' she goes. 'And stick some bog roll in your bag, will you, love?'

'Allow it, mum.'

'What? We're nearly out.'

'Mum!'

'All right, I'm joking. I'll get some at my interview. Bound to be a bog there somewhere. Joking! Come here, tell me, Don …'

'What is it? I'm late.'

'How did I get a son what's so much smarter than I ever was? How did that happen, eh?'

I cross the road and don't look back going into school because I want it to be like I came in on my ones. I don't mean to but I can't help it; at the last second, when the doors slide shut, I look. A lorry's waiting in traffic and I think mum's gone. But it moves on and she's there where I left her. She got one hand up and she's smiling, the way she done at primary school and I pray she ain't still there at three o'clock.

They brung down the old school here when I was away down south in Peckham and it cost something like five billion to put it back up again, only in glass like them City towers. Every wall's got glass so it'll take bare skills to bunk. I look around. There ain't no place to blaze, no place to trade snacks, no place to play money-up for the chicken shop after school.

The playground ain't the same as when I walked this way to primary school. They've put up MUGA cages, laid down astro and planted a friendship garden with trees you can tag in biro because the bark's white like paper and peels. They planted nice bushes by the student entrance, though one got burned. Luckily, them kids what torched it weren't no good at lighting fires so new leaves is already sprouting out the top. Kids stick Red Bull cans and Lucozade down the water tubes they got by every tree. Looks a bit like flowers if you don't stand too close.

By the end of my first week there I find out bare things, like how the fence paint is anti-climb. It don't never dry, so when your ball goes over, you got to shout, 'Oi! Sir man! Excuse me! My ball!' to grown-ups what ain't teachers. Then it's up to them if they kick it back or act like we're ghosts and there ain't never been no school here.

Everything's changed up except the kids. The plasterboard soon cracks, screws unscrew, locker doors come off and hard drives get jacked or hacked. About the only thing what don't break is the glass. It won't matter what's dashed – bags, chairs, hole punch, Mohsun in Year Ten and he ain't light – them glass walls don't crack.

I see bare peoples from my primary. We bump fists when we go by, but plenty other kids I knowed from primary don't come here. They move out of London, or go to some boarding school where you sleep and you can't go home for time. I know how they feel.

I seen Seb from primary kicking a ball with his dad in the park, but he don't lime round the chicken shop after school. His dad acts like he don't know me no more. He don't remember he lined up the ramp for me at Archway Bowling so I don't waste my balls down the gutter. He forgets I been round his big-up house for birthday parties and played with Seb in the kitchen and he laughed at me when I asked, 'Why's there nothing but a kitchen in your flat?' and he told me all their other rooms was upstairs and I could go see. I remember the heated floors they got, what make your feet sweat, and their yard grass what's like a park, except it got no needles because they don't share it with nobody else.

And it turns out it's the same with them mums from primary I knowed. They forgot they heard me read when they was parent helpers. They all said I was the best at reading because I was. Now they look at me like I ain't there and I'm wondering if I changed up so much, or was it them?

So all this goes to say, I'm glad of Kasim because, except for tagging himself K, he ain't changed. When I call round after school my first day, his mum unlocks the bolts.

'Donny!'

'*Foulard, maman*,' Kasim goes, 'put on your headscarf.' He pushes past her, grinning at me. He's gone tall in the time I been gone but his face is still primary.

'*Mais, Kasim*,' Mrs Zidane says, '*c'est Donny*.' It's only Donny.

'*Tout de même, il a treize ans.* You're thirteen now, ain't you, Donny?'

Mrs Zidane puts on her headscarf anyway. She don't speak much, but she smiles a lot and I always liked her. She don't need to keep putting her hand over her mouth when she smiles but that's her way.

Me and Kasim played here since time, since nursery, since we was babies. Mum used to leave me round his yard when she needed to be somewhere so I know his four brothers and now he's got a baby sister and all. Their flat's got two bedrooms. Kasim and the twins got one, his bigger brothers the other, and the sofa in the sitting room flips out into a bed like a Transformer, but without the weapons. That's where they sleep, Mrs Z and the baby.

'Dad comes weekends. We go Alton Towers,' Kasim says. 'Next year he's taking us to Disneyland in America. But he's got to work, you get me?'

His big brother looks up from his phone and snorts.

'It ain't always going to be like this,' Kasim says. 'I got a trial with the Gunners so when I go professional, I'm going to buy a house and another house next door for maman and Ghislaine. But my bros can do their own thing, you get me? I ain't keeping them.' I nod. If I could play like Kasim I would do that too. He looks sideways at his brother. 'But maybe I would get them a season ticket *if* they was bare nice to me. I don't think big-club players pay for season tickets out their own money.'

'They don't,' I say, because what kind of club is going to make their pros pay for their fam? 'Get me one too?'

Kasim grins and gives me his fist and I feel dumb for even asking.

Kasim's uniform's lent down from his brothers, but his creps is fresh from the box and I know how he's going to style himself when he's playing pro.

'*Maman*,' Kasim goes. He acts a cup to his lips. 'Get my friend a drink.'

I tell him about South London. 'Peckham's not as frit as mandem say,' I go. 'And my foster mum was bare nice.' I don't say nothing about Michael.

Mrs Z comes back with a gold tray and gives us mint tea and sugar. She smiles at us and I know she's happy to see me again. Kasim totally blanks her, so I say, 'Thank you, Mrs Z.' I don't think she hears me though.

'You got no manners, K man,' I say when she's gone. 'Show your mum some respect.'

Kasim shakes his head and says, 'I don't need to thank no one. I treat her good.' He shows me his paper, a handful of five spots. 'I'm just a roadman, come in on my own. Don't judge me, man.'

113

We play Fifa and Mrs Z's cooking smells proper nice. Kasim tells me I can stay and eat if I like. That's what should've happened but it don't because his phone dings.

'London Fields is paying out twenty for a ped. We can go halves. Come,' he says, and I think about how mum would smile when she comes home and finds the meter clocked up to ten pounds. I'd tell her, 'Maybe it's them lekkie fairies?' and she'd know it was me in real life and wrap me in one of them hugs she got when she's bare happy.

We dash down Cally and wait by the petrol pumps. A couple of motorbikes roll up, but people ain't dumb. They take their keys with them when they pay.

Then this Ped Lady comes. She lifts the seat and fills the tank, and she's about to lock her tank when her phone rings. She tries answering it but she's holding way too much – bag, purse, keys – so she gives up and puts her keys down. She's still chatting on her phone when she goes into the kiosk.

I take the helmet, make it look like it's mine, no rush. It flops, straps too stiff to change. Man looks at us like we're too young to ride.

'What?' Kasim says, screw-facing him. 'Wasteman!'

Black Cab Man rams his horn. We're on the wrong side of the road and Kasim don't even know he's playing chicken. He jerks the ped to the left, pulls down the accelerator and tries a wheelie to show he meant it and he don't care. Suspension makes it feel like them wheels get air but they ain't never left the tarmac.

Kasim don't care about red lights and yellow junctions but I'm glad he knows Hackney; he don't take Dalston Lane, too

114

much feds. We do Richmond Road all the way to the Fields. We're nearly there when the street goes yellow and blue and we hear a siren.

'Lose the helmet,' Kasim says.

Easy. Mine just slips off. Kasim walks the ped round till we're facing a police car on its ones. He holds his helmet up.

'Dash it!' Kasim orders and them helmets roll like ten pin under the car. 'Strike!' Kasim laughs and spins the ped. Down the road, we look back. They ain't moved. One's got gloves on. He puts the helmets in plastic bags like he's CSI.

'They ain't allowed to follow us now,' Kasim says. 'Yo! Wasteman!' he shouts at them and looks at me. 'You know we is bare lucky?' he says. 'If this was State-side, we'd be smoked. US Feds packing and they don't like Black people.'

'But Kasim, man, you're white.'

He looks hurt. 'No, blood. I'm African. North African, innit.'

'But you got white skin, man.'

'Allow it,' he says. 'I ain't white.'

Kasim pulls away and we're gone.

'You got green eyes though. Blond hair. Why's that?'

'French soldiers, innit,' he goes. 'Back in the day. Maghreb still counts as Black, innit.'

'Only saying, bruv.'

And we go back to saying this line we always had, back in primary after we heard it one day from some big kids on the street. 'Don't call me bruv, bruv!' he goes and then I go, 'I ain't your bruv, bruv!' and we start up laughing.

'Allow it, man,' he says when we get to London Fields and ride over the grass. 'This is business. Grow up.'

London Fields crew is in the middle of the park where there ain't no streetlights. Kasim tries to spin the bike in front of them boys, but the engine stalls and they think it's funny.

'Mandem wanted a ped,' Kasim goes. He pats the tank. 'Got a nice one for you.'

'Seriously?' some boy says, frowning at us. '50cc? You think we're mugs? You trying to mug us off?'

All them crew boys laugh. Kasim looks at his feet. I don't think he done this before. He never knowed there was an engine size we got to find.

'Allow it,' Kasim says. 'There weren't exactly time to say, "Excuse me, miss, but how many ccs your ped got?" before we jacked it.'

'Safe, blood,' Topboy goes, putting his arm round Kasim. 'It'll do.'

He gets on the ped, picks a henchman to ride behind and gives him a bottle of OneShot what says on the label there ain't no drain it can't unblock. I ask Kasim why they unblocking sinks for but he don't know neither.

Them boys, Topboy and his henchman, ride over the grass and out of sight and the crew boys get happy, saying they're going to come back with bare dollars.

'What they doing with drain stuff?' I ask one of them boys I know from my school. He's in Year Ten, I see him with the learning mentors in the library going over the Easy Readers.

'Don't sweat,' he goes. 'They ain't even going to open it, guarantee. Uber mans keep bare cash in their taxis. Topboy only got to show them the acid and they ain't going to say no.'

116

That still don't answer my question but I don't like to ask no more.

'So can we get our twenty now?' Kasim says, quiet because most of them boys is big, like sixteen or seventeen, and he don't want to piss them off.

'Blood, chill,' my Year Ten goes.

'Please?'

'Allow it. Wait up for them to come back. You get your money when you lose the ped. You have to do this mission. You have to do it. Then you move up.'

I can hear them white peoples laughing outside the pub, the other side of the park. I don't know why they're laughing for; their bikes don't even got gears and I swear down, I will never get why they don't buy nice cars when they got the dollars.

'Man on!' some boy goes and we see the ped come back. Youngers start getting happy but their faces soon drop. The ped tips and henchman rolls in the grass, no care for his threads.

'Shit!' he goes, holding his arm. 'Jesus, it hurts!'

I don't want to be here no more. I shouldn't never have come.

Topboy tries to get the plastic glove off henchman's hand but it's stuck and henchman boy screams like his hand is on fire even though there ain't no blood.

'What you crying for?' Topboy goes to him, getting vex.

White people at the pub go quiet. This beardy man stands up to see. His lady friend touches his arm but he blanks her. I know what he sees – a ped on the grass, Youngers in hoodies, bandanas, bike masks. He ain't going to do nothing.

117

'What?' one of them boys spits at the man, arms out. 'Bring it! Wasteman!'

Beardy Man jumps on his phone. His lady friend pulls his sleeve, says something that makes him lay down his phone on the table, in the open, like he don't care nobody could jack it. Like he don't care the London Fields Boys is right there.

Henchman's proper crying now, yelling for his mum. Them gloves is for medical people what got big-man hands, like for protection against Ebola. But they don't work against acid. Skin peels off with the glove and it's like meat under. I throw up but nothing comes because I last ate at school lunch and that was time ago. Kasim looks more whiter than usual, shaking like he's cold so I tell him he don't got to worry because Topboy's nearly a grown-up. He's going to know what to do.

Topboy gets a bottle of water and tips it over the boy's hand. He screams.

'Call an ambulance, man!'

'No,' goes Topboy. 'Are you dumb? You want to get arrested?' He gripses henchman's shoulder and shakes him. 'Idiot, man! Are you dumb, blood? Are you dumb?'

Topboy's eyes go red. His nose is running. I think he's going to cry.

Them peoples outside the pub laugh louder. It sounds fake, like they're pretending we ain't here and this ain't happening. People is good at doing that in London.

Topboy wipes his face on his bandana and points at me and Kasim. 'Why you jokers still here for? Lose the ped, man,' he goes. 'Burn it out by the canal. Police soon going to be all over the shop.'

'Come on, D-boy,' Kasim says. He climbs on and starts the engine. I don't like getting on the ped in case I get burned up and all, but I don't see no way to get back neither and them postcodes between here and home is raw. 'Let's split.'

Kasim turns to the canal path and we pass them pub tables.

'Hold up,' I say because I clock Beardy Man.

Kasim skids and I run back to the tables to find my man. I pull back my hood and them ladies what flick long yellow hair when they laugh go quiet like they're scared of me.

'Sir man,' I say. 'Can you call an ambulance, please?'

He nods. I tell him thanks but I don't think he hears me.

'What the hell, Donny? Do you even know him?' Kasim says when I get on the ped.

'Mr Headley,' I lie. 'My old Tutor Man.'

'And you pick now?'

The ped hits the cobbles hard down the towpath and I don't like it at all. I pray Kasim ain't smoked too much weed today because I can't swim and ain't nobody seen the bottom, not even them policeman divers when they was looking for that lady. 'Oi! Diver Man!' I ask the diver man that time. 'What can you see?' and he says nothing but black and he don't know a trolley's even there till it smacks him in the face. And after three days they pack up and go home and that lady ain't found for time. A dredger brung up her bones hooked up in bike wheels and them Iceland trolleys people jack for their pound. She been in there so long her skin was leather. I ain't seen that with my own eyes but that's what people said when they put up the forensic tent and taped off the towpath. I thought it was some Younger shanked again.

We go by canal boats covered in all kinds of shit. They got their whole lives living out on the water: bikes, plants, canoes, firewood, sacks of coal, wet clothes and everything. Kasim revs the engine at people and they stand back to let us pass. Some bridges is so low they could take your head clean off your shoulders so we stop and push. Ain't no warning, just signs saying, *Be More Turtle, Less Hare*, and on the next bridge, *Share the Space, Less Haste*. Council should build them bridges higher.

Next sign says Islington Canal Tunnel and I know them trees and yellow bricks all crumbling. This is where the canal goes down into a black hole and there's no more path.

'What we going to do now?' I say because this is a proper dead end and we're going to be dead and all if we don't lose the ped.

'Dump or blaze. You choose,' Kasim goes. He ain't smiling. We both know the greens ain't coming.

'Dump it,' I say because I don't like fire that much.

We push it to the water. The front wheel drops but the frame's hooked. We try lifting and pushing. It won't move. The water won't take it.

'Light it, then,' Kasim says. He gives me matches and backs off to the steps up. The first stick fizzes and goes out. Kasim's already at the road.

'Matches are wet, man,' I say, but he's gone.

I knock on a canal-boat window. Inside they got a fire burning and candles and this lady's reading a book because she don't got lekkie for TV or nothing. She looks up and I wave.

'Can I borrow a light please, miss?' I ask.

She grins. 'You're too young to smoke.'

I shrug and try the next boat. Man comes to the hatch and gives me a lighter just like that and I think, Grown-ups should be more careful giving youths fire, no questions asked. It ain't responsible.

I cover my face with my hood and use the lighter to light a match. That way, I can dash it down the petrol tank and my fingers don't get burnt.

And I think, Maybe if I lose this ped I can still get the meter filled up for mum because there ain't that much I do for her. It's time I stepped up.

I drop the match. Sprint the steps.

Kasim's at the top, hands cuffed. Police Lady helps him in the car, all gentle so he don't knock his head.

Ped explodes. Thick black smoke comes up the side of the bridge and I think of my half of the twenty, blazing in the water.

Chapter 9

After the ped burns out and that, I got to stay down Clapton police station all night. They can't get hold of mum and don't believe I'm almost thirteen neither, on account of my tallness, so I sleep in a grown-up cell. To be fair, they ain't got spare time for me; they got some next level stress going down because that place is like JDs in the riots. I don't know if you ever seen them riots but they was mental: sirens screaming, smoke choking, orange and yellow and blue lights blazing. Hackney, Tottenham, Brixton, Peckham, every place was the colour of everything vex and in pain and on fire on account of the Feds killing another Black man for no reason.

I was maybe seven or eight when our endz caught light and stuff in them shops walked. It was like the man what got smoked – Mark Duggan, he was called – was some kind of zombie Santa bringing peoples Christmas and Eid and Diwali one-time. As well as protesting what the police done, there was some next-level teamwork, like coordinating Co-op trolleys and double-buggies to jack washing machines and microwaves and sofas from BrightHouse. Mum was smiling at them shop windows wide open – glass on the pavement twinkling like snow – because she was still paying off a mini-fridge we had to leave behind since time, since when I was a baby, and now nobody had to pay for nothing, it was all for free. No 99.9% APR, no pay-day loans to see you good; people was taking what they dreamed of getting, arms full of threads, creps no matter what size, you can sort swapsies later. They was getting what they always walked past before, thinking, One day, one day.

On the positive side, Clapton can't keep me in Custody if the duty solicitor can't see me so they let me bounce. I send mum a message and she don't reply but then I see the time and she's probably sleeping. Ain't even 6 a.m. and that bus is rammed. I don't know why them Clapton ladies go down City endz for on the same bus. Must be a church there. One big-up African lady gets on and she smiles at me bare nice and she can't hardly walk so I let her tax me my seat.

I see Torvill even before I press the stop button, and I think, Why's he sleeping on the junction for? Why them cars driving round him and he don't move? Lady crosses her buggy over the street and starts pointing at birds and planes so her baby don't see him lying there. No blood, so he can't be dead. I get off, run to him, say his name, tell him, 'Get up, Torvill. Ain't safe here,' but he don't wake. Cars go round us. People walk by us. I pat his head, try to pick him up but he's too fat. I try pulling him a bit so he don't get knocked by some idiot driver texting on his phone, only he's more heavy than he ever was. I don't want to leave him but I have to sprint home because I need mum.

'How'd he get out?' I say to the entry speaker.

'Where you been?' mum goes. 'Get in here now!'

I don't go in like mum says I got to. I'm proper crying. Every bit of my skin itches and I scratch the eczema on my elbows till it bleed. Mum comes down and drags me up the steps. I go to the window.

'A dog's got to pee, Don. He took his chances. We'll get another one. Promise. I'm calling the school. I'll tell them you're sick today.'

Council comes at nine to take him away. Weren't nothing on him, no cut, no blood. How can you die when there's no cut, no blood?

'But I want to say goodbye.'

'You're not going out there, Don,' mum goes. 'The council will only charge us for taking it away.'

'Allow it, mum! He's got a name!' I say. 'And it ain't It. Call him by his name!'

Greener Hackney van mans dash him in the back like when they find a mattress on the pavement and my heart is hurting so bad I want to mash up everything. Kasim's waiting for me on the street, hanging where Torvill was lying, like he's paying his respects. I watch him send a message. Next second my phone dings and *Mental. Some dog like T got smoked!!!* comes on my screen. More messages follow: *That was gas last night!!* and *But did you got let out yet bruv?*

My door buzzer goes. Last message Kasim sends says, *Waiting for u ok?*

I don't answer. I go on my bed and hide under my cover. Mum comes in and starts screaming about the voicemails she's been getting from Clapton cop shop and how she don't need my shit. I ain't lying when I tell her, 'I hate you.'

125

'Don,' she goes, like she's speaking from the bottom of the most deepest ocean.

'Piss off!'

Front door goes and I know she ain't phoned the school and we're going to get fined but I don't care. I start thinking it weren't never mum's fault about Torvill because it was me what was supposed to take him out and I weren't there. I should've thought about it more. Mum's in one of them weeks when she ain't been in her brain so she ain't got stuff sorted like making me get up in time for school or taking our threads down the laundrette or going down the food bank. Torvill started peeing inside and I knowed we could lose the flat like that and he didn't like it neither. He put his ears back like he was proper sorry and never meant it on purpose.

I text mum saying all that but she don't reply. I'm bare hungry because I missed breakfast club what gives toast for no money, and if I go school they ain't going to turn round and say, 'Come in and get lunch early and don't worry about Maths if you ain't feeling it today.' They don't do that.

I wait in for mum all day and stay awake all night till the sun come up, till I can't keep my eyes open no more. She still don't come home and I still don't eat. Ain't nothing but a few broken sticks of spaghetti and a KFC ketchup in the cupboard and I ain't in the mood to start cooking. I look in the money mug what we hide so we can go out Saturday and get pizza, but it's cleaned out so I go sleep, my head stinging and dizzy. I sleep on mum's sofa bed so I know when she comes in.

Next morning, flat's still empty. I look at my phone; nine twenty-two. I check my messages; nothing. I'm merked

126

because I missed breakfast club again. I hope Kasim's got some Beef McCoy's.

School don't feel right. I'm a ghost floating down them corridors like nobody can't see me. I can't think about History when I don't know where mum is and she ain't even text me to say where she's at. And I ain't going to English neither, because we're only doing some made-up language about dumbarse peoples in Athens what get lost in the woods. So what? That's why you don't go Epping Forest neither.

I stay back in the playground when the bell goes and watch Year Tens running the astro for a bit, trying to make like I forgot my kit at home because fresh teachers always think I'm in Year Ten.

I check my phone and message mum, saying, *Where RU I'm sorry.*

PE teachers start to clock me so I bounce. I go two times round school and don't get stopped. That's got to be a record. I start feeling like I ain't there at all but my luck don't last.

Two teachers is on the other side of the Maths doors, blocking my exit strategy.

'Skiing in my state?' one goes. 'Not this year! Of course, sod's law this is the year we'll have a huge dump of snow. I'll be knitting teeny jumpers at the bottom while Phil's enjoying himself ...'

They laugh their heads off like that's funny and it goes quiet. I think they gone and it's good to go, but the door opens and Ski Lady's in my face, shorter than me by long, looking like a sixth-former except for the flower dress ain't no sixth-former going to wear. She stands her ground.

127

'Where should you be now, young man?' she goes, eyebrows up like she ain't never seen nobody out of class before. She can't have been here long.

I don't say nothing. I go up the stairs to the Science floor but she follows, goes by me and blocks.

'Stop,' she says, voice hard. 'I asked you a question. What's your name? Show me your ID. You should be in a lesson. What year are you in? You're truanting,' and rah, rah, rah, like that.

I split and she follows more, chatting some next shit, like I'm getting in more trouble because them new academy bosses don't like it, Ofsted neither. She says they'll penalty charge mum if I don't go class and I don't know why they don't leave us alone.

'You're making a poor choice, young man. Ignoring the instructions of a member of staff. I think we need to call mum, don't you?'

She got no right.

That teacher don't even know mum.

She ain't even met mum.

She don't even teach me.

'Hey?' she goes. She tugs my sleeve to make me look at her.

'Don't touch me,' I say, screw-facing her. She swallows like she knows she just made a mistake. I ain't sure how this is going to go. She takes in a slow breath and lays a hand on her big-up fat belly.

'You're here to learn, not wander the corridors. And you're using a mobile device.'

She takes my phone and I weren't expecting that so it sort of slips away. I act too late and it's sitting in her hand.

And I tell myself, No tears, man. Do not cry.

'Mobile phones are banned. Your parents can collect it after school on Friday.'

Do not cry.

Lady sees the way I am and backs off. She shouts at the Maths office door, 'Can I get some help? I've got an extremely aggressive boy here!'

'You don't get it, do you?' I say, stepping to her. 'I want my phone.' I know mum's going to message me soon. I want to grips up that lady's hand and bend back her fingers. I want to shake her the way Torvill shakes a stick to tax it off me. Or used to. 'I ain't joking. Give. Me. My. Phone.'

I can't hardly see no more because my eyes is full of water. Lady laughs in my face but it ain't a happy sort of laugh.

'Jack my phone and I will mash you up. Watch! I will get my cousins! I will get my crew! Give me my phone back!'

Deputy Head calls the Learning Mentors on his radio. Teachers close round her because she's crying now, saying she ain't never been so scared. Maths Teacher Man puts his arm round her like she's a baby what fell over trying to walk. Long bit of yellow hair gets caught up in her snot and he smooths it away from her face. He says he's going to get her in the Maths office for a cup of tea et cetera, and they'll write down what I done. He says she's safe now. He tells her she don't need to be frightened no more. They going to sort me out, he says. Academy don't stand for assault.

'Donny,' one of them Mentors says. 'Come, blood. Let's go.' For a moment I forget myself and where I am and almost hold the man's hand by accident down to the office.

'My head's twisted, innit,' I say. 'But I never touched her.'

'I ain't going to lie,' Mentor man says. 'It don't look good.'
He gets me water and a tissue and I really want him to stay
with me. 'It ain't easy,' he goes. 'And I swear down, it'll get
worse before it get better. I been through it. But it will get
better, blood. Trust me.'

I lay my head down on the table and watch him. He acts
like he's boxing, fists close to his body, ducking his head left-
right.

'You know, life's going to keep throwing you shit, you get
me? Now you keep ducking it and sending it back.'

My eyes start up but I ain't letting them.

Don't cry.

Don't cry.

Don't cry.

I start up crying.

I wait for time. Secretary Man puts his head round the
door to see I ain't trashing stuff. School Liaison comes in
wearing her stab vest like she thinks I'm carrying a shank
or something. Headteacher Man comes in. Small time later,
Children's Services Lady sits next to me, thin lips, tight
smile. Academy Directors turn up and all, grey old white
mans in suits, and this lady I ain't never seen before they
call the Trust Executive. She don't look like you can trust
her. Olu was right about secondary and I got to keep my
dignity.

They play the CCTV first, look sideways at each other like
I'm some dangerous animal, chat words like 'intimidation'
and ask if I got comment.

I kiss my teeth.

Don't cry no more, I think, and I start up laughing and all the time I'm laughing I'm thinking, Are you mad? Why you laughing for? Stop laughing, man!

Children's Services Lady touches my hand and says, 'Do you have anything to say?'

I don't know why but I point to the TV screen and go, 'Look at me staying up. Yeah, boy. I stand my ground.'

Them Directors shake their heads and shut their laptops.

'Oh, my days,' I say. 'Can I have my phone back now?'

'When you assaulted her –'

'I never!'

'Donny, that's enough!'

'But it ain't enough. It ain't even nearly enough. Ain't never been enough!'

Liaison Lady swallows. Her police radio crackles and she turns it down low. 'Were you aware that Mrs Anderson was pregnant? Did you intend to hurt her?'

'Excuse me, but this is hardly appropriate,' Children's Services Lady says. 'If this is a formal interview, he has a right to a solicitor. Donny, don't say anything.'

But I do want to say something. I want them to listen.

'Can you please give me my phone back now?' I say. 'I'm asking bare nice.'

Secretary Man comes in again and gives some paper to Headteacher Man. He looks at me, thin lips making a sad smile and gives it to Children's Services Lady. They got some secret sign I don't know because they all leave the room one time. They say stuff outside and Children's Services Lady comes back in on her ones. She takes a deep breath.

131

She got that look in her eyes what squeezes my heart. I know that look. I seen it time and time after again.

'I'm not going to dress this up. I think it helps if I'm absolutely straight with you, so no surprises later. Your mother's been arrested,' she says in a careful, slow voice. 'I'm very sorry. She's been remanded. That means she's not coming back until after a trial date, or her sentence has been served. Last Monday, you were cautioned for the theft and arson of a motorbike –'

'Moped! It was only 50cc.'

'Moped, then. You've been put on the Operation Shield list. Do you know what that is?' I shake my head and laugh because this is one big heap of bollocks and I ain't in the mood. 'It's a list police draw up of young people involved in gangs, at risk of offending. And today, Donny, you've assaulted a pregnant member of staff. The Academy Directors have suspended you. Permanently. I'm sorry.'

'They can't do that. They ain't even seen mum.'

'Donny, the academy's got the power to do it with immediate effect and without appeal.'

She looks at how I take it.

'Can I have my phone?' I ask. 'Can I go now? I don't want to be in this shitty dump anyways. This place is messed up.'

'I'll take you home. We'll get your things.'

'No, I'm staying at Kasim's. Till mum gets home.'

'Donny, I'm sorry, but the council has terminated your tenancy. It's policy where there's evidence of,' she frowns and looks sorry for me, 'criminal activity. You wouldn't be able to go home, even if –'

'I need my phone!'

132

'Donny, you're in an extremely vulnerable position. It's our – my job – to look after you.'

'You ain't hearing me. I want my phone!'

'We've got you a place ready in a residential home. You'll get your own bedroom, television, an ensuite – that's your own toilet and shower, like in a hotel. You'll stay there for however many months pass before your mother's case comes up at court. If your mother's given a custodial sentence, we'll find you foster placement outside of London, as soon as we can. After what happened in Peckham, and your recent involvement in the London Fields incident, we need to get you away. Gangs exploit children like you. You're being groomed and we need to take steps to protect you.'

Now, the London Fields Boys ain't my affiliation and they ain't no paedos grooming nobody neither; all I wanted was a ten spot for mum, and I don't even really know what went down in Peckham with Michael because ain't nobody said shit about it.

But I do know I ain't moving again. I'm tired of moving and I ain't going.

'This is bullshit. I don't need no ensuite shower. I need my phone. I need to call mum.'

Flower Dress Lady comes in smiling. I don't know what she's been smoking.

'I want you to know I forgive you, Donald,' she says, turning a gold ring round her finger. 'You've made some bad choices, but you're not a bad person. I've decided not to press charges.'

She waits for me to say something and I want to tell her she's chatting shit because I never touched her. But I know

133

what I'm supposed to say. She wants me to go, 'Thank you, miss. I done a wrong thing, miss. Sorry I scared you, miss. Sorry I messed up your nice day, miss, only I weren't myself but it won't happen again. As well, thank you for allowing it and giving me a chance and I won't never let you down.'

And I can see she got a baby inside, swimming round that fat belly. I don't know how I missed it. I can see everything now; like when it gets born, they'll probably call it Sebastian or Edward. And her husband's going to carry it through their house to the garden. He'll stick it on a blanket on the grass under the swing and before it goes school they'll quit London and go someplace nice. Someplace me and mum ain't.

I see it, wrinkle-up pink thing on a blanket, looking up at the swing and laughing because it ain't never going to cry over nothing what matters.

'I hope your baby dies,' I say.

PART 2

County

Chapter 10

Hertfordshire lanes run skinny like some side alley to nowhere. We head north out of London, go for time seeing no shops, no flats, nothing at all; and when you do see people, mostly all of them is white. Except Laura ain't. I'm glad of Laura. She's my new foster carer. Don't get me wrong, I ain't got nothing against white people but county endz, I don't know, it's different.

Laura shows me a tree.

'That's the bus stop,' she says. 'School bus stops here at eight. If I've got a meeting scheduled, I'll need you to catch the bus.'

The quiet stings in my ear. Laura's car ain't got no engine, only a battery. Doors shut like they whispering and ain't nothing else making much sounds. Even them cows don't say nothing; they just look at me like I'm dumb.

Laura gets a bottle and some manky wrapper out a hole in the bus-stop tree with her bare fingers, puts them in the back of her car.

'So you work for the council?' I say.

'That's right.'

'Rubbish?'

'Sometimes.' She smiles. 'Ah, it's not that bad. I'm Head of Legal. Contracts, due diligence, those sorts of things.'

I nod like I know what she's just said.

We drive some more and trees grow both sides. Branches shake hands over the road and even though it's day Laura turns her lights on. She parks up by a footpath sign. I spy with my little eye these houses the other side of a field and I know I can run faster than she. Find a bus. Get out this county.

'If you're coming from the canal,' she says, 'this path takes you straight back home –'

'You got a canal here?'

She nods. 'The towpath's one of my cycle routes. Take a look. I'll wait for you here.'

Council should do something about this footpath. I get stung through my trackies, and my nice creps get all scratched up. I start to loop back but then I hear this ticking – *putt-putt-putt* – and a boat slides through them trees like it's floating on air. I find the towpath and another one comes. It sucks at the canal. Later, when I do Work Experience at my new school, Andrew who is teaching me calls that sucking sound 'displacement'; it's when the water at the front really wants to get to the water at the back, and it rushes the long of the boat trying to get where it wants to go. Looks like it's steaming along but it ain't going no more faster than a walk.

'Good?' Laura says when I get back in the car. There are scrapes down my arm and I think of the cuts on mum's arms. 'I see you've had a tangle with a bramble. There'll be blackberries in September.'

I don't care. I won't be in this dump in September. Before I came up county, when mum went prison again, they stuck me in residentials for another two years, but this September, when I turn sixteen and mum gets out, no one ain't going to tell me I can't live with her no more. No one.

'Is this grass all yours?' I ask when we get to her place because Laura's house got wrap-round astro. Tell the truth, I'm playing refugee; I know that ain't no park. No Youngers is going to kick there. Ain't never going to be no forensics tents, no police tape round them trees. I just want to hear it said.

She presses a button and that garage door rolls up. 'You forgot to lock your car,' I say because she don't roll it down again when the car's parked inside.

'There's nothing worth stealing in it,' Laura goes, 'unless a burglar's looking for empty sweet packets dropped by our local teenage litterbugs.' She sighs. 'I'll take it in for a clean. You hungry?'

Her front door swings open like she's been done over but she don't go, 'Oh my days, we been done over!' She goes in like that's normal.

First room's where coats get left. I ain't brung enough creps to fill the rack she gives me. There's another door and that one's locked so I feel better, though I still don't like my best creps back there on their ones.

'I've made pizza for lunch. You like pizza?'

I nod, but I don't know why she's asking me for when they already typed up what I like. She got the print-out on the fridge: McDonald's, Domino's, Nando's. As well, I don't know why they put Nando's last. Maybe they don't got no Nando's in Hertford.

Laura opens the oven and takes out the food. It ain't any pizza I know about. She says it's homemade: brown bread with tomato and cheese and roast courgettes. Courgette makes me want to throw up but I ain't been raised like that so I eat and say thank you. We sit on high stools like at a chicken shop, except ain't no street outside to watch. Only plants and trees and maybe wild animals if you wait time enough.

'I grew the courgettes,' Laura says like you might say, 'I shot ten straight hoops in a row, both eyes shut.'

Laura's sunglasses get tangled up in her hair when she takes them off. Her curls look like mine, if my braids was out, and I know people here are going to take her for my mum. That ain't never happened before.

'Is your mum or your dad Black?' I ask.

No lie, except for the sky and the sea, I ain't never seen so much white as in the photo she got on her phone. White lady in a white dress on a white boat what's got white sails and a white-hair white man in white trousers holding her lily-white hand. It's like looking at heaven. Only I'm looking for the Black man and he ain't there.

'That's my mum. The yacht belongs to Tony, my stepdad.'

'Where's your real dad at?'

'I never knew him, actually. Mum met him at university in the seventies. They were both reading Law. Things got tough, politically. He was sent home.'

'Illegal immigrant?'

140

'No!' I don't mean no offence so I feel better when she smiles. 'Well, yes. I suppose you could put it like that, after his embassy closed. He was a junior diplomat by that point. He couldn't stay in London and mum wouldn't leave. He got married eventually, to someone else.'

'Sorry.'

'Don't be. Mum and I are good. We got on with it.'

Upstairs she shows me the bathroom what's only for me because she got another one spare. She bought donkey kind of Lynx for me. No joke, it's like she looted Superdrug and she ain't forgot my hydrocortisone neither. Vaseline and Palmer's there and all, and a razor, except ain't nothing on my chin yet. Towel holder's heating up towels, blue like the curtains I seen in my bedroom and the cover on my bed.

I open the window because my feet is sweating.

When I visit mum in prison and she says, 'What's the sticks like, Don? You happy?' I ain't going to lie. Laura's nice. She ain't trying to be no mum and the way I see it, her yard's fine till summer and I know my life's going to be better when I'm sixteen.

I tell mum Laura's house is like being on some next island; ain't no 4Gs, no PlayStation, only plants and trees and all kinds of alive things round it. Laura's got this outside camera what takes photos and videos at night so you can see deer and rabbits, and sometimes foxes and badgers. It's infrared, so them animals don't even know they been papped. They move through her garden like roadmans; timecode is like 2 or 3 a.m., and they're looking over their shoulders and sniffing the air like they got themselves in the wrong postcode, smelling for the wrong crew. In the morning, they're gone. Only a pile of feathers or some Malteser-shape shits to say they ever been and the garden starts up with birds singing in it and bare flowers.

I want to tell mum I miss her. But that ain't nothing new. I don't think I ever ain't missed mum, and when I miss her most is when she's right there in front of me but ain't. Them times.

As well, I hear London calling me and I miss Kasim and my peoples. I don't even got no digits because they took my old phone for evidence, but I can hear London still. It's like, you know how when some mental neighbour calls up the antisocial hotline at 9 p.m. and a Special turns up and cuts the music but your ears keep hearing bass even though the party stopped? That's what London sounds like up county.

'Don?' mum goes. 'It's all right though?'

'It's okay. Bit white, innit.' She don't get what I mean because she ain't even been as far as Walthamstow. 'It's like being in History. You ever seen Hitler Youths? I'm doing it at school. Germany: Democracy and Dictatorship, 1890 to 1945.'

'Hark at you!'

'Well, it's like in them photos.'

'Don, they being racist to you because I ain't standing for that.'

'No, mum. I don't mean they're no Nazis or nothing. What I'm saying is, most of them kids is white. Blond hair and uniform. No lie, mum, county Year Tens wear blazers and ties and white socks like they're Year Sevens, even when they don't got to because they're only on the bus. They frit about rules and no lie, county teachers is bare soft.' Mum laughs.

She's getting better again and I'm glad of it. 'Anyways, they ain't all white. There's five Asian, three Chinese and one more like me – Marlon in Year Thirteen. He's sort of like my friend.'

'You got a mate already!'

'Not exactly. But we chatted and Laura's going to do me bantu knots; she searched it up on YouTube. Marlon's got bantu knots. He says county people find it non-threatening and girls reckon it's cute. He works at a restaurant Saturdays, in Hertford, saving for university because he's got a Science place at Loughborough. Says he's worked there a year but when he got bantu knots he started getting bare tips. His mum's a librarian.'

'You tell me if anyone gives you any shit, Don.'

'It's cool, mum, it is. Ain't no Olders here. They all battymans, anyway, even ones what got girldem.'

'Don't be 'phobic, Don. I ain't raised you to be that.'

'Allow it! I'm only saying they got white socks.'

'Don!'

'Allow it, mum. My bad.'

My most new friend thinks he's ghetto. He's called Josh and he asks me for weed and chats like he's from the Bronx. He goes, 'Cool, homey,' and shit.

'You're new, Don-no, right?' he says, first time we meet. 'Tell me, Don-no-AS-BO, you fish?' I nod even though I ain't never been fishing, unless you count watching down the Regent's. 'Eight o'clock tonight. At the canal. Night fishing. I'll lend you a set-up.' I don't say nothing but I think he clocks I'm dumb because he goes, 'A rod and line, pillock. You bring the weed. I'll teach you how to catch carp.'

I ain't got no weed but Laura's got a bottle of whisky in a box what says it's eighteen years old. And then I'm like, are you mad? Laura's safe. I ain't jacking nothing from her.

'Don-no-AS-BO! Nice one, Josh. Ha, ha!' one of his crew goes.

'Anyone got spare socks, like proper white socks for our new friend?' Josh says. 'Banter, mate, just banter. See you at eight.'

Turns out, I don't have to worry about no weed. Laura's been cooking.

'Delicious flapjack,' I say. Laura makes out like she won *Masterchef*. 'I made a friend at school.'

'Great. What's his name? Or is he a she?'

'Nah, Joshua. He's asked me to go night fishing later. Eight o'clock at the canal. Can I go, please?'

'Sounds exciting! We'd better wrap up. Very cold weather forecast.'

'The thing is ...' I start to say. This is going to be easy. Laura's already had a chat with me about what she calls masculinities and how she can't fill that gap and I got to find strong male role models. 'It's just sons and dads going.'

'Oh, I see. A man thing.' She smiles. 'Okay, young man. Make sure you're home by nine-thirty. Take these flapjacks to share.'

It's a no-cloud night and back home I ain't never seen so much stars. Down Hackney endz, it's more satellites and planes, on account of the streetlights and diesel that fuzzes up the sky. Back in the day, mum used to go, 'Look, there's

Santa. You better be a good boy,' when some plane went by. By the time I was eight I learned she was chatting shit but most times kids is better off acting like kids. They got to say their lines.

But here, it's like looking out a window on the big-up universe and if Santa did roll by, you could probably see what colour his eyes is.

There's a line of orange where the sun's gone down. Grass goes white and the moon lights up the footpath so I don't have to get out my new phone what Laura gave me and I'm glad of that, even though I know there ain't no Youngers here on bikes looking for mugs. I don't think this county even got Youngers.

Josh and his crew's at the lock, sitting in camp chairs, three rods hanging over the water. Straight away I clock a blade – proper commando one, camouflage handle – and my heart goes a bit cardiac even though I know it ain't for me. It's more like for shanking fishes.

'Oi! Don-no! Got the weed, mate?'

'No. Laura gave us flapjacks though.'

'Shame. We thought you were gangsta,' he goes, stuffing his face.

I ask for a turn on the rod but he says it's fine-tuned, calibrated. I wait bare long and nobody catches nothing. I can't say how deep the canal goes or how cold it is at the bottom, or what they think's swimming down there, but I know they ain't even going to catch no supermarket trolleys. No crackhead's going to push a trolley eight mile through county bush and dash it here for its pound.

'I got to go. Laters,' I say because I ain't come here to catch cold and all the flapjacks is gone.

Them boys stand up.

'Ah, come on, Don-no. Don't be wet,' Josh goes. 'Now that's not very sociable.' He looks at his crew. 'And we're being so nice to the new boy.'

They block me both ways. The canal looks like you could just step out on it but you can't. Maybe there's bits of the Regent's where you could probably run on the trolleys they got stacked up, but county canals is clean and deep. Nothing but brambles and nettles the other side and I don't like this no more.

A dog barks and some man's yelling, 'I'll call your parents again, lads!'

Josh laughs. 'It's Andrew. Watch out, Don-no. He'll set his vicious dog on us. But we'll be fine. His dog's only trained to bite pikeys and Blacks.'

My belly flips and I want to run but I can't shift my legs. That dog barks again. One of them boys behind me goes in his pocket and I swear down, I see a flash of silver. I see what Michael would've seen in Caterham.

'I won't stand for drugs and litter! Go home, lads!'

'Please?' I say and it comes out lame like I'm frit. I go weak when I should be vex. I'm supposed to be safe here. This place is why I don't see mum more than one time a month. I might as well be in Clapton – Tottenham even – seeing her every week if this is how it goes up county.

'Let him have it,' Josh goes and I brace.

'All right, then,' the boy says. He drops a bit of silver paper on the towpath and gives me a fruit pastel.

'Come on, boys. Pack up,' says Josh. 'Let's leave Don-no to the doggy. He's fast but I doubt he could outrun Ziggy for long. Shall I call an ambulance now to save time?'

The dog pisses on the Canal and River Trust noticeboard. Josh slaps my shoulder.

'Of course, you could always swim to safety,' he says, looking at the canal. 'Andrew's dog can't stand water.'

'But I, I can't –'

'Can't swim? Time for your first lesson!'

One of them boys puts his shoulder into the back of my leg like a rugby tackle. Josh gripses up my wrists. My ankles go up and I think, This is it. This is the end.

'One! Two! Three!'

They swing me over the water but they don't let go till the last swing and the last swing drops me flat on my back on the gravel.

'Banter, mate, banter!' they go and they're gone.

It don't hurt much, only a bit of blood on my ear. Next up, claws scrabble the towpath. I shut my eyes. Dog breath blows in my face and I think, I ain't no Traveller! And, How can he see my skin in the dark? And, He ain't going to bite if he thinks I'm dead. So I don't move and he don't bite. He starts up licking my ear and then my hand, tail whipping my face. He does this little whine, ears flat and sits with me till a whistle goes and he's off and I leg it out of there like Bolt in the Olympics.

I open the door. Laura's smile drops when she sees my face.

'What on earth happened?' she goes and I tell her it ain't nothing, we was just gassing. 'Are you sure? You might need stitches. Why didn't you call me?'

'It's nothing. It don't hurt.' I go to the stairs but she looks so sad I got to make it better for her. I lie. 'We caught two

147

carp. Joshua's dad's going to teach me how to swim and fish. And I want to learn rugby. There was this man called Andrew and he's got a nice dog.'

'The lock-keeper guy?'

'Yes. Can I have a shower please, now?'

I wash for time. Water keeps on going pink and I know what I got to do. I take a breath and turn the thermostat down cold. In a little time it runs clean but my mind don't. I'm full of spite, thinking, Watch! Tomorrow, them wastemans! Do they even know who I am?

But when tomorrow rolls up, and them fishing boys is all playing Fifa on their phones in the playground, there ain't no beef.

'All right?' Josh goes. He chucks me a bag of Haribos. He ain't trading; it's his birthday.

I go back with a letter in my bag about Work Experience. Laura reads it out loud. My transfer was late in the year, so I missed out on choosing a placement, only it ain't over. School got an offer from the Canal & River Trust.

'No way, I ain't doing that,' I say because I ain't picking up nobody's litter and that's the first thing the letter says I got to do.

'Wait. Let me finish,' says Laura. 'Outdoor clothing essential, conservation work, bird habitat, operating canal lock gates ...'

'Sign it, Laura. I'll do the canal thing. But I ain't touching no rubbish. Might get bare sharps. Might catch Ebola.'

I don't know this yet, but Hertford Union Canal ain't got no Ebola. But what it do got is boats and if I catch anything on Work Experience, it's boats.

Josh tells me I got no chance when he clocks me looking at this girl in Maths. I ain't looking at her that way, but I go with it.

'Zoe only dates men, twenty or older. You wouldn't know what to do with her. She's been around.' He smirks. 'She's what you call experienced.'

'So?'

'So, give up.'

After class, Teacher Lady's telling Zoe to remove her make-up, saying, 'There's no rush to grow up.' And Zoe's using the window for a mirror, wet-wiping her face. Mascara messes up her cheeks like she been crying or like when mum comes home after working nights.

'Don't mind me,' Zoe goes to no one but I know she means me.

'I was looking for the canteen,' I say.

'No, you weren't. You were looking for me,' and she stares at me funny. Not funny like I seen here before, the way they look at me like they think I'm tooled up or ghetto or something. The only way to say it is, she looks at me like I got all the outside and away in me. And I look at her and I know she got that too.

We go to the canteen and get our eats. She takes the stool next to me and we both don't say nothing for time.

'Six o'clock,' she says. 'Six okay for you? Don't be late. What's your number? I'll text you my address.'

Now first off I think she's taking the piss and then I get a bit angst because maybe she's not and maybe I don't know what to do if she likes me like that. I don't know about girls but I say yes anyway and I'm glad I did because Zoe is Zoe

149

and now that I know her I can't think about not knowing her.

Zoe's manor's at the end of this track. Laura spins her lekkie car round a tub of flowers what thinks it's a roundabout and parks up next to an Audi TT convertible and a Range Rover, one of them low-pro cut-downs.

'Nice house,' Laura says as I get out the car. 'You've got school tomorrow so I'll be back at nine. Have a great time. I'm thrilled you're making friends.'

Laura's gone and there ain't no bell, no intercom neither. I bang the door and wait. Nothing. There ain't no numbers, so I check my phone. It's the right manor, I know, because she text it me. The Grange. But Zoe ain't said what flat is hers. I dash a metal knocker down to tell them I've come and check myself in the glass.

This lady answers the door in high heels. She's wearing an apron over a little dress.

'Donald!' she goes. She holds up a wine glass and a bit spills. 'Donald!' she goes again like she knows me and she gets up in my face and kisses both my cheeks. 'My, you're handsome.'

'I've come to see –'

'Zoe!' she yells. 'Your gorgeous friend's here!'

Lady goes and Zoe comes to the door. 'Did mum just kiss you?' she goes. 'God! She's so embarrassing.'

'True that. Both sides.' I wipe my cheeks. 'She French?'

'No. She's drunk.'

'She going to a party?'

Zoe don't answer me. She goes off all vex and I get left in her block's entrance hall. I still don't know what door's her flat.

150

'Coming in?' she goes, sticking her head round a door. She's wearing a kangaroo onesie, stuffed baby kangaroo in the belly pocket, and I see Josh's gone and mugged me off again. I follow and it's a sitting room; widescreen TV, log fire blazing. I'm deciding which of them three sofas I'm going to sit on when Zoe walks out and I don't know if I'm supposed to go too.

'I'm in the kitchen,' she says.

I try four rooms before I locate her. First's an office. Second's got boots and coats, and they got a private laundrette with its own washing machine and dryer, no coins. Last room's got a long table and chairs in it so bare people can all eat at the same time if they like.

'Your flat is massive! This ain't all yours?' I say when I find the right door and she's waiting for me, two pizza boxes on the table.

'Mum's burnt supper. I hope you're not hungry.'

It's Zoe's idea to stream *Paddington 2* even though she says she's seen it a million times. It ain't the kind of film I watch, even if it was streaming for free, but I don't say nothing. We sit on one of them big-up sofas and Zoe sticks her legs on my legs, and even when her mum comes in bringing hot chocolate and popcorn, she don't shift them.

At the end, Zoe goes, 'God, I love that film,' and starts chatting about living in Kensington because she's going to be a model. 'The Big Smoke,' she goes.

I feel like I got to explain.

'It ain't like that, Zoe. That ain't London. You see sleeping bags? It's Kensington, man. There's going to be sleeping bags, you get me? You seen Black people? I counted two. One's a binman and he's bare happy. The other's in prison and he's bare happy and all.'

'It's only a film. It doesn't mean anything.'

'Kensington, Zoe! I don't see no burn-out tower –'

'For God's sake, it's a children's film!'

Door knocker goes clack. Time's over, but I ain't giving up.

'I don't see no youth out on bikes. I don't see no one getting jacked for their creps. I don't see no policeman stopping no Black mans. I don't see nobody getting shanked. It's gas, that's what it is.'

Zoe acts like I'm joking, dashes a pillow at my face and says in her posh voice, 'I have no idea what you've just said.'

I ask her when was the last time she went to London and she goes, 'Dad keeps promising but it never happens. He's always busy. Mum says he even checked the stock markets on their wedding day.'

'Why don't you just get on a train?'

'I wouldn't know where to go.'

'Trocadero. That's where we'll go.'

She looks at me like I've just given her my pound for no reason.

'Trocadero?' she says. I open my mouth, but before I can say shit she goes on, 'Dad recommends the Science Museum, followed by Buckingham Palace, a ride on the Eye, lunch up the Shard. He takes clients there when he really wants to impress! But I bet you've done all the touristy stuff to death. I'm up for the Trocadero. What is it?'

Back in the day, Mama Folu showed me the Science Museum but I ain't confessing to Zoe that I ain't been up in no Eye, Buckingham Palace neither, so I go with it.

152

'Troc's wicked, trust me. Forget the Eye. Forget the Shard. I used to see the Shard from my manor, by the way, when I lived in Peckham.'

That gets her smiling. She got the sweetest smile.

'So, tell me about the Trocadero? Is it like the one in Paris? I love the one in Paris! The gardens lead onto the Seine ... so romantic! The Eiffel Tower and –'

'It's like eight floors. The 38 bus goes there direct. You got bowling, cinema, arcades. You can play Fifa, or Gran Turismo sitting in a little racing car like it's for real. You got these grab machines and you grab a toy, but they're a bit shit because the power always cuts out when you're about to get it. Like the penny ones, you know, where you put in a coin and the shelf pushes the coins. They're shit too. You always think, This is easy, man! But no way, it ain't – I mean, it isn't. Easy. At all.' Zoe ain't following me so I slow it down. 'There's five pool tables and you can sit and watch skateboarders do tricks and free-runners do their stunts for time. It don't cost no money and they keep it bare hot in winter so you don't got to sit in your coat. Mum used to take me all the time, you know, when the meter ran out.'

Zoe searches it up on her phone. She bites her lip.

'Looks like it's closed down.' Her eyes go big. 'But they're turning it into a pod hotel. Cool! Have you seen those Japanese pods? Would you ever sleep in one of those? I mean, claustrophobic or what! Like sleeping in a coffin. I'd do it for a dare, though. Would you?'

'Don't matter,' I say, except it do. They should keep it the same, not make some next hotel. London got enough hotels. I liked it how it was.

'Donny? Are you all right?'

Laura puts her hand on my shoulder to the car and I don't say nothing all the way. It ain't till we get to the house she goes, 'I take it it didn't go well, your first date?'

'No, and I'm starving. And it weren't no date neither.'

She dashes me an apple when what I need is a family bucket.

'What happened?'

'For a start, there was no food. So I was already merked. We watched this kid film.'

'Did you not get on?'

'She's from some next planet,' I say, but I know what's really up. 'Can you take me to London? I want to see mum. I want an extra visit. Four weeks is too long.'

'Of course, if they say it's appropriate.'

I should get a pound for every time I hear that word. That word does violence to my ears.

'She needs me, you know.'

'And you need a childhood. It's not your fault. It's not your mum's fault either, but it's not your job to fix it.'

'So whose fault is it?'

I think she's going to say them Olders, but she don't.

'It's like David Lammy says – he's an MP – we should stop arresting boys in tracksuits and start arresting men in suits.' Laura opens her tablet and searches up Top UK Drug Dealers. The first eight photos is white men.

'These criminals control the market. They smuggle in a hundred tons of cocaine on private jets and luxury yachts. More than ten billion pounds a year. They keep profits in offshore accounts and arms-length property trusts. Some

154

went to the same schools as FTSE 100 directors.' She jabs the screen so hard it's going to crack. 'They're the start.'

Her eyes is proper vex now. 'It's like tobacco in Africa. Sales are falling here, all over the developed world; advertising's banned, high taxes, health warnings. So Big Tobacco's going hard into developing countries. They're targeting children, turning them into addicts. The white men in suits strike again.'

I ain't never heard nobody speak like this and I am proper listening.

'It's the profit motive. Their aim is to keep us in chains,' she says. 'And the only thing we can do to break free is to not buy what they're selling.'

I don't say this, but it's like, she got some bits of the jigsaw and I got the others because I seen the things she ain't. I seen Olu chatting to that man in Bognor. I seen youths turn into Youngers, hungry for green, and it always ends up same-same; slides and climbing frames wrapped up in Do-Not-Cross tape, forensics tents keeping it clean so we don't see. It ends in cuts Olders say don't hurt bad, only stinging on the outside, because ain't so many nerves inside. And they say we all done it, part of life, innit. This is your mission. When you done it, you move up.

And I don't know if it took one cut or twenty to bring Michael down. I don't want to know. I shut my eyes, hearing the blood going between my ears. I open them again, look at Laura and say, 'What if people stop selling what they're bringing in?'

'Have you heard of the Chinese Opium Wars?' she goes.

'I thought we was talking about London?'

155

'Two hundred years ago, at the end of the slave trade, the British grew opium in India, heroin poppies, and forced China to buy it. The Chinese realised it was turning their people into addicts so they passed a law to make it illegal. So the East India Company – a private business, you understand? – bought themselves an army. They fought China for the right to sell drugs to the Chinese. They forced them to buy.'

'Turf war,' I say because that's what it is, if you don't dress it up and call it History.

'Right. The East India Company were the original drug barons. Corporate gangsters. White man wins.'

Laura's right; them mans on screen is white. I ain't got her down for hating whites, not like Olu. I mean, she got white friends and neighbours. Most of them lawyer peoples she hangs out with is white and all. But this is different. She's chatting facts, history, showing her education. Bossman weren't never no topboy – I can see that now, sleeping on some rank mattress in his mum's flat – not even close. Olu thinks he's playing to win but he ain't even in the game. I want to tell him he's being mugged off, but I ain't got that Nokia no more, only the SIM.

But I totally get Laura. She ain't saying History repeats itself. She's saying when History spits, them lyrics rhyme.

Chapter 11

X marks the spot in Downview. I searched it up on Google maps at school. If them drones could drop photos as well as phones and smack and spice, they'd know that. All them prison buildings is made like Xs and I don't know if it's because that's where they buried the treasure or if they're making kisses on the ground for planes to see.

It takes three hours to get there on account of the M25 and all them other road miles but that don't mean they give you more than an hour for your visit. It don't make no difference to them if you walked there because you live down the same endz or if you came all the way from the next-along-next-along county.

Same hour. Same sixty minutes. Same three thousand six hundred seconds.

'I'm getting a job,' I tell mum. 'Down the canal. Going to work on boats.'

Mum don't say nothing. I've started thinking she don't want to be out. I understand. They make it nice here. Not nice-nice, but at least you don't have to think about nothing, plan nothing, lose nothing; ain't no meter to feed and the food's free. I know she works in there, and she's always learning some new thing. They got a nice library and all, but it's not the same as outside.

Outside is hard. I feel her slipping away in the kind of nice they give here and I can't reach her. I don't know if I'm enough to make outside the place she'd rather be.

'Me and you's going to be okay,' I say.

She don't say nothing because she's watching the TV they put on in there for little kids.

'I'm going to look after you.'

I hold her hand.

'I ain't a kid no more,' I say.

Maybe that was a squeeze. I ain't sure.

'Come September …' I say.

She looks at me like she ain't never been more sorrier and I want to tell her she don't need to be. It's cool, because when I'm sixteen, they can't tell us shit no more.

'Please, mum,' I say, but it don't make no difference if getting here takes three hours or five little minutes. You ain't going make nobody talk if they don't want to.

'You know you're living in a massive X?' I say. 'You can see Downview from space. Serious! International Space Station people wave at you every hour when they go by. They go, "Hi, Mrs Samson! Nice weather we're having," except weather's always nice in space, innit.'

I get the littlest smile but that's okay. I'll take that.

'No shit. Google it up, mum. Next time you do IT and the teacher ain't looking, search it up. You only can't see the X because you're living in it. You got to look at the big picture. It ain't all here. This ain't all it is. There's more, you know.'

Andrew yells at me from the other side of the lock gate. I ain't done nothing wrong, it's only that the water's bare loud.

'Harder, lad. Give it a shove! Turn it!'

I try, hard as I can, and the cog starts to move, millimetre, centimetre … and I see it's working so I go hard on the metal.

'No! Slow down … easy … slower,' Andrew goes. 'Keep a tight hold on that windlass. Don't let go or it'll fly off the ratchet like a shot and kill someone.'

The lock gate opens and water flows in. First it's dead leaves and a brown water trickle. The mechanism shifts; cogs and gears doing what they done for hundreds of years and the trickle goes white with foam.

'There's three and a half tons in each gate,' Andrew goes. 'How much have you just shifted?'

'Seven tons, Andrew.'

'Bloody right! How does that make you feel, eh?'

I flip the windlass in my hand and start up smiling. No motor, no electricity. Only me. You learn about pulleys and gears in Science but trust me, them textbooks don't make sense till you move seven tons of wet wood and metal on your ones.

'Hench!'

'Great,' Andrew says. He must have opened this lock a million times and every time it's like he's won the lottery or something. His eyes go twinkle and I start wishing Work Experience don't never stop. If they allowed it, I'd quit school tomorrow and work for Andrew, because he ain't like no man I ever knowed before. He tells me about the people living on the water back in the day, and kids what never went to school because they travelled the canal and their job was the horses. Them quiet horses, he says, heavy horses. They pulled bare coal, hundreds of times more heavier than their own size.

And he says about the navvies what built the network with their hands and arms; no JCB diggers, no front loaders, none of them heavy plant machinery you seen on a building site. Only shovels, wheelbarrows and horse carts. They was mostly English workmen and some of them was Irish, but all of them was a long way from home.

'They had to dig seven cubic yards every day, six days a week, just to keep their jobs. Put your phone away a minute. Do you know how much rock and earth that is? Can you picture it, Donny?' I don't mind putting my phone away for Andrew. He points to the yellow skips where they put canal rubbish like paint cans, bicycles, bedframes, and I was wrong about trolleys: they got them here and all. 'That's eight cubic yards,' he goes.

'So they fill that?'

'Right. You were listening. It was dangerous and hard. Three navvies died for every mile of railway and it wasn't much better in the canal trenches, maybe worse. Think what happened if the bank collapsed or the trench flooded.'

The way he says it, I can see them navvies' arms built like Bossman, covered in mud and sweat.

'They drank hard, fought hard. The locals used to complain. They spent more money on beer than food and lost their strength, so the engineering company started paying meal tokens instead of money.'

Sounds like food bank vouchers. I imagine them navvies necking tins of peas and carrots with their spaghetti hoops, except they ain't invented microwaves then.

Andrew flips a coin. 'Heads or tails?'

'We playing money-up or what?' I remember the brick wall round the back of assembly. I remember what losing meant.

'Heads or tails?' Andrew says, eyes going twinkle.

'Heads.'

He takes his hand away. The coin's brass, seven straight sides. He laughs because there ain't no head and gives it me. There ain't no tail neither. Just HUC both sides and I don't know even what country it's from.

'HUC stands for Hertford Union Canal. They swapped this for food,' Andrew says.

'Is it!'

'Not much use if you want to send money home to your mother. What's money-up, by the way?'

'It's a game,' I say. 'You pick heads or tails and dash your pound up a wall.' I don't say that's the same as throwing your eats up a wall. 'If you win, you get both pounds. If you lose, you give it up.'

I tell him about Lamar, pockets full of other people's pounds. There was days when most of the boys in my year owed Lamar. Now, wise ones give over their coin in the game and walk away. Dumb ones play credit and lose that too. Then they sell their credit to other kids and Lamar keeps the numbers inside his brain. One time, Lamar was owed

161

sixty pound by this boy in Year Eight. Nobody can't explain how he won so much pounds when them odds should have been fifty-fifty.

'Well, you boys had fun,' Andrew says, smiling. 'We had games like that, when I was a lad.'

'That's what Headteacher Man said. Money-up was banned before he came, but then he let us do it. He even played with some Year Tens once. All them teachers was bare vex, because we were like, "Mr Howard said we can play so you can't say nothing."'

I tell Andrew about him coming round the back after school, sucking in his belly.

'Kids start thinking they're in trouble, but Mr Howard waves, all smiling and friendly, and instead of "Stop!" he goes, "Wait up," and asks us to teach him how to play. Teach him, you get me? We're thinking, Is this Teacher Man for real? He tries to make friends with Lamar, don't even know who he's dealing with. Lamar was always nice to teachers. The kids with the biggest outside reps are like that. Lamar played him, I mean, played him as well as played him. He told Mr Howard no pound changed hands in real life. It was only a game, he said, and the man bought it. They played for a bit. Mr Howard lost and Lamar let him keep his pound.'

'Why did your teachers want you to stop?'

'Not all. Some did. Some teachers knew what was really going down. They'd walk past the chicken shop and clock Lamar eating a family bucket. Some snitches in Year Seven went crying to their tutor because they lost their pound and weren't going to get no food till breakfast club, or if it was Friday, till forever. There was bare beefs over it. I mean, fighting, loads of fighting. Mr Howard didn't understand you had to work off your credit.'

'How?'

'Doing favours and stuff. Like running, delivering, looking, keeping stuff safe. Youngers' stuff, so you can move up.'

Normally, when grown-ups stop to listen, they only see and hear what they done when they was kids. They think they're so smart with their qualifications but they get the wrong answer to bare easy sums. But when Andrew don't get something, he asks.

'So tell me, I'm confused. Did you boys want this game banned?'

'That's the thing. It can't be. It just is. If they banned it, bare people wouldn't never get their money back. They'd be fu–' I check myself. 'Basically, if you're up, you want to go on. If you're down, you're always looking for the chance to get back up. You think, Next time, I will be up.'

I flick the coin. Andrew strokes his white beard and looks downstream.

'See them birds hyping?' I say, pointing at two coots on the offside bank. 'Beef's about to go down!'

One coot sticks out its neck and goes at the other. Big splash and wings go slap, slap. Loser one does this run-fly thing on the water and hides in the reeds.

'Rah, boy! He got shook!' I say. 'He got owned!' County's brutal like that sometimes.

I give Andrew back his coin and he polishes it up on his sleeve, looking at it funny.

'Weighting.' Andrew sits up and tugs my arm. 'Here, Donny, did anyone ever look closely at Lamar's pound?'

163

'What?'

'Over time, even a small amount of extra weight on one side changes the odds.'

Mum finally starts talking. When she says, 'So, first week of Work Experience. How did it go?' I tell her it's better than school because Andrew makes cups of tea and gives me biscuits. I tell her all about lock mechanisms, stripping engines and boat licences and she makes out like she's interested. I slag off all them dumb leisure punters what don't even know how to operate a narrowboat, and put everyone at risk. And I tell her about the fishes I catch, which ones you can eat and which ones you let go.

'Andrew's got a canoe. He keeps it by the office and lets me paddle it. We use it to get to the places the work flat's too big to get to.'

'Work flat?'

'It's a type of boat. It's, like, flat. Anyway, the canoe's good for fishing because it gets your line out further than you can cast from the towpath.'

'You wearing a lifejacket, Don?' mum goes. 'Does he know you can't swim?'

I don't tell her I lied when the Work Experience Coordinator Lady done the risk forms.

'Yeah, mum. I always wear one. Andrew looks out for me. He was a sailor back in the day, in the Merchant Navy. And when he quit that he took Dutch barges across the Channel. Do you even know how dangerous that is? They don't have the right hulls for seafaring – they got no keel, flat like creps

– so you choose a dead calm day to cross, wind under three knots. It takes hours, mum. Seven hours.'

'He sounds nice.'

'I like Andrew. He asks what I think. He listens. I don't want it to stop. I don't want to go school again neither. I don't even want to go back London no more. Me and you should get a place up county.'

She don't say nothing for time and I start to think something's gone wrong but then she goes, like it ain't nothing at all, like she's telling me she had sandwiches for lunch: 'Don, they're putting my date forward. I got two little weeks and that's it.'

And now I don't know what to say.

Zoe's on her MacBook again. I try to see the man she's talking to but she slaps me away and hugs it close. She looks bare happy. As well, when she smiles her silver braces flash because they're studded with pink bits. Like grills, except pink.

'Donny, butt out!'

'He can't see me. You've got privacy switched on. I want to see.'

'Don't spoil it for me! Okay, how do I look?'

'All right, I reckon,' I say and smile and make like I don't care. When she kicks back, I jack the MacBook out her hand.

Talent Man is old, same like Zoe's dad. He's wearing a white shirt, open at the neck, and a leather jacket. His hair's thinning, face orange down to his neck and then it goes pink. There's a gold ring on his little finger but it ain't that.

Something else about him makes me go frit and then I get why. His eyes look like them men mum used to know, like Marcus, and I don't like him one bit.

'Turn your video on, beautiful. I want to see you,' he goes to me, smiling.

'Donny, give it back! Butt out!'

'Babe, let me see you. Turn your camera on. I bet you're the prettiest young lady in your college,' he goes again.

'Donny, please? This is my chance.'

I give it back and sit on her bed next to all her Beanie Boos. Their big-up eyes is wide open like they don't get it neither.

'No, Donny. Right out!' she tells me. I go in the hallway and sit on the carpet, knees up to my ears. 'I'm going to turn on the video and sound now,' she says. 'If you come in, I'll never speak to you again. You literally cannot ever be my BBF if you dare come in or make a sound. Do you understand?'

'Okay,' I say.

'Pinky promise?'

'What's a pinky promise when it's at home?'

'It's a promise you can't ever break, stupid.'

'That's gas. I'm going to say, I swear down,' I say. 'I ain't making no pinky nothing.'

'Really? This is Hertfordshire, not Hackney. Say it! Say, "I pinky promise". It doesn't count if you don't say it.'

She sticks out her little finger.

'Sweetheart,' goes Talent Man. He don't sound happy. 'I'm a busy man. I have other young ladies to see.'

'I pinky promise,' I say and our fingers curl together. Zoe smiles, goes, 'Thank you!' and she's gone.

I shake my head because I know this ain't right. I can feel it. I feel like when that man stuck his stinking feet on me and mum's bed and never asked if it was okay.

'That's better,' Talent Man goes. 'I was starting to think you were a time-waster. I can see you now. So, tell me about yourself. How long have you been interested in modelling?'

'I've always wanted to be a model, since I was, like, five years old.'

'And how old are you now?'

'Um … nearly eighteen.'

'I have to say, darling,' he says, 'you don't look eighteen.' And I think, Finally! 'You look at least nineteen. My niece is nineteen. Are those your little sister's Beanies?'

'Yes.'

'Beautiful. Beautiful smile. Tell me about your hobbies, your interests? I like your profile, but it doesn't really say who you are, the real Zoe. Who are you, Zoe?'

There's quiet for time.

'I don't know really what you mean.'

'Do you do your own make-up?'

'Yes, no … um, sort of. Sometimes my friends do it for me.'

'When you go on dates, clubbing?'

'Yes, I suppose.'

I know she's trying to sound more sure than it comes out. Her voice goes squeaky. She wants him to think she's a grown lady but she's messing it up big-time. She sounds more like she's twelve or something, only it don't put him off. It makes him get more happy.

'Do you have a boyfriend?'

167

'Um ... no, sort of.'

'I'm asking because modelling sometimes involves a lot of travel. Paris, Milan.'

'No. I'll dump him.'

'What do you weigh, sweetie?'

'I don't know. Seven, nearly eight stone.'

'Height?'

'I'm not sure.'

'Bra size?'

'Wait.' Zoe's in her cupboard. '30A,' she says. I'm glad I ain't in there. My cheeks go bare hot.

'Beautiful. You've got a strong look and a sweet personality. I think our agency can work with you. I know these questions are personal, but in this business we rely on trust. Do you understand, darling? I've got to be able to trust you. Can I trust you, Zoe?'

'Yes.'

'So, are you able to meet me at our headquarters for a contact strip shoot?'

'Yes! What's a contact strip shoot?'

'Sounds dodgy, doesn't it? But it's strictly professional. You come in your own clothes, no make-up please – our artists will do that – and we take a series of strips to get your face on the books. Simple headshots. Tasteful. I'll message you the address.'

'Thank you, Mr, um –'

'Gorgeous, you can call me Uncle Nico. Let me tell you a little secret, darling: my niece still likes Beanies.' Zoe laughs like that's gas. 'She's got hundreds. I'll tell you what, when we meet, I'll buy one you can take back for your little sister.'

'Thank you!' she says again.

'Before you go, babe – do you have a school uniform you could borrow from your little sister?' He clears his throat. His breathing's gone like he needs a toke of Ventolin. 'Sometimes companies like to see versatility.'

Now when grown-ups start chatting uniform, I know it ain't right. Go county lines? Bossman say uniform. Shirt in. Tie up. Go school? Tutor Man say uniform. Shirt in. Tie up. You try crossing the wrong endz in the wrong blazer. Adidas more safer. Now this Talent Man wants Zoe in uniform.

Ain't right is what it is.

The call ends. I want to say something but Zoe's got a big-up smile on her face and she says, 'Donny, it's actually happening! We're going to London!'

'We? Zoe, I don't think –'

Her face drops and she goes, 'We've got to get cash. Will you help me?'

Laura leaves her purse sitting in the kitchen because county peoples nearly never get done over. She's probably got enough for a train ticket, but I ain't going there and besides, the station's miles away and it's bare dollars to get a taxi. I tell Zoe this and she hugs the folds of her duvet like she's going to cry.

'I know.' Zoe grabs my arm. 'Call Joshua.'

'Joshua?'

'Let's go beating!'

I admit, hearing it shocks me. I didn't think Zoe was like that. She acts so posh all the time.

'No thanks, Zoe. I ain't beating nobody and neither should you. It's nasty.'

'It pays well, though.'

'I don't care what it pays. Are you mental? It's dirty, man! I ain't doing it.'

Zoe's face goes blank. Little second later she starts up laughing like I made the funniest joke. 'Did you think I was asking you to beat someone up?'

'No.' I don't tell her I was thinking of worse. 'What's so funny?'

'You, you dingbat. Beating means beating pheasants.'

'Beating what-ants?'

'Pheasants. Game birds.'

'I ain't beating no birds neither!'

'You know, shooting parties?' Zoe goes. 'Twenty-five pounds a day, plus tips.' I don't say nothing. 'You beat the bushes and shout. That scares the pheasants out of the bushes, into a field, and the guns kill them. They're syndicates.'

Syndicates, game birds, shooting. To me that sounds proper merky, like the worst kind of Clapton shit and I been there and done that and I ain't going back. But the greens . . .

'Twenty-five quid?' I say.

'Plus tips.'

'To scare birds so they get killed by guns?' I think about it. Sounds good, but, 'Nah. No way. That's got to be illegal.'

'It's not. City boys come up from London to do it. Businessmen, stockbrokers. They pay thousands. Twenty-six thousand, in fact, for one weekend. They tip their beaters in twenty-pound notes.'

When she says it like that, I get it. It's like county lines, except it's businessmans going out there on trains, throwing their twenty spots at kids.

'Let me get this straight: big-up City mans coming Hertford to shoot up little birds, for fun?'

'Yes.'

'That's sad, man.'

'It is. Didn't you read *Danny, the Champion of theWorld* when you were little?'

There it goes again. One of them questions showing up what I don't know, ain't seen, ain't done. I got bare catching up to do.

'I don't agree with hunting, either,' Zoe says, 'but it pays cash. And we need cash. Wait there.'

Zoe runs upstairs, comes back with a book and dashes it at me so I nearly don't catch it. The cover's got a bird flying over this boy and his dad walking through a wood.

'Just hold off reading it until after we go,' she says. 'Or you won't do it.'

But I'm thinking this ain't legal, shooting birds for fun. In fact, I know this ain't legal and I tell her some Hackney youths got community sentences for the same shit.

'They broke into City Farm, where you go stroke guinea pigs and see a goat. One that ain't in a curry,' I laugh. Zoe don't. 'They smoked all the chickens with a BB gun. All of them. Then they got caught trying to blaze a rabbit hutch. The rabbit got away though.'

'God! What is it with some people?' Zoe goes. 'Last year, boys from St Mark's College – you know, the boarding school out by Tanner? – they snuck out of their dorm and into the copse behind the school, in the dark, and killed hatchlings.' I shake my head like that's bare merky, except I don't know what hatchlings is. I don't have to ask because Zoe goes,

171

'Hundreds of baby pheasants, dead. The gamekeepers thought it was foxes, but then they found bottles of gin and joints.'

'Is it!' I say. 'So why they kill them for?'

'I don't know. They were drunk, I suppose. Mum said it's the kind of thing boys do when they're away from home, when they don't have parents looking after them. Dad wanted me to go to boarding school but she wouldn't let him. What's the point of having children, she said, if you don't see them growing up?'

I don't say nothing more. I'm thinking about them baby birds and BB guns and I start up thinking about mum, coming out on her ones, no one to meet her and nowhere for home except some rank hostel.

I ain't waiting to sixteen till I can go be with her, look after her properly. I ain't waiting no more.

'I'll talk to Josh tomorrow,' I say. 'He owes me.'

I sit through the Canal & River Trust team briefing with half my ear open, checking my phone under the table for an email. I don't want much, only a time, a day, an address, but mum won't give me nothing. Maybe she don't got nothing to give.

Andrew says we going to take out the dredger and he teaches me a marine diesel engine – how to break it up, clean it up, oil it up and put it back – so I know how them little bits work together. Exhaust farts smoke and that makes me smile.

'You did that,' Andrew says and I think, Too right. I did that. Then he starts on football again like he does but I play rugby now I'm up county. I'm a fast left flanker, I tell him, and I think what Kasim would say if he was here. 'Rugby?' he'd go. 'Now I know you're chatting!' and I'd say, 'Nothing wrong with rugby,' and he'd go 'Except for being bait,' and I'd go, 'Try it yourself, bruv. You won't last five minutes,' and he'd say, 'You're all right, blood. Keep your rugby, posh boy, my threads is going to stay clean.'

We're on the work flat now, on the canal and I'm still thinking about mum and Kasim and then I hear: 'No, Donny, not the nearside bank.' Andrew is laughing and my ears tune back in. 'I was meaning the offside bank. That's the bank opposite the towpath. What are we going to do about it?'

He gets me to reverse the work flat so we can see what reeds and grass is growing there.

'Looks okay to me,' I say. 'It's nice with all them pink and yellow flowers. The birds need this for their home, don't they?'

'Right. It's a balance. You and I've got to decide. The canal users are going to want to turn here, and the birds are going to want to build their nests. What've we got here? Iris.' he brushes a yellow flower. 'That's what my granny used to call Flags. Here's what we want, Himalayan Balsam.'

He snaps off a bit of a pink plant. See-through blood comes out the end. Balsam is invasive, Andrew says. It chokes other plants and weakens the banks so they erode.

'Then we cut that and leave the rest?' I say.

'Right. Start pulling.'

The stems come up easy and my hands go sticky. 'Put your back into it, lad,' Andrew goes, laughing. He rocks the work flat and I drop to the boards so I don't go in the water. I

173

forget he don't know I don't swim and my belly goes tight and I want to deck him because he ain't got no right to laugh at me.

'Wasteman,' I go, 'if you wasn't some old man I'd –'

I check myself because I'm glad of Andrew and instead my eyes go heavy and I nearly start up crying but I don't. Andrew cuts the outboard.

He looks at me strange. 'I think I see now,' he goes, and then he swings his feet over the boat so his legs is up to his knees in water. 'Let me show you something.'

He smiles and slides off the side but he don't swim and he don't drown neither. He walks round the work flat like that's normal and the water don't even come up to his chest and he ain't even wet on account of them plastic trousers he wears.

I swear down, I never knowed a canal was like that. I never knowed you could walk, just like that. I never knowed I didn't have to be frit.

'Now look at this,' he goes, and gently opens up some reeds at the back of the work flat. 'See? A heron chick.'

A proper rude boy is what it is and he don't care about us. He stabs his beak at Andrew's hand, yellow eyes hard, then folds up his neck and sulks.

'Better leave him in peace before his mummy comes back, eh?'

I fix a lure and he sets a waggler float. There ain't no knot I can't fix now: line, twine, cable, rope, nylon, hemp, polypropylene, coir. I want to get one of them pike out the canal. Andrew says the word pike like it's something bad. He says they can swallow a duck whole, even a teenager if he goes in at the wrong time.

174

'You're chatting now,' I go.

But we don't never catch one. Andrew says the names of what we got in the keep net. Bream, mostly, but sometimes trout. I even hold them fishes a little time before they go back, but we don't let them all go.

'Supposed to put them back,' he goes, wrapping one of them fishes in newspaper. 'But I like a bit of trout.'

My line twitches and bends.

'Pull him in,' Andrew goes and drops the newspaper. I wind in the line.

'It'll snap,' I go. Rod makes a U. 'Andrew!' I say when the fish comes.

Andrew gets his triangle net under the fish and brings it to the bank.

'You've got a carp there, Donny. Biggest one I've seen in this canal.'

We lay him on the grass and he pants and gulps like he's drowning. Andrew's out of breath and all. He holds his side like it's sore.

'Put him back,' I say. 'He's dying.'

'Not yet. We must get the hook out first.' Andrew gets a towel out his kit bag and lays it over the fish. He wraps it up like a baby. 'Like I showed you. Go on.'

I clamp down on the hook with pliers and feed the metal through the fish's mouth. Carp's mouth starts bleeding, like when mum's earrings got ripped and I got bog roll for first aid, like at school, and told her it would stop and she was going to be okay. I concentrate on the hook. It comes out the same way mum slides out earrings at night, except the times she don't bother and goes to bed, same clothes on and all.

175

'Wait,' I say because Andrew starts peeling off the towel. The fish struggles. 'There's more.'

I work them pliers down the other hooks and each one got line still tied up in the hook's eye. Not all them hooks is the kind Andrew says is legal. Some got barbs and I cut them first before pulling the hook out his mouth.

'He's got the old kind of hooks. This one's rusty. Could've been swimming thirty years with all this,' Andrew says. 'Looks like this fish doesn't learn from his mistakes.'

'But he fights,' I say. 'He don't give up. He breaks the line every time.'

'Every time, except this one. Perhaps he was meant to find you? Perhaps he was looking for you, eh?'

I get the last hook out and kneel by the water to let him go. I watch my fish slide down into that murky dark and I know we ain't never going to meet again.

We use Zoe's landline to call Josh's dad and she says it's better I talk because gamekeepers is better dealing with men and, if they have to, boys. Josh's dad talks rough, like his time's already been wasted. Two of his usual beaters let him down, he says, dropped out of the Saturday shoot, so yes, he does have space. He says, 'good etiquette' a lot, which basically means say nothing to the guns, don't look at them and keep out of sight at lunchtime. He's worried we got no experience – we might drive the birds too quickly or too slowly – but he takes our names anyway. When I say Zoe's name, he asks me can she take it? He don't want no silliness, no girls crying over pricked birds.

'Well, friends-of-Joshua, I'll give you a go,' he says, like he ain't got no choice. 'Harpingdon Estate, Banyards Copse, tomorrow. Eight o'clock. If you're late you can go straight home. Bring your own bloody sandwiches and for Pete's sake, leave your blasted telephones at home.'

'Thank y—' Line goes dead.

Zoe runs downstairs and pulls coats out the coat room till there's a heap on the floor and she finds what she wants. Next, she's digging out shoes and boots.

'You've got to fit in. Try this on. And this. And these.' She dashes me a navy-blue Barbour, flat cap and a pair of green boots. Jacket makes me look like I'm a Green Lanes Young Turkz, but I know she won't get that so I say, 'I look like Jay-Z.'

'The queen, more like,' Zoe says. 'Actually, I was worried you'd find it too feminine. It's mum's.'

'Females don't wear these threads down my endz,' I say. I try the cap and look in the mirror. 'Ha! I look like a local now. Off to lime with my rich white friends.'

'Okay. If anyone asks, you're my adopted brother. No, you're on the Africa exchange. We get exchange students every year.'

'Allow it, man. Do I even look African?'

'Duh, yeah.'

'Duh, no. My dad's Caribbean.'

'Hey, well, they won't know the difference. They'll just see your skin.'

'My skin is brown. And I ain't pretending to be no African. Can I just be who I am?'

'Don't get all touchy. I don't care what colour your skin is.'

The thing is though, she do care. County people always care and I got three things to say about that.

177

One: I don't belong here. I want to lime with Kasim and get mashed by him at football and share a packet of Beef McCoy's and get chucked out of Maccy D when it's raining because we ain't bought nothing for time. I want to hear him spit lyrics at breaktime, half-Arabic, half-French, but all of them sick. I want to be how I am when I ain't trying to be nothing else except me.

Two: I want my mum.

And three: I changed up my mind. I want to go home.

Chapter 12

Andrew's brought a roll-up map to show me. It's like some kind of ancient scroll because they don't make maps like that no more. They make donkey kind of maps for road, motorway, alleyway, footpath, mountain, train line, tube line, ferry line, river and stream, but I ain't seen no map like this. And I done a PGL school trip to Wales so I know these things.

We're sitting on the grass by the lock-keeper's cottage eating lunch, except Andrew ain't touched his sandwiches and he's so skinny I don't think he's filled his belly for time. He taps the scroll, pours a cup of tea for me and stirs in three sugars. I unroll the scroll and he tells me it's a navigation chart for the whole of the Hertford Union Canal. At the bottom I see endz I know: Lee, Stratford, Regent's Canal, King's Cross. This chart goes all the way.

Andrew drags a finger down the line. 'There's the cut to the Thames, here at Globe Town.'

I shut my eyes and let that information rest. I listen up for Tottenham, Hackney, Islington but I don't hear nothing. I try again, concentrating. A plane's doing that air-brake thing, low hum, high whine; closer to me, willow branches clack in the wind and there's blackbirds, crows, a car engine a long way off. A coot hoots once in the reeds. Nothing else. Mostly silence.

'Are you okay, son?'

'How far is it? My mum's going to be in London soon. How long does it take you on a boat?'

He gives me a formula: count the number of locks, add the number of miles, divide that by three. That's the number of cruising hours.

A river snakes top to bottom down the middle of the paper. Ruler-straight lines connect up meanders, like in Geography, joining the river at the straightest points, cutting off a bend to take the short way. Them straight lines is the canal. My finger goes south and the Lee stops. No more river. It just ends.

'You've found the culverts,' Andrew says. 'Ask me what you're going to ask me.'

'What happens to it here?'

'Goes underground. You won't find it on an *A to Z* but it's there. They built tunnels under the roads and houses – culverts, they're called. They smuggled the Lee, its streams and tributaries into the Thames under everyone's feet. City folks are living on a river their whole lives and they never know it. North, south, east, west: home is best. Where was your home?'

'Me and mum ain't got a home exactly,' I say. 'But we had donkey number of rooms.' I start at the beginning. 'Mare Street, Clissold, Hackney; Queen's Road, Peckham;

Islington; Coventry – don't count, that was only a week; Hackney again; Clapton, Lower Clapton, Homerton, Haggerston ...'

Andrew looks at me funny for a little time, a sort of frown. He writes down some code, goes to his office and comes back with a book.

'Hackney Brook ... There! You see? It goes subterranean at Clissold Park. The ponds are the only part of the river above ground now. It runs right under Mare Street. You were sleeping on a river, lad. They call it a brook, but before they took it under, it was more of a river. See here.' He reads, '*1830: ten metres wide in Hackney, thirty metres when it met the Lee*. That's a substantial body of water, Donny.'

That book don't lie. I know because I lived it. Bodies of water what hide bodies in the water, all them rivers and streams, tunnels and culverts. They was always there underneath. I heard them sounds when I was little; the split and the crack, like having no weight no more, like the building's floating away.

The canal feels different now I know it goes south, goes home – right here, where I'm dashing Laura's manky bread in the water. Most people don't even know that. Canals move like ninjas, getting where they need to go and most people don't even know any of them is there.

I know Maths. I count the way Andrew says:

Twenty-nine locks on the Union Canal.

Add twenty-five miles, according to the map, equals fifty-four.

Divide it by three.

The answer makes me eighteen hours from mum.

A narrowboat comes out the lock gate. The skipper waves at us. Andrew nods and smiles like he do. The man's dog jumps on the cabin roof, getting bare happy to move, finally, after waiting at the lock where they got to shut him inside, on account of safety rules. He's wearing a lifejacket for dogs. They got them things for real. Skipper pulls back on the accelerator lever, motors round the bend and he's gone. Simple as that and I think, What if I took Andrew's canoe? What if I jacked his flatbed? I know where the diesel's kept. I know the codes on them padlocks.

And I think, Twenty-nine locks off-grid. Eighteen hours under the radar.

Andrew gives me his sandwiches and I'm glad of it because Laura cooked bread again. I dash a bit more in the water. Them ducks ignore it because they ain't dumb. Next up, there's a splash and Andrew's dog Ziggy jumps in. He comes back full of wet, shaking duckweed over my creps and dashes the bread on my knees. I dash it back, and he only goes and gets it again and it's proper soggy now.

'No way, Zigs!' I say and Andrew says sorry, he don't know how Ziggy got out. I remember when I thought that dog was trained to attack but most days he only sits next to me and we're tight. His nose gets up under my elbow a couple of times and he looks up at me so I stroke his wet head. I think he likes me.

Andrew calls time and takes him back to *Zuma Jay*. All them boats got their own names tagged both sides in curvy letters and shadows for everybody to see. *Zuma Jay*'s got another name I know – Camden, where she came from – and pictures of flowers and castles. That paint job don't suit Andrew.

Cabin stinks of fags and looks like the inside of a tree but it's still the best thing for living in I ever seen invented. For a start, there ain't no other kind of place what's got a hatch in the kitchen you can open up, and sit and look at birds on the water. You can even put a line in if you want and catch something from your window. And Andrew's got his own library in there, shelves what's built so books don't fall out when *Zuma Jay*'s moving. I pull out the biggest book, a World Atlas.

'Cup of tea?' When I nod he goes, 'You make it.'

I go round the galley looking for teabags and I can't find shit. Andrew kicks the seat panel.

'In there, son.'

'Where? There's no door.'

'Come here. You'd make a terrible Customs Officer. "I can't find the drugs! There's no door!" Thump it, lad!'

The seat comes away and there's a big hole in there where Andrew keeps tins and packets of stuff and a bottle of rum. That's the trick they done with these boats; they got secret stashes and holes all over the shop so it makes a little place big.

Andrew tells me about them pirates he had to watch out for back in the day, what tried to take his ship. They wanted money mostly. 'Hungry-looking lads with machetes,' he says. 'Your age, and younger. Blood-shot eyes from the drugs they were given.' He shows me on his atlas where he had to run his ship past them pirate boys up the Gulf of Aden and along the Red Sea to the canal at Suez. I know how that feels. Running out Vicky Park way into Newham, you got to keep your eyes open. You don't know for sure if you're going to get home.

'My daughter lives there,' Andrew says, pointing to the page on Australia and a photo of a red rock sitting in the desert on its ones.

I never knowed he had a kid. She must be old now. 'Have you been?'

'No.'

'Why not?'

'I don't want to bother her.'

He keeps postcards in that book. One of them's the same red rock as the encyclopaedia.

To Dad, hope you're well, it says. *Weather nice here. Having a lovely time. See you in June. Love, Kat x* The date on the stamp is May, 1989.

'I didn't see her in June. She never came back. Met an Australian. Stayed.'

Next postcard's a beach and people sitting on towels. I read it out: '*To Gramps, Happy Christmas, love Lacklan.*'

'What kind of a name is Lacklan?' Andrew goes.

The stamp says December 2017 and there's an address in little writing and then just *K* and *X*.

'You got a grandkid! Do you write him? Got any photos?' I say.

'There's no point now,' Andrew goes. 'It's too late.'

'No, it's not. Send a letter. Tell them how you are.'

'No point.'

'There is. I know what it's like. I write to my mum and she writes me,' and this is when I normally start chatting all kinds of shit about where mum is. But lies is starting to merk me so much now, so I tell him the truth like I ain't saying nothing at all.

184

'She writes me from Downview. That's a prison. She keeps getting into trouble and getting done. She don't mean it but trouble keeps coming back on her. She can't shake it off. But she's doing better now. This time I'm going to make sure of that. I'm going to look after her. I know when I'm sixteen my life's going to be better. I know she loves me and misses me because she writes it down in her letters. She'll be out soon and I'm going to go get her in town.'

He don't budge, so when I get back to Laura's I write it for him because sometimes grown-ups don't know shit about nothing.

Dear Kat and Lacklan, I go. *Andrew won't say it but he misses you. Please write him.* And I sign it, *Andrew's friend.* I write down the address of the Canal & River Trust office, in case they ever write back.

'You smell of cigarettes again,' Laura goes. 'I can smell it on your clothes.'

'I swear down, it's not me. It's Andrew. He smokes in his boat.' She sniffs round my face. 'And I know,' I say. 'Lung cancer and all that. We've been told at school a million times. I don't go there, for real.'

Laura's eyes is angry. She don't believe me.

'It's not about cancer, Donny. It's about chains. Mental chains.'

With Laura, things ain't never only things. Things always mean more than things.

'Donny, addiction and cancer is one thing, but look at the big picture. Look who's owned tobacco production around the world for four hundred years: big business, white

185

business. In my father's country they're still in control. The chains are invisible but they're there. Look at history! White Abolitionists in the North of the United States claimed to believe in emancipation –'

'Is it!'

'Yes. They were the first to free slaves, if you don't count Haiti – and General Toussaint Louverture is a whole other story – but the truth is, it wasn't until the tobacco fields in the North were exhausted by over-farming and stopped making a commercial profit, that the slaves were emancipated. In the South, where cotton was still growing, still making a profit, it didn't make economic sense to abolish slavery. Do you understand?'

'Slavery and smoking go together?'

'Yes. British-American Tobacco was founded on slavery and tobacco turns us into slaves. Consider it your duty, Donny, as a Black man, to never pick up those chains and put them on yourself.'

'Can I go now?'

She twists a lock of her hair and smiles. She knows I get it. I just never heard it said.

Laura's got smart things to say about all kinds of things, like being female and Black. And to be fair, it plays out good for me.

Because my life's like *Avengers Assemble* or all them *Oceans*; bare skills is needed and ain't one person got them all.

I keep that feeling for time, like I know what's what and my mind ain't twisted no more. I go over what I know and can do and what's coming soon.

Last day of Work Experience comes and they're all thinking I'm going back to Hillingford when they don't know shit about where I'm going. I been all right up county, but soon now I'm going to bounce.

Andrew gives me a present he wrapped in paper with boat knots all over and I'm keeping that paper safe, even if the present is lame, because I don't intend on forgetting them knots.

'You've been the best Hillingford boy I've ever had,' Andrew says. 'I'm nominating you for the prize. I'm very sad to see you go, so I want you to have this, for luck.'

But the present ain't lame. It's the coin; HUC. The one them navvies couldn't send their mums and which made the canal some kind of next slave gig. Forget zero hours, this was zero dollars.

'Thanks, Andrew.' I feel my eyes go wet but I don't let them.

'Look after it. There's not many of them left. I'd like you to think about coming here Saturday mornings, if you want to. I can't pay you, but when you've done your GCSEs, you can apply for an apprenticeship with the Canal and River Trust.'

I want to, but I can't tell him I ain't going to be here Saturdays nor no other days. Not because I don't want to, but because I got somewhere else to be and my mum needs me more than he do.

He smiles and we get on with it.

'Now,' he goes, 'the enamel paint is in the workshop. Off you go.'

Chapter 13

The field at Banyards Copse looks like steam's coming up off the mud. Spider webs criss-cross the ground, and everything – sand, dirt, silver-birch bark, the backs of new beech leaves – is gold from the sun coming up. Big-arsed buzzards do turns in the sky. Maybe they seen the cars. Land Rover Defenders in the wood. Lame Micras on the lane because they don't got off-road wheels. Maybe them buzzards know what's going to happen.

The birds me and Zoe's come here to beat is hiding for sure and I hope we find them because we're going to need that twenty-five quid.

We lean our bikes on a hedge. Skinny dog runs to me because most times dogs like me. He lies on my feet and looks up at me and his tail goes wag when I stroke him.

'Don't touch,' this man says like he's vex. 'That's a working dog, not a pet.'

Dogs is running round everybody's feet, whining and barking and I want to tell him, 'Your dog come to me, man, so it ain't my fault.' But I ain't saying nothing. These county mans is green like soldiers, all camouflage jackets and ammo pockets, and packing serious weapons. Guns, knives, clubs. And no lie, there's a little kid playing with a *Rambo Zombie* shank and ain't nobody calling Social Services.

Josh's dad tells us we got to drive them birds steady and me and Zoe got to split up. I take up my position in the copse like I'm a sniper in *Call of Duty*. I know a copse sounds like something what goes with robbers, but county endz it means a wood. And the trees in the copse is mostly dead-looking, sawn-off stumps, but them stumps sprout up fresh branches and leaves, long like cutlasses. When the wind knocks them about, shadows and sunshine change up warm and cool on my face.

'Don't let any get past the hedge to the lane,' a man says. 'If they do, they'll fly into the woods the other side and we'll lose them. Drive them back to the guns.'

'Yes, boss,' I say.

'I'm not your boss. I'm Bill.' He takes out a bag of tobacco and starts rolling. 'Going to be a nice day for you, son, nice and hot. I imagine you'll like that, coming from where you're from.'

'True that,' I say. 'I'm from Hackney. City's always more warmer than county, on account of the pollution.'

He looks at me for a second like he's got a question.

'City?' he goes. 'Today's guns are from the City. Business syndicate. They'll turn up soon; all the gear, no idea. No etiquette. Couldn't shoot an automatic camera.'

Six polish-up Range Rovers drive round the field cutting up circles, like in Maths when you describe a circle with a compass. City mans get themselves and the weapons out, stand by the bamboo sticks, shotguns split on their elbows.

It goes bare quiet like the wind's holding its breath. Even the dogs stop their whining.

They load them guns up and snap them guns shut: *click, click, click*.

Blackbird clocks us in his endz and sings a warning song. Bounce, then, I think. Mandem packing serious pieces.

Some man blows a trumpet and it all kicks off, shouting and barking and sticks beating up them bushes, and I ain't never been so shook. Pheasants start flying up but ain't no escape. Them guns fire, *pop-pop-pop*, though not exactly *pop* like a BB gun or PlayStation shooters or Lower Clapton at 3 a.m., more heavier. A bit of me's waiting for sirens, but no police come flashing their blues and I'm listening out for that noise what makes you go mental; you know, when helicopters sit in the sky for time and you're trying to sleep, but that don't come neither.

And them birds start dropping.

One.

Two.

Five.

Ten.

Exponential, you get me?

They fall and fall and fall some more, and the dogs collect, leaving birds at their people's feet. Most birds is dead but some try and get free. Mans get their clubs out and smash up still-alive ones on the head. They flap for a little time and go floppy and they go on the pile and all.

A trumpet sounds. It's lunchtime and my man Bill says this was a good morning.

I pick up one of them yellow tubes what comes out the guns. Bill says they're full of metal shot so they don't need

191

a good aim to bring a bird down, on account of the little bits of shot ball spraying everywhere. Them birds got no chance; needs only one little bit of metal to bring them down.

The syndicate mans give their guns to Josh's dad and drink fizzy wine by their Range Rovers like they won the Premier. Everyone's bare happy and you can see for miles and the sun's warm and everyone's laughing and chatting about all that death they done.

Zoe asks me how it was. 'Bit merky, innit,' I say and she squeezes my hand. She looks a bit more whiter than normal and lets me eat her sandwiches. I ask her where people go toilet round here and she points at the trees and says, 'Anywhere you like. I went behind the Range Rovers. You can pee on their tyres if you like.'

'Serious?'

'No, course not.' Zoe laughs at me. 'But they are dickheads. One of them's got a misogynist sticker on his boot. That's the kind of men they are. Spearmint Rhino and groping waitresses at charity suppers.'

'Mandem touched you?' I say. 'Tell me which one and they ain't never doing it again.'

'Relax, Donny. I can handle them. Besides, my dad probably manages their boss.'

I go round the back of them shiny new Range Rovers to piss and I'm thinking I'm going to ask Laura what misogynist means when I get back because she knows all the words in the dictionary. I clock the sticker. It's a pink cartoon lady what's wearing long heels and rabbit ears and bends over like she forgot something on the ground. Big hair flows down her back like sea waves and her arse is sticking in the air. It don't look comfy, standing like that, and something about her makes me think of LaShawna. I pick up a stone and scratch her off because it ain't nice to ladies to have that on your motor. It ain't polite.

I go back to Zoe and I'm still hungry so I eat the sandwiches Laura made even though they taste dry.

A banana hits my head.

'Sorry, mate. Slipped!'

Them boys behind us start up laughing.

'That's okay,' I say. I dash it back so it lands by their feet.

The banana hits my head again. I look round and they're laughing. 'You can have it, mate,' one goes. 'It's yours.'

I tell him no thank you and I ain't hungry and he goes, 'Not being rude or anything, but I thought you people liked bananas.'

My belly goes tight. Zoe's on her feet in a little second, standing over him.

'What's your problem?' she goes in his face.

'No problem. Just being friendly.'

'Stop being a tosser, then,' she goes. 'Leave him alone.'

'Who? Your new boyfriend?'

His friends laugh.

Zoe dashes my bread crusts right in his face. Laura's home-made brown rye ain't soft like sliced white. They could do some serious damage, so I'm glad for him he got reactions and bats them away before they hit. Them boys is laughing at her now, rolling in the grass, so I stand up to sort it but she pushes me down and says, 'Leave it. They're not worth it. Remember why we're here.'

Trumpet goes for the next bit of killing. Zoe looks like she's trying to say sorry so I go, 'It's okay. We all done it. Do the mission and move up, nah? Twenty-five quid.'

'Plus tips.'

'Plus tips. Then we're out of here. You're going to smash that modelling interview, innit. Man, them idiots is going to see you on the TV and wish they showed more respect!'

'And we're going to find your mum.'

Trumpet goes again and them guns start firing. Bill's got a smile on his face. He says the tips is going to be big today; they must've shot fifty, sixty birds. Says he's going to take his wife to dinner on the back of this day.

A dog drops a bird at my feet, wings is still flapping.

'Use this,' Bill goes, dashing me his club. 'Give it a knock.'

I don't think about it too much, just bring it down the way I seen. Pheasant tries to stay living for a little time but I know he's dead when his eye slides back. And it don't feel right at all. I don't know if you ever touched a pheasant before, but they're probably the most softest thing in the world. As well, feathers is more warm than you think, like your bed in the morning when you don't want to get up. And close up, pheasants got bare colours like a tropical bird and them colours change up in the light. Neck feathers go green and purple. Brown body ain't brown at all; it's gold, with bits of black at the top of each feather. And he's got a clean white necklace and a red eye-patch, which goes to say he don't belong here. He should live somewhere safe. Some nice tropical place.

I lie him down gentle and my hands is blooded up. A dog comes, collects my bird and goes down the hill. Soon as he's gone, this brown lady pheasant thinks it's time to bounce and she got more brains than all of them because she goes the right way for a change, flying low over the lane. More birds run flapping their wings and running like they ain't sure they want to take off and they're all coming my way and all.

'Go,' I say. 'It ain't safe here.'

I know where I'm meant to drive them and I know there ain't much time left and the more them mans kill, the happier they get, and the happier they get, the more dollars they tip. But still. It don't feel right. I drop my stick and press my back on a tree like I ain't there at all. Them pheasants go by, under the hedge and start up flying, hooting their metal songs like they're taking the piss.

Trumpet goes and I run down the hill, counting my twenty-five quid, counting my tips and all. But it don't go the way like we planned and I should know that by now. Things don't never go the way I want.

'My car!' one of them City mans goes. He's gone purple, yelling in a gamekeeper's face. 'Can't you keep your bloody beaters under control? Find out who did it!'

'Sir, I assure you this is unprecedented,' Josh's dad says but the man's already walking away from him. He checks out the Range Rover, running his fingers down them scratches.

Beaters is bare vex an' all, their tips gone for the day. They start chatting about how it was such a day and a shame. But Josh's dad ain't dumb. I don't know how but he clocks it was me.

'Allow it, sir man. It weren't me,' I say, but them boys from lunchtime say I'm lying, they seen me. They say everyone best check their bags and pockets and all, because they heard I was from Hackney.

Zoe steps up. 'It was me,' she goes. 'I did it. It was demeaning to women. He's a dirty old man.'

'Bloody feminazis!' Range Rover man roars. 'This is criminal damage. You'll pay for this, mark my words!'

Josh's dad tells him this ain't never happened before and he's going to think about letting untested girls on the drive again. He swears down Zoe and her darkie friend won't get their pay. Range Rover Man ain't listening. His wheels carve up the dirt.

Beaters do get paid though. Josh's dad got a roll and he gives them their paper and two dead birds each. They go off to their crappy cars and he just looks at us and I know there ain't no point arguing this one. Zoe's vexed up and crying but she ain't going to let nobody see.

'Hold on, son.' My man Bill's got something for me when we get our bikes, though it ain't exactly what I wanted: two birds tied up by their necks. 'Take them,' he goes but I ain't touching them dead things no more. I look at Zoe because she knows county.

'Thanks,' Zoe goes. 'Put them in here. I'll carry them for Donny.'

And them birds curl up in her panier like they got no bones, like they're sleeping.

We freewheel down the lane, our legs sticking out sideways, weaving like we don't care if nothing's coming and I don't know if it was not getting our dollars or the wind but both of us is crying by the time we get to the main road. And one mile later, we start up laughing for no reason.

'Your face!' Zoe says. 'When that bloke gave you the dead birds …'

'Allow it!'

'You looked like a bad extra in a horror film. "Take this, Donny, my severed hand!"'

Back at Zoe's yard we dump the birds in her garage and work out what we going to do.

'No taxi fare. No train fare. No bus fare,' I say, 'and do pheasant blood ever come off?'

'We'll find a way,' Zoe goes. 'I promise.'

I call mum and tell her about the beating and collecting and picking and shooting and little boys with shanks and City mans wearing diamonds on their timepieces and taking the life out of them pheasants with a club on the eye. She goes, 'Oh my days! Sounds like Clapton.'

'Yeah, mum,' I say. 'I don't think I need to be here no more. I think I'm better off in town.' And I ask her where she's going to be and what time, because soon it's all coming to an end and I want to be there. She tells me the name of the women's refuge at King's Cross.

'I want you to be there, Don, I really do, but –'

'I don't care what they say. I'll be there,' I say because I will.

I try but mum ain't having it. I don't think she believes what I said about beating and all them guns and knives. School sent her my June report so she knows I got put up to top set in Maths and I won the best Work Experience prize and teachers is now saying I got to stay in sixth form after Year Eleven and do A-levels and shit. So she ain't having it.

197

'No, Don. You stay where you are. You're better off there, babes. You're more better off than you've ever been.'

'Don't say that mum,' I go.

'It's true though. Say some of that Latin you been learning.'

'Like what?'

'I don't know. It's all Greek to me!'

'Do I have to?'

'Go on. Anything.'

'Okay. *Te amo mater*.'

'What's that when it's at home?'

'I love you, mum.'

'Aw! Teach me to say it back, Don. Go on.'

'Something like, *Te amo filius*, maybe? *Filius* means son.'

'*Te amo filius*, that right? Did I do it right?'

'That's right, mum. *Semper*.'

I was going to tell her *semper* means the same as 'always' but her fifteen minutes of call time is up and the line goes click and we don't even get to say goodbye.

I plug in my phone to charge and start up reading the book Zoe gave me. That story happens like I'm watching it. I don't stop till it's done and when it's done I think, Donny the Champion of the World! And I see them pheasants flying over the lane to where they're safe and I'm glad of that.

As well, I make a promise because I can't do some things no more. So I swear down: no matter how skint, no matter how low, I ain't doing no merky shit, begging off of no big man.

Not town.

Not county neither.

And I know what I got to do to make this work. If we ain't got no money, we ain't getting no taxi. And if we ain't getting no taxi, we ain't catching no train.

Whatever, man. Them twenty-nine locks is calling me. We're taking the canal.

Sunday morning I start scoping for a boat what ain't lived in, the keys left in the Canal & River Trust office. I scope the winter moorings first, the long-let ones. I'm still looking for shut curtains and padlocks on the outside of hatches when Zigs comes up wagging his tail. I kneel down so he can lick my face because that's what he likes.

'Hey, Donny!'

Andrew leans out *Zuma Jay*'s swan hatch and I must've gone soft or something because I start feeling shaky like he can see what I'm trying. I jump on board and drop down the hatch so my feet don't touch the steps, the way Navy sailors do.

'All right?' I say.

'There's a poem I want you to read to me,' he goes. 'It's by A.A. Milne.'

'Poem?' This is a bit weird and I ain't got time for no poem. I got to get to town so I say, 'Bit busy now. And I'm no good at reading poems,' but he jams the book in my hand anyway, folds my fingers over. 'I mean, I don't like reading,' I say. 'And I've got bare stuff to do.'

'Look up "Disobedience",' he goes. I don't know what he's chatting about. My behaviour been just about nearly 100 per cent here. 'Go on.'

'Okay.' I read the poem to myself first before I read it out loud to him. It's about this kid called James who's only three

199

and he tries to take care of his mum, only she goes down town on her ones and gets lost.

Me and Ziggy jump because Andrew suddenly goes, 'Tell me,' and I think the man's tripping, 'what can anyone do?'

'I don't know. I'm sorry, but this is bullsh– I mean, it makes no sense.'

'Well, think about it. What would you do if you were James?'

I don't need to think about this one.

'I'd go down the town and get her.'

Andrew looks like he's chewing something what don't taste right.

All of a sudden he says: 'I'm going in for an operation. Tomorrow morning.' I sit down by him. 'They think I'll be in for three weeks at least. Ziggy can't come. They want to stick him up in a cage in Hertford dog pound. I can't leave my Ziggy.'

When he hears his name, Ziggy jumps up and licks Andrew's white beard and I swear down Andrew looks like Santa. 'You're too big, hound. Get down!' he goes and Zigs jumps down and sits on my creps. 'I told them Ziggy's my seeing dog. I can't do without him.'

'Yeah. He's your seeing dog, all right. Sees your food and takes it.'

'Right,' he laughs. 'But they didn't believe me. I've never even had glasses. So, I was going to ask you. Can you take care of Zigs for me? And keep an eye on *Zuma Jay* until I get back?'

And I get it now. Andrew don't need no beard to be Santa and I don't need to wait till Christmas. He's giving me the best present ever, right now.

'Yes, Andrew, I will,' I say. 'I promise.'

'Keep her head clean. Empty the cartridge every day. If I learned anything in the Merchant Navy, it's to keep your heads clean. And your oil checked. And your ropes tidy.'

'Yes, Andrew, yes.'

'And don't get too attached. I'll be back in three weeks.'

So it ain't exactly a lie when I text Zoe and say, *Andrew says we can take Zuma Jay to London. Meet U 2moro B ready*.

Laura's looking at one of them newspapers you have to buy with money. 'This is interesting,' she says. 'Men called Edward earn an average salary of sixty-two thousand pounds a year. And the lowest average wage-earning name is, of course, a woman's name.'

'I know averages,' I say. I don't need the *Guardian* to tell me there ain't no Jades or LaShawnas out there getting greens. 'Averages lie though,' I add. 'Especially in this country. You got a couple of people holding everything, so the inequality is probably even more bad.'

Laura smiles at me like she's finished one of her flowerbeds and she likes what she done.

I wash up and say I need a packed lunch for school. Laura asks me why, because I get free school meals, so I tell her it's on account of a match I'm playing in. I smile the way kids here do; the smile county kids give parents what ain't theirs.

I send Zoe another text. *Getting pasta bring money*. She pings back in a little second. *Got money numpty. Don't panic xxx!* Emoji boat. Heart. Flowers. Sunglasses. Wine bottle. Cake. I don't know why girls do that shit.

'That's some lunch,' Laura says when she comes back. 'Are you feeding your friends as well?'

'No, I'm just more hungrier on Mondays. Actually, the match is after school. I'm going to be rather late back,' I go, and I pray I don't say words like *actually* or *rather* by accident when I hook up with mum and Kasim and my own peoples.

And I want to see the look on Kasim's face when I roll up King's Cross endz in some next-level narrowboat. I ain't got his digits no more, but as soon as I pick up mum we're going round his yard. Mum and Mrs Z can chat mum stuff and baby Ghislaine's got to be four years old now, so me and Kasim can take her down Barnsbury and she can laugh her head off in the park.

I ain't got much time. I put all them dried pans, plates and stuff in the cupboards and take biscuits, tins and a whole bread. When my school rucksack's full I use my rugby bag. I work out we need enough for three days but I ain't got a clue what three days looks like in food. What we need is enough money. If we got enough money, we don't need much food. We can just buy it when we want it. Proper food, like chicken shop or Maccy D's.

Laura's got three ten spots in her purse. Them notes feel good and new but my brain spoils it. How many deliveries Michael done for this? How much would this buy mum? I put them back, one by one, because I lived more than one life already though I ain't sixteen yet, and I ain't going back.

I set my alarm before Laura and put on my uniform like nothing's different. Olu's SIM card goes in my pocket because, I don't know, maybe I might need back-up. And I act like there ain't nothing going on, home threads and my best creps in the kit bag. I run to the bus-stop tree and carry on going till I get to the canal.

Andrew's on the towpath, taxi waiting. He stops to breathe like he's proper sick which he ain't. Or maybe he is, but I know he can walk faster than that.

'I've come to get Ziggy,' I go.

Andrew puts some keys in my hand and says, 'Take care of my boy.'

'I will,' I say. 'Just until they kick you out. Man, they don't even know what they're getting, do they? You'll get excluded in no time, watch!'

Them keys is attached to a tennis ball; one key for the hatch and one for the engine. It's smart when you think about it. Keys ain't going to sink if they ever get dropped, and Ziggy can swim for the ball.

The taxi goes and I ain't said thank you or bye or nothing and now there's no point even waving.

I check the time on my phone and write a text: *Where RU? Hurry* but before I press send, Zoe rolls up with a rucksack.

'This is so exciting!' she says, laughing and hugging me up. 'I can't believe we're actually going to London.'

Before we go, I leave a message on mum's voicemail because after now, I ain't letting them track me on no GPS. When I get through, I say, 'I tried this county life, mum, and it ain't for me. I don't care what they say, I'm going to be there: King's Cross, Monday. Don't worry about nothing because I got it, and what I don't got, we can work out. I miss you, mum. I'm coming home.'

PART 3

Canal

Chapter 14

Zuma Jay starts up like she's been waiting for me. I idle the engine a few minutes to warm up while I sort the mooring ropes. Each rope off the bollard makes me more lighter, like we're going flying. I curl them in neat coils on the roof the way Andrew showed me, the way they do in the Merchant Navy.

'Time to embark,' I say. I boss the first manoeuvre off the mooring like I been a skipper before I can walk, and when we're on open water, I say, 'You can pilot her now.'

I give Zoe the tiller arm because I don't think nobody ain't better off for getting boat skills.

'Aye aye, Cap'n!' Zoe goes in some kind of pirate voice.

County kids act so much like kids. A little smile starts up anyway on my face. Ain't nobody else around except Ziggy on the prow, barking at swans and coots, so I say, 'Aye aye, let's be getting us to London Town.' Ain't nobody watching.

We motor on the legal limit, four miles an hour. This engine can do six. Problem is, if you go too quick, you only drag the hull on the canal bed and that's what Andrew calls counterproductive, because it ends up slowing you down when you think you're going faster. As well, I ain't going to damage the banks and mash up *Zuma*'s prop and stern gear. And I ain't going to be responsible for pulling out no mooring pins neither.

'I feel sorry for Andrew,' I say. 'What if he gets complicated? What if he's got to live for time in hospital?' I ain't said this to Andrew, but I know what it's like. 'The problem with places what ain't home is they ain't home. The walls ain't your walls. The bed ain't your bed. It belongs to other people and you're only staying. They don't have to keep you neither. They can say, "Go now. We don't want you no more," and you got to go.'

I don't think Zoe gets it; she only lived in the one house, so I'm surprised when she don't say nothing, just squeezes my shoulder.

'I know, Don,' she goes, rubbing my back. 'I know.'

'That's what my mum calls me. Don.'

The diesel motor goes *putt-putt* and we go down a tunnel of willow branches that cuts up sunlight so it dances on our faces and *Zuma Jay*'s fine ceramic paint. A heron takes off, hanging on his wings, legs dangling for a few beats, before he hides them the way you see landing gear fold up on a plane. If you ever go Richmond Park, you can watch them planes do that. Moorhens sprint to the balsam me and Andrew ain't cleared yet. Black water and white scum gets sucked under, halfway down the long of the boat, as if the canal's downing a Guinness Punch.

Zoe gets boat skills in no time. She sits up, watching, holding the tiller steady, so I can kick back and stare up at the branches and the sky, maybe sleep a little between the flower tubs and the coal pile.

'What are you thinking?' she asks.

'Nothing,' I say, because I ain't.

Minute goes by and I tell her, 'Innit, phone's dead.'

'That's a good thing, isn't it? They can't track us now.'

'I know that, only ... I wanted a message back from mum.'

A leisure widebeam comes up. You can't say it's coming fast, but four plus four makes an impact speed of eight, so it ain't nothing.

'Shit, Donny, which side again?' Zoe says.

'Port.'

'What?'

'Left.'

'That's on a road, you dingbat! This boat is coming towards us on the right.'

'That's their left.'

'Donny?'

'Relax, fam.'

Two old people in the barge smile at her. I seen that with Zoe before. She's the kind of girl grown-ups smile at because her face makes them feel good. She even looks like she can do nothing but good. Them freckles on her face and yellow hair do the opposite of my tallness and brown skin.

I should be on the tiller because our fenders touch.

'Sorry,' Zoe says to them old people.

'No problem,' they go.

She goes red and says, 'I'm not very good at this yet.'

Next second, they clock me and a different kind of smile sits on their faces, like they think we gone and nicked a boat.

I see it happen in slo-mo. Zoe sees it too and I catch a flicker of panic in her eyes.

Zoe is quick. 'Daddy?' she whines into the cabin. 'Can you come up here and take over, please? I need the toilet!'

When we don't see them no more, I do my best county accent. 'Daddy, I need the toilet.'

'Rubbish,' Zoe says. 'You still sound London.'

'Teach me, then. Teach me to speak Hertfordshire.'

'If you mean RP, you just have to make your vowels longer and –'

'Yes?'

'Wait! I know a joke. Say, "Air".'

'Air.'

'Say, "hair".'

'Hair.'

'Say, "lair".'

'Lair.'

'Put them together and you'll sound like the queen.'

'Air, hair, lair.'

'Air, hair, lair to you too. Charmed, I'm sure.' Zoe waves a little circle.

I try again. 'Daddy, I need the toilet!'

'Better. But you have to believe it.'

'I know that,' I say. 'It's called Stanislavski's Realism, innit. I done it in Drama. To act the character you got to *be* the character.'

'Close your eyes,' she goes. 'You're fifteen. Your dad's a stockbroker. You never see him because he works all week in the City and he's having an affair with a woman, not much older

210

than you, who he keeps in an apartment in Chelsea. Your mum drinks a bottle of wine every night to forget she knows that. You live in a big house, with a drive that has a turning circle.'

I open my eyes. 'You're describing your yard,' I say.

'Shut up and pay attention.' Her fingers run down my face to shut my eyes. 'You've never sat in a car that's more than a year old or didn't have leather upholstery and walnut dashboards. You use your cashcard all the time and you never know your balance. You don't need to know. It's always topped up anyway, by your dad who feels guilty. As he should do. You have three holidays every year. One of them's skiing. One of them's at your grandparents' place in Provence. The other could be anywhere really, but usually long-haul; India, Caribbean, the Maldives. And you're bored. You're so bored that a shitty little trip on a stinky narrowboat is the most fun you've had in your whole life.' I open my eyes. 'Now talk. Talk like me, Donnislavski!'

'Daddy,' I go. 'I need the toilet!'

'Perfect.'

And it was.

Slow miles and some more slow miles and some next slow miles and all. Soon, every time the boat gets near the bank, Ziggy starts up whining, leaning out, paw in the air.

'Dogs don't really like boats,' Zoe says. 'Look, he wants to get off. He needs a pee. Have you ever looked after a dog before?'

'No,' I say because that ain't no lie. Truth is, I never looked after a dog good enough so it stayed.

'Hey, Zigs! I like you, Zigs. Yes, I do,' she goes, and I try to remember what we did when Torvill needed out and I was little. Sometimes I can't even see his face.

We stop by a field and moor up to a tree. Ziggy's on the bank already. After he's done a long piss up a tree, he runs tight circles, throwing sticks for himself the way he does when he's bare happy. Cows clock him, stamp and snort, and they start coming over so we leg it to the boat. Inside, yellow lights make the cabin glow, like shop windows down Oxford Street at at Christmas-time, except this time I'm on the inside.

'So,' I say, 'we got a switch here and here. The alternator charges the leisure battery all the time we're motoring. And if that don't work, there's kerosene for back-up.'

'Stinks a bit.'

'I like that smell,' I say, and I think, If me and mum lived on a barge like *Zuma Jay*, we wouldn't never miss no room. 'You can sleep there. I'll take the galley bench.'

I start opening tins and light the gas burner. Andrew ain't the sort what parties. He got two chipped enamel bowls, one tin mug, a spoon, a teaspoon and a knife and that makes Zoe laugh.

'Not quite *Bake Off*, is it? What we need is a centrepiece.'

She comes back with cow parsley which, if you don't know, looks like somebody's been cutting up a wedding dress or christening clothes. She puts them flowers in the mug on the table and it looks nice.

'I'm gonna have your back, you know, when you hook up with Talent Man,' I say.

'I know you're worried, but I'll be fine. It won't look right if you come too.' She taps the table with them long nails what mess up proper basic stuff like tying laces or sending a text. 'It's just not your world. These guys are fashion professionals. Paris, Milan, New York. They don't want to see a teenage boy; you'll put them off.'

'Nah, but they want a teenage girl though, don't they? They know you're only fifteen?'

She don't look at me. She dashes the teaspoon in the food she ain't started eating.

'I'm nearly sixteen. This is something I have to do on my own.' She pushes the bowl my way. 'Do you want this? I'm stuffed.'

'You ain't eaten nothing.'

'Well, anyway, I don't want to be all fat and bloated tomorrow.'

I ain't never not hungry so I don't mind eating her food. I knock the wooden panel under the seat and find Andrew's bottle I clocked.

'Secret stash,' I say.

We don't need no *Bake Off* no more so I take the flower out, dash the water out the swan hatch and fill the mug up with rum.

'Let's get rat-arsed!' she goes. First taste and she coughs and goes pink.

I copy her, saying 'rat-arsed' in her county accent. 'You ever seen a rat's arse?' I say. 'Because I have, when I done Snowdonia PGL in Year Nine. Me, Kasim, Little Hassan and Tommy, we was in the same team. We seen this fence in Wales made with bare pointy bits of wire, and stuck in them twists of wire was three little rats, like them ones what live on Tube tracks. Instructor Man said they was moles. The

213

valley was flooded, he said, and they tried to escape but they got stuck on the fence and drowned. I thought about them all frit, legging it from the water rising up, chasing them. Teacher Lady from my school's thinking the same because she goes, "God! Really?" and the Instructor Man just laughs at her. He was joking. It was the mole catcher. Used poison. Mole Man stuck them there to show the farmer he'd done the job so he'd get his money.'

'I'm going vegetarian.'

'You don't want to eat rats no more? They taste like –'

'Dingbat.'

'Joking! Seriously though, did you ever go Outward Bound? One time the Instructor Man says he lost the map and we got to get back on our ones. No map, no phone. "Rah, boy!" we said. "This is raw!" So we had to look out for clues, listen out for water, look at what the sun's doing.'

'So, exactly how many years were you yardies wandering round the mountains?'

'No, we smashed it. We found a path down, like Bear Grylls.' I don't tell her I was frit at the start, hands in my pockets in case them sheeps bite. 'And you're thinking we ain't made for them mountains, ain't you? Now that's what Laura calls making an assumption. You're thinking that because most of us was brown we don't know mountains.' Zoe laughs. 'Let me tell you something. My man, Little Hassan, he was made by mountains. Turkey mountains. He dropped a kid once. It was the Eid when he was twelve and his mountains back home was still white. It weren't a kid like you think, though. It was a goat and he dropped it like Ibrahim with his grandad's blade in the neck. He showed us

214

what it looked like. Don't know how he'd stashed it all week; they was contraband.'

'Oh, my God! He had a knife?'

'Nah, an iPhone 6s. He showed us a photo. Little Has said that blade was like a thousand years old. His grandad put a hand on his hand and showed him how.'

I can see Hassan cutting through the alive thing's neck, holding down its struggle.

'God, Donny, stop. You're making me feel sick.'

'He said he stroked the kid all the time it was dying, said it took bare long to bleed out and hot blood made holes in the snow and it was quiet because the kid couldn't cry because its throat was cut. No one said nothing to Little Hassan after that.'

I tell her about lying on my belly in the grass and moss to look down a mine shaft. I say how the rock smelled the same as rusty swings or blood. And I want to ask her, because sometimes she's older than me, though she ain't by months, how comes we never see left-over blood when some youth gets shanked? They clean it up quick so we don't see.

And I tell her about mum getting me from the coach and walking me home because I got to cross N5. Zoe don't get what I mean so I say, 'It's a postcode thing. You don't cross N5 when Youngers know you're supposed to be in E2. Not without your mum or a grown-up.'

'Was she not scared?'

'My mum ain't scared of nobody. She'd do time for me.'

I tell Zoe how Mum got us a Maccy D on the way home and we stayed up late to talk about everything and nothing and next day she called me in sick so we could lime because school ain't everything.

'She's nice like that, my mum. Bare nice.'

But I don't tell Zoe about the dreams what still come in my brain, like baby sheeps down the mine what ain't crying because their throats is cut. And sometimes I dream there's blood all over the streets, because the grown-ups have given up. Because that's what would happen if they did. London would surely turn red.

And I still dream about Michael and what it feels like if your lung fills up with blood and what inside-the-skin things look like when they spill outside. As well, I'm older than him now and that hurts and all. He ain't never going to be older than me again.

Zoe starts up smiling and claps.

'This is going to be so brilliant! We'll find your mum, you can eat a celebration McDonald's and I'll get so rich from my new modelling contract we'll literally have to buy a swanky flat in Mayfair. No, an apartment. No, a penthouse!'

'Can mum come live with us and all?'

'Of course! Oh my God, your mum sounds amazing! She's definitely not the sort of parent who tells the bloody au pair to switch off the WiFi at eight. Donny, this is going to be awesome! We'll give parties to beautiful fashion people and super-talented recording artists.'

'And footballers?'

'And footballers, yes.' She's going to like Kasim then, because he's probably scoring for the Gunners by now. 'They'll park their luxury cars outside and get parking fines they don't mind paying because they've got so much dosh.'

'Bentley Continentals?'

'No. Probably Range Rovers.'

'Balotelli drives a Continental.'

'Whatevs.'

I get a blanket out the cupboard, turn the lights off and lie on the bench. My feet stick out over the end and though it got foam and stuff, it's too cramped for my shoulders and I think, Look: big man like me! I grown bare much since the last time I looked. Ain't no way but to turn on my side and bring up my knees. I hear Zoe in the bow pulling the cover over and put out the light.

The moon shows through the swan hatch and all the wood in the cabin goes silver and I only have to sit up to see the water. Zoe sees it too and comes over.

'It's beautiful,' she says. 'The water looks frozen. Like you could step out on to it and skate all the way to London.' She laughs at my knees sticking into the table. 'You don't fit. Let's swap.'

'I'm okay.'

'Come in with me and Zigs.'

'All right.'

I turn so my back's to her. I lie still and don't say nothing in case it stops. I ain't slept like this since me and mum had that room in Dalston. It's weird and I know my breathing ain't normal and I hope she don't clock it and think I'm dirty or nothing. It's like I been holding my breath or I'm trying to hide that I just been sprinting, but it ain't about her. I feel my

217

legs jumping. Ziggy's sleeping on my feet like a dead weight, but it ain't that. It's because I want this bit to go quick. I want to get there.

And I think there's Science going on here. The long of the galley's got light what started in the sun shining on the moon, and next thing it gets split by a willow on the bank, hits the water and goes on in the cabin and on us. Zoe's right, it's beautiful. And *Zuma Jay* rocks us or maybe some deep current goes under the hull, or maybe it was only from my own feet walking down the cabin. Bare Science going on, anyways.

Most people think a canal's a still thing. They look at it like it's some long puddle or thin pond, thinking it don't move like a river. But it do. Andrew told me about the time the Union section went dry, on account of peoples leaving the lock gates open. I don't know if they did that on purpose or they just forgot, but one night the water kept going and going. It carried the stars on its back and it didn't stop till it found the sea. Next morning, cormorants and herons picked out their eats for free in the mud, and when them boaters woke in their little narrowboats and Dutch widebeams and big-up static houseboats, they was proper stranded.

Back in the day, maybe I was like them birds getting what I can. But now – watch! – maybe I'm all that black water slipping out them locks.

'Can you hold me?' Zoe goes. I shift round, fold the blanket so we don't exactly touch. I wait a bit and put my arm on her shoulder. Not under the cover though. My hips go to the edge of the bed, away from her. We don't say nothing. It's only our breathing and my heart beating and the Union Canal on *Zuma Jay*'s hull.

'You know this doesn't mean anything,' Zoe says.

'I know,' I say.

But it do.

It means everything because it's like I'm six and mum's next to me on our mattress and I hear the crack and water going under us and I know we're going to keep floating till we find home.

When I wake up Zoe's gone and I hear the engine. I go through the cabin to the tiller hatch. Zoe don't see me straight away. She's checking her speed round a bend like I said to her and like Andrew said to me, because you can't know what's coming round the next corner.

'You got her started. She's tricky,' I say, except she ain't no more, not really, because I stripped the engine and did the servicing myself.

'Morning,' Zoe says, concentrating on what's coming. 'Donny, please explain why blokes always call boats and cars she. My dad does it, too.'

'I don't know.'

'I think it's because they secretly want to have the same kind of control over women; drive them, ride them.'

'Like Talent Man?' I say.

'That's different. He's giving me an opportunity. And stop calling him that. His name's Nico.'

Zoe knows herself and I ain't going to change up her mind. She's always one thing and another. Sometimes at the same time. One minute, she's rolling up her skirt, contouring her face and telling everyone about her fake boyfriends. The next, she's in a onesie, all, 'Don't look at me, dirty old man.' And whatever she is or ain't, she knows herself and for that moment, it's the truest and only thing. Ain't nobody can argue with that. But when I hear Nico's name, my belly goes tight and I want to dash her school clothes over the side and watch them fill up with water and sink to the silt at the bottom. But I don't do that because I know what them dredger-mans would be like if they think they're going to get a bike or a trolley and they get a blazer and some schoolgirl skirt rolled up at the waist.

'Last night ...' I start to try to tell her about me and mum but maybe I should've put more oil on them bearings because the crankshaft sounds like there's metal contact on the loading. *Zuma Jay* jacks what I say.

Zoe's braces shine when she smiles. 'Stop worrying,' she goes. 'It's going to be fine. In fact, it's going to be better than fine. The difficult bit's over. We got here okay, didn't we, on our own?'

I don't say, but I got a feeling the difficult bit's coming up in about ten locks. But I ain't worried about the locks. Andrew taught me donkey kind of locks: paired locks, staircase locks, narrow locks, broad locks, barge locks, stop locks and boat lifts. There's even a lock in Scotland what can make a barge fly and I want to see that one day with my own eyes. So I know I'll smash it. And anyway, we already done Ware, Hardmead, Stansted, Feildes, Dobbs, Carthagena, Aqueduct and Cheshunt. I ain't worried about Waltham and Rammey, and maybe Enfield too. But we still got Tottenham, Walthamstow Marshes and Stratford.

The Housing Association tried giving us Stratford one time, saying it had Westfield shopping centre and all that nice new Olympic stuff, but mum turned it down, saying – though she weren't exactly saying, she was more screaming at the man in Housing: 'You trying to kill my boy? I won't let you kill my baby boy!'

So, yeah. I think the hard bit's downstream and coming our way.

I only got a little thing to say about night number two.

I decide I need to tell mum, when I see her, that them barge lights by Enfield lock look like searchlights, the way they spread out in long triangles on the water.

And the way they touch, it's like all our boats is threaded together.

Chapter 15

Zoe's in her school uniform before we even get there. Her mum's cleaning lady ironed her shirt flat and she ain't forgot her blazer neither. Logo's on the pocket, same place it always is, all the schools I been to. The Hillingford one has kids with their arms growing into tree branches where their hands should be. And that's just messed up. You're always better off having proper arms.

At St Pancras Lock, Zoe says she's going to come with me.

'Okay, but only to the door,' I say. 'When I go in, wait up outside with Ziggy,' and his tail starts up beating the table. He runs to my creps and looks at me and I swear he ain't never thought even one time about Andrew.

Before I slide the hatch shut and snap the padlock, I get Andrew's kitchen blade. It ain't nothing against some cutlass or Samurai shit, in fact it's only good for potatoes and carrots, but it makes me feel better because I know these endz, and I know the Women's Centre at King's Cross because we been there before, me and mum, when luck was low.

But first I got to do something I should've done before, like time before. I go to the booth on Cally Road what sells and unlocks phones. Phone Man knows what I'm talking about. Two seconds later, he hands me this thick, vintage Nokia, 2006, and a BlackBerry. Some roadmans still rate them kind of phones, like old-school BlackBerries, because they ain't got tracking and BBM don't got cell location so basically, the CPS can't do jack. I give the man one of the twenty spots Zoe swears down her mum don't even know about because she drops paper all over the house when she's drinking. Olu's SIM works in the Nokia and I switch both phones on. The batteries is still full even though they was probably last used years ago, which also goes to show that iPhones ain't all that. I give Zoe the number and make a text on her BlackBerry, ready to send.

'Keep this on you,' I go. 'If you need me, press send and I'll come.' Zoe looks at it like I given her dog shit to carry. 'It's only for the case of emergency.'

'The only emergency here is your taste in phones.'

I get a new padlock a few shops down, fix one of them new padlock keys on the tennis ball and give the spare to Zoe. You see, I got it all set out in my brain and, like I said, my life's like all them *Oceans*.

'We better get a float for that soon,' I say. 'Don't let me forget we got to switch up the lock when we get back.'

And when all that's done, we go round the back of King's Cross. I take a deep breath, go to the desk and ring the bell. Lady looks at me like I'm suspect. She's smiling, but I seen her face shift and her shoulders went stiff when she first clocked me.

224

'Excuse me,' I say. 'I've come for my mum.'

'How old are you?'

'Fifteen.'

Lady lets out her breath. Maybe I best call Zoe in from outside, but I don't want to say what I got to say in front of her.

Behind the desk there's a poster of a random Black man with cornrows, and a white man with his head shaved. They look proper vex and their heads is PhotoShopped to look more bigger than their bodies. The poster got a number for help with domestic violence and I could've been the actor for that poster. Only got to screw my face up a bit. I wonder what life's like for Zoe, what it's like to never be looked at like you're the problem.

And I think, Olu was right. That's how people see us: big-up Black man danger.

They don't even know me.

They ain't even tried talking to me.

They look away, move seats, cross the road.

Lady twists a pen in her fingers. 'Do you have photo ID?'

'Like what?'

'Passport, driving licence.'

'Driving licence? I'm fifteen.'

'Travel ID? Oyster photocard?'

I got my junior library card from Hertford Library, but that ain't got a photo so I find my old Oyster. I'm maybe twelve in the photo. That's three years ago when I was in Year Eight; before Hertfordshire, before Andrew, even before me and Kasim got done.

'I moved out of London. That's why my pass is out of date.'

She puts her glasses on and looks at my card, trying to find the boy in the man what's standing over her front desk.

'What's your mum's name?'

'Mrs Samson. Jade.'

'Address?'

'Downview Women's Prison, till yesterday. She said she'd come here, after.'

'I see.'

Lady taps the keyboard with her pen, clicks a file.

'Listen, I'm not supposed to say this, but she hasn't presented herself.'

'That ain't right. She was coming here! She said she was!'

'They don't always make it if they're not picked up at discharge. We have the probation referral here ...' Lady looks up. 'I'm sorry.'

I feel my eyes going and I swallow hard so they stop.

'Can I leave a message, please? Because she will come here. I know she will.'

I write the Nokia digits and a note what says, *Mum, I'm in London phone this number. I got a place for us to live. Don't worry. all sorted. Call me. Love you, D.*

The pen she gives me keeps running dry so I got to scratch them words over and over till little lines of ink turn into proper shapes you can read.

I think the lady thinks I'm crying because she says, 'I'll do my best. If she turns up here, I'll make sure she gets your note.'

'Thanks, miss.'

Zoe's waiting for me. I wipe my eyes with my sleeve and she says, 'Okay?'

226

I say, 'Okay.' But it ain't and I ain't. I don't know why mum done this and I don't know where she is. And London's some next big place, you get me?

But Zoe's interview is in an hour and she acting like it's her birthday.

'I'll come with you,' I say.

'Just to the door, like I did with you just now, right?'

Zoe says this is the international HQ, but I'm looking at a sign saying *cheap office space, no contract, pay by the hour*. It ain't what you think an international modelling agency is going to look like, but Zoe ain't down. She skips up them steps, presses the intercom and wiggles her fingers at me. The door unlocks and she's gone.

Me and Zigs wait in the park. He sniffs the flowers and wees on some plant and I think about back in the day when these paths and pavements get covered in leaves and then it rains and I used to think that was the most beautiful thing I ever seen. Because when you look close, they ain't leaves at all but prints of leaves in red and yellow and brown, staining up the pavement. The council already collected them real leaves, but they left a bit of themselves back and it's nice.

I want to know what's happening inside, behind the glass, because I don't trust Talent Man. If my phone goes, I don't even know what floor she's on or what room to go to if she needs me. I don't even know what I'd do. Office is probably full of CCTV. Maybe I go to the lady and say, 'Parcel for Mr Nico,' and she'd buzz me in. Probably she'd clock Ziggy or maybe she'd be chewing gum, scrolling up and down her screen with her glitter nail and me and Zigs could go by like ghosts.

Forget *Oceans*. This is more like *Jason Bourne* and I'm writing the script, thinking, How can I protect her, how can I get her out? The problem is, county's made me soft. I need more street. I need some swagger, like Jordan when I was in Year Seven, red eyes like he been punched in the face or smoking crack. Back in the day, no one stepped to Jordan because he used to sleep behind his grandad's widescreen by the plug and he shanked his little brother over a bike and one time, he dropped the Deputy Head, broke his jaw with a kick. I cheered and felt sick at the same time. I think most of us felt sick even if we was cheering. 'Jordan, watch!' people say. 'He's going to switch.'

So I think I'll make like Jordan if I have to, dig at my eyes till they go red and swell-up, pull my jeans low, belt below my hips, hood over my head. It's like a film: *Let's Go, Jordan!* And in my film I hear Talent Man grunting inside. Music goes loud. *Dan, dan* ... I open the door a little. I'm only on a bench in the sun, but I feel my blood move, and it's like this film's already out there, waiting for me in the universe. All I got to do is turn up and tune in.

Stanislavski's Realism, innit.

'*What the hell do you think you're doing?*' Nico would say when I grab Zoe.

'*She's coming with me!*' I'd go in his face so he knows I'm truly gangsta.

But what if he's more gangsta? What if he pulls a shank?

Ziggy's wet nose goes on my fingers so I know what comes next. Ziggy comes next! He would snarl because he ain't going to let no man hurt Zoe. That's what dogs do; they protect. I shake my head and suck my teeth for long. I look

228

left and right, like all my crew's in the room, and I say my killer line. Trust me, it's a proper end-the-movie line.

'I'm only hoping you never went and brung that little shank to a gun party, blood.'

Ziggy does a long, low growl and I say, *'Blood, if you ain't got no dibs with Jordan's girl, I ain't got no just cause. Let she back with me and we call it quits.'*

Nico drops the shank but he ain't giving up easy. *'Who do you think you are?'* he goes.

'Jordan's blood, blood. Get in the lift, before I mash you up!'

I know that don't sound nice, but I got to make him believe. She'll thank me later.

Ziggy whines and licks my fingers. He don't like waiting so we leave the park. Zoe's back with the reception lady. Talent Man's there too. They shake hands and he brushes her cheek with a finger like he's her dad or something. Door clicks and Zoe's out, spinning a new purse and smiling.

'What?' she goes when she sees my face. 'I wasn't that long.'

'Did he – you know? I should've been there! I could've protected you!'

'What?'

'Did he touch you?'

'For God's sake, Donny. He's not Harvey Weinstein. He's a nice man. Chanel!' she says, waving the purse in my face.

'Right. You know I could've got you three of them for a five spot down Chapel Market?'

She opens the clasp. 'Beanie!' Rocking it, she goes, 'Hello, Donny. My name's Tiny and I was born on the first of April.' Next thing out is an iPhone 10. 'It's on contract. He's paid

229

for everything. Oh, and he wants me to deliver this to his business associate.'

It's a present. The label says, *Lawrence, Enjoy! N.*

'So what happened?'

'We talked. His photographer took a few contact strip photos. He emailed them to a man called Chapman who has the final say. So exciting!'

'It don't sound right.'

'Stop worrying. You're worse than my mum.' She gets the BlackBerry out and dashes it on my chest. 'So you can have this piece of shit back.'

'Wait up, Zoe. Don't you think you should tell your mum?'

'Look, he treats me like an adult.' She kisses her new phone and wipes off lip grease. 'Which is more than I can say about you.'

'Zoe, wait up,' I say again. 'I'm sorry.'

'Listen. Help me find Limehouse Basin. It's in East London. Nico's already paid me to go so I can't let him down. We have to find a restaurant on the marina called the Roundhouse. Please, Donny? We can get chips on the way!'

Zoe don't get it. She's grown up soft on mud and grass; more trees than lamp-posts, more sky than ground. When she walks these streets, she got no idea what monsters lie beneath.

King's Cross endz is all changed up where we moored *Zuma Jay*. Everywhere's growing and still more flats getting built. People in them glass balconies look down on the low-rise council flats down Copenhagen Street and it's like soon they're going to have more flats than peoples.

I plan on filling my belly at the kebab shop, except my eyes is taken by this pile of plastic on the corner of York Way.

'Aren't you coming in for chips?' Zoe goes when I walk past the door. She tugs my arm but I can't move. 'Come on,' she goes.

I ain't going nowhere. I want to see who this is about. When you see that much dead flowers and plastic and notes you know it's *somebody*. Them flowers is dried up if the plastic's open, rotten if it's closed, and ain't none of them the colour they supposed to be. Zoe picks up a card some kid's covered in lines and lines of Sellotape so it don't get wet when it rains. So it lasts forever. Them notes must've taken bare time because they been drawn out with felt tip pens in bubble writing. Buses blow them scraps, knock the paper down the pavement, but ain't no street cleaner going to touch them. They ain't going to lay disrespect on some next-level hurt.

'What does Jannah mean?' Zoe asks.

Air sticks in my throat. My chest goes tight. Eczema burns my arms.

'Heaven. It's a Muslim thing.'

Then I cannot breathe. Kasim's picture is taped round the streetlight. My lungs go so empty I start thinking they ain't never going to fill again, like I'm going to die right here, and I got a million questions all at once, like, Was this what it felt like for Kasim? Did he die in the gutter, right here, or was he knocking on the kebab shop glass, begging for a grown-up to come? Did his crew give him back-up, or did they get frit and split on their bikes? I don't blame them though, if they did. Was the traffic light red or yellow or green when

231

he looked through his eyes, last time, or was it them new balconies he saw?

And did he make it back to his mum? Because sometimes they do and it's better that way. This boy down Peckham got shanked, but he could still run. He ran across his estate and up three floors to his mum so she could hold his hand when he died. So that does happen and it's got to be better that way.

Adrenaline goes down my belly to my legs. Instead of running though, I drop down by all them flowers. Businessmans see me flat out on the pavement. They check for buses and cars so it's safe, because they got to step out on the main road if they don't step on me. I'm glad they don't step on me.

Zoe kneels down and puts her arms round me and I start proper crying.

'I knowed him,' I say when my breathing comes back. 'I knowed him. I knowed him. I knowed him. I knowed him. Kasim was my friend. He was my friend.'

She pulls all her friendship bracelets off her wrist. 'Pick one,' she goes and I take the purple because that was the colour of our endz.

I have to stand on people's cards and paper to hook it on a photo of Kasim because they're everywhere.

K Bro may you live in Dar al Salam

rip lil kasim

neva 4get ya

Kasim's photo must've been taken at his club. Big shorts make his skinny legs look more skinny and he's wearing all the kit: keeper gloves, shin pads, mouthguard. You can't see

232

who he's playing against. Only his hand out, saving them goals. I leave the bracelet and back off, trying my best not to stand on all them notes in pencil and biro and some was even printed out on a proper printer like the ones they got in schools.

And I think, I'm standing on bare people's feelings. And I think, I never knowed he turned keeper.

I don't know I want to smash shit up. Not yet. Not until Limehouse.

Truth is, as soon as my breathing comes back, my head goes quiet. I'm on my own mission and when it's done, I can move up.

Chapter 16

The Navigable Canals & Waterways of London chart don't fit on the table so I let everything north of Tottenham drop. I put a teaspoon on Battlebridge Basin on the Regent's because that's the start. I move my finger east where the canal drops down Islington Canal Tunnel, coming out again to Hackney and the Vickie Park junction. It splits just after Old Ford Lock. Union Canal carries on east and Regent's goes south to the Thames, to Limehouse. Where the canal hits the river is called Limehouse Reach and I wonder what all that water feels like when the last lock opens.

I put Andrew's kitchen knife on Limehouse Basin, the sharp end of it on the marina. And I count seven locks and five miles. Seven plus five equals twelve divided by three equals four hours. I ain't dumb. I work it all out. If we moor *Zuma Jay* and walk the last mile it skips a couple of locks and that's twenty minutes each. I check the time on my phone. We could be there by four o'clock. No buses. No tube. No Overground. No CCTV.

There's bare room to turn in Battlebridge Basin but I screw up for no reason.

'You're in a hurry,' Zoe goes.

'We got a package to deliver, innit.'

Islington Canal Tunnel makes a big O like it's surprised. It goes under Angel for miles and miles; so many, the light goes dark and Zoe turns on her phone torch but that only gets eaten up. I say to take the tiller arm and drop down the hatch to get Andrew's torch. It's a metal one, takes batteries the size of my fist and when I switch it on, light floods down the tunnel. I lie on my back and touch the bricks on the roof. I keep my head down and I'm glad I got bantu knots in my hair because there ain't no room for a mighty 'fro.

And I tell Zoe, 'You know back in the day when they didn't have marine diesels and you can't fit a horse down a tunnel, do you know what they did?'

'No.'

'They walked the boat.'

'There's no towpath. You can't walk if there's no path.'

'Andrew said they lay down on their backs and walked with their feet on the roof. They walked, innit. On their backs, like this.'

I'm chatting like I ain't seen what I seen, like nothing's happened and Kasim's still kicking at his flat, getting vex because Ghislaine's watching CBeebies when the Premier's on. It's like I'll see him soon, no hurry. It sounds wrong, but I start up thinking I got to do something about my hair.

'Can you do me a fat favour?' I ask Zoe and I know she's going to like this one. 'Fix up my hair?'

I'm in the footwell now, Zoe's on the side, tiller under her arm so she can work at undoing them tight bantus Laura did.

236

By the end of the tunnel, half my head's flat and the other half's mighty. Untamed.

'I think we should stop there,' Zoe goes. 'That looks so cool.'

'No. Go on.'

'Okay, Mr Samson. Going anywhere nice on your holidays?'

'I went Bognor once.' I bend back to look up at her. 'I'm going back there with mum when we're sorted.'

A boat horn blasts down the tunnel. A narrowboat's coming towards us.

'Holla! Straighten up!'

Zoe pushes the tiller hard away. *Zuma Jay* bumps the bank but we don't hit the narrowboat. The skipper looks at my hair and says, 'I've seen the pizza boat, the bookshop boat and the bakery boat. But the barber boat?'

'Pizza boat!' Zoe says. 'Where's that?'

'Offside bank, Wenlock Basin. You're nearly there,' he goes, and he's gone.

We're now down past the start of the tunnel, where the towpath stops, and I know this place.

'Slow down,' I say. I run the long of the boat, looking down the towpath for the burned bit.

'What is it?' Zoe goes.

I keep looking. There's got to be a burned stone here. They only leave them flowers and notes till the letters bleed like that Science experiment and stain up the paper so you can't read nothing and then there'll be nothing to say he ever was. So I'm looking for a burned-up stone what's here forever.

'What's wrong?'

'I been here before. Back in the day. I – someone I knew jacked a ped and blazed it out by the tunnel.'

'You're not speaking English.'

'A moped. They stole a moped and burned it. It was here, I'm sure it was.'

Zoe reverses the engine so we stop. Them cobblestones, brickwork and bollards is clean and it ain't right. Maybe they better start up one of them poppy displays they do, so you can see how much youths died.

'Okay,' I say. I give up and go back to the hatchway. 'Take me to the pizza boat.'

'I'm sorry about your friend.' I know she's trying her best. She gets the last plait out. My curls spring up and out. 'You look like Bruno Mars. I like it!'

We moor at Johnson's Lock and I switch the padlocks. I ain't sure if we're coming back together. I might have stuff to do what don't involve her.

Before I close the hatch, I put the windlass in my school bag and Zoe goes, 'What d'you want that for?' and I say, 'You never know when you need a key.'

I run the afro comb through my hair and tell Zigs to guard the boat.

'What are you doing? Lawrence Chapman's meeting me, not you. Forget your hair. You're going to make me late.'

I offer to carry the present but she says, 'No thanks, I'm the delivery girl.' True that. 'We're meeting at a gastropub, you know,' she goes like that's something.

Limehouse marina is full of houseboats and Dutch barges and manky narrowboats, same like *Zuma Jay*, but their owners ain't never been in the Merchant Navy, you get me? They're continuous mooring people, which goes to say they're basically hippies and make the marina look bait. But Limehouse ain't only about them manky boats and I start to feel better when I see some got class, like this nice white cruising yacht, moored up under the Harbourmaster's office where it won't get trashed. It's three times higher than a narrowboat and two times as long. The stern's fitted out with seats, and garden tubs and plants twist round four pillars holding up a sun-shade. It looks like it should be motoring some blue Caribbean waves, not hanging out at the arse end of the Regent's where the water's rank with plastic shop bags and wine bottles and all the other nasty shit Andrew calls flotsam.

We're at the harbour mouth where the canal turns into the Thames. The last lock.

The pub place is at the end of the marina but first we got to cross a road what ain't a road. I work out it's a bridge on wheels so fixed masts can get in the marina and the rest of the time the cars own it. The last lock plays at being mentor to the water. One side is smooth like glass, wanting to talk. The other's proper high-tide Thames, bare vex and in some mad rush to be somewhere else.

'I won't bother you,' I tell her. 'But I'll be here.' I point to a platform floating on the river, chains creaking and screaming like strange birds. 'That's where I'll wait.'

I thought that'd make her happy, but she frowns and it don't look like she wants to be on her ones no more.

'I'll be here,' I say again. 'If you need me.'

Zoe walks straight up to the first waiter she sees. I can't help smiling. Waiter points to a table outside: bottle of wine, two glasses and a fat old white man on his phone. When he sees Zoe he stands up, puts his phone down and pulls out a chair, so he's got to be Chapman. She gives him the present. They laugh. He pours a glass. She giggles. Then she drinks a bit and wipes her nose with a white napkin. Small time later, he gets out his wallet and sticks notes he ain't counted on the table. He puts his arm out for Zoe and she hooks hers in his.

I climb up off the platform and follow Zoe and the old man back to the marina, past the lock with all the nasty floating shit trapped in it. They stop by that nice white yacht. Man puts his manky hand low on Zoe's back to help her up the gangway, like she needs help getting on a boat. He don't even know she can skipper one. And his hand goes more lower, like she's going to fall in the water if he don't nearly hold her arse. They go in the cabin and I don't like it and I don't even think this is right, but I wait because this is her opportunity.

And I never planned on trashing nothing, except just then I clock a Younger. His hoodie slips off his cornrows coming down Chapman's gangway and I know straight away he's just collected because back in the day that could've been me.

He's like twelve, thirteen tops. He comes off that boat with bare more important shit to carry in his school bag than homework and he's taking it serious. He looks left-right for the next crew's soldiers and I know he's got a shank in them trackies. But when he gets to the dock, he's thinking, Don't step on the cracks, or mum's going to die. So his creps go pat-pat, legs giving it spring like a trampoline the long of the dock to his bike. And I swear down, them flagstones is more longer than you ever seen, but he's proper flying. He don't hit a single join.

I'm so vex, it's about all I can do not to switch right there. That kid should be a youth, not a Younger. We all got a right to be a youth but they make us into Youngers.

I ain't watching no more. I aim for the yacht and I'm over the gangway in three steps. Close up, them deck pillars ain't nothing; the first Samson, the one from the Bible, he would've pulled them down, mashed up the yacht till it sank and killed himself. The first me would've done that and all, but not this one.

I open the door. The cabin's full of cushions, a soft sofa and a low table with a black box and magazines like *Vogue* and *Wealth Collection*. Chapman's got his back to me. He's pouring a drink when he turns, saying, 'My dear, would you like ice?' He clocks me and he don't like what he sees. 'This is private property. Leave immediately.'

'Go back to *Zuma Jay*,' I tell Zoe. 'I'm sorry but you ain't no model. I swear down, there's no modelling contract. It's you he wants.'

Chapman looks at Zoe and says, 'Do you know this young man?'

She shakes her head like she ain't never seen me in her life so I land a kick on the box on the table and it drops, spilling white over his nice red carpet like someone's been gassing with talcum powder in the PE changing room.

'He only wants a line of coke and a nice delivery girl,' I say, and I ain't taking my eyes off Chapman for even one little second. 'Go back to Zigs, Zoe. Call your mum

241

and dad and get them to pick you up. I can handle this joker.'

'This is outrageous!' Chapman says, cheeks flapping. 'Get off my bloody boat!'

Zoe pulls her blazer round her front and stares at the powder, mouth open. Fat tears is running down her face. She looks like a panda and I'm nearly going to laugh when I remember this is a bare serious situation. She wipes her eyes and mascara gets on her school blazer and it only makes her eyes more black.

And she looks at me like she ain't never hated nobody so bad. 'Go to hell, Donny,' she goes. 'I thought you were my friend!'

She takes one last look at the powder and heads for the door. I know she's safe and it's going to be okay when the gangway cables go *clink-clank* and it's quiet again.

'I know who you are. I know exactly who you are,' I say to Chapman. I'm looking at him straight. I ain't taking my eyes off him. 'I know what you been doing and I know what you want.'

'Get off my boat before I call the police.'

'You ain't supposed to be here, are you? You're supposed to be getting your white backside tanned in the Virgin Islands or raping some little girl in Thailand. But you can't keep away, can you?'

'Get off my boat, I said!'

'You miss it here, don't you?' He looks at me like I'm dumb. 'You miss going up county shooting parties. Killing little pheasants make you feel like a big man? You're not a big man. You're pathetic.'

'Who the hell are you? How do you know about my shoots?'

'What? You think because I'm Black I don't know about no pheasants? You're racist, man!'

I flip Andrew's coin on the back of my hand.

'Heads or tails?' I smile. 'Guess right and I'll tell you. My bad! I'm joking, man. Ain't no heads on this coin. It's a con. Like you.'

'You don't know me!'

'Hertford. I scratched the sticker off your Range Rover. Criminal damage, remember?'

'I have no idea what you are talking about. I don't own a Range Rover! I shoot in West Sussex! This is absurd. Right, I'm calling the police.'

He gets out his phone. Like I want him to.

'Go on, call,' I say. 'Get me arrested. Ain't sure yet? Look, I'll make it easy for you.'

I take the windlass out of my school bag. Chapman looks like he's going piss his pants when I start up smashing them seat panels.

'What the hell are you doing? Stop!'

'Stop what? This?' Marine ply panels shatter no problem. I peel back the wood. 'I think you know this is called criminal damage. You better call up the police.'

'You can't do this! This is my boat!'

'Don't worry. I ain't going sink your boat. That would be dumb, you get me? It's got a steel hull, right? And a reinforced keel? What is it, triple laminate? Quadruple? And the ballast chambers, eight? Self-righting?' I nod. 'Exactly what I thought.'

'How do you know all this?'

'Year Ten Work Experience, you fat shit. I won the prize!'

'What?'

'Every prize! So don't worry about me mashing up your boat. It's you I'm going to sink.'

The windlass goes right through the next panel and plastic packages fall out. 'Go on then, call the police.' He don't make no move and I say, 'See? I already knowed you ain't going to call.'

'Stop, I'll pay you,' he goes. 'How much?'

He gets out his paper, a roll of fifties and you ain't going to believe it but he gives them all to me, all them dollars like I never seen since Bossman's flat. I dash them out the porthole. They flutter like seagulls and float where they land.

'That don't work on me no more. Back in the day, you could give me one pound to be your Younger. I jacked a ped once for a ten spot I never even got. Know what happened? Mandem got burned. I ain't dashed the acid myself, but I've been carrying that.'

'Why me?'

Chapman starts bleating like them sheeps they got in Wales. One time, me and Kasim clocked this baby sheep, tucked up in a peat bed, standing in water the colour of piss. His mum was bleating a while away and he looked up at us and told us his need.

'These walls is too high for me,' baby sheep went with his eyes.

'No worries, cuz,' I said without opening my mouth, keeping vigilant-like for them eagles in the sky in case they was coming for him. So Kasim lifted him clean up out of the water, clear of them twisting roots, so he could get back with his fam. But this baby sheep was like, 'Nah. I'm following you now. Anywhere you go and further still.' He ran to us and the other boys and the Instructor Man's dog and all; no fear, nothing. His mum stamped her feet and cried, but he paid her no heed. She ain't taken him by the wool and set him down to live. That was us alone.

Instructor Man waved his arms and told him to go away, which he did after a bit, and started drinking up his mum's milk so hard it must've hurt.

We wanted so much to keep him, Kasim and me. He wanted so much to keep us.

'Why?' Chapman goes again when I don't answer.

'Why? I'll tell you why. As long as men like you is around, my mum ain't never going to be free. She keeps beating it but you make sure it comes back, innit. "Free sample, try before you buy, three for one." Look at what you got here. How many kilos? How many lives you wrecking? Me and mum was all right, you know. She was all right. She looked after me. We was all right, but —'

'I expect your mother had choices,' Chapman dares tell me.

This is the bit where I kill him but I don't. I take a deep breath.

'Let me lay it down for you. Zoe's fifteen. Did you know that?' Chapman shakes his head. 'Don't lie! Yes, you knowed it! Man, there's bare shit you ain't going to go down for. The girls you rape. The boys you kill. But when they get you today, it's going to be for this.' I kick them packages. 'You're a killer.'

'I haven't killed anyone.'

'Shut up! You killed Michael! You killed Kasim!'

245

'I don't know these people. I don't know who you're talking about!'

'*Shut up!*' I smash the glasses off the table with the windlass. 'I ain't wasting my time. If you don't call them police, I will. This is a crime scene, innit.'

I dial three nines on the vintage Nokia and press call. I ain't never called them numbers before.

'I'll say you assaulted me and tried to rob me,' he goes. 'Think they'll believe you over me? A little yardie gangster with a crackhead mum and criminal record?'

The line connects.

'Police, please.' I look him in the eyes while I talk to the operator. 'Yes. My name's Mr Chapman, Limehouse Basin Marina, Pontoon B,' I say in my county accent. 'Thank you.' I breathe hard in the phone like I been running. 'Yes, thank you so much. There's a Black man on my yacht, threatening me. I think he intends to rob me. He's armed. Yes. With a windlass.' Emergency Telephone Lady needs educating so I tell her, 'That's a metal key for opening canal lock gates, like an iron bar – it could kill a man! He's damaging my property! He's in the bedroom now. He must be on drugs, some kind of,' I look at Chapman and smile, 'crackhead. Please come now! Please help me! Limehouse Basin. Hurry. Yes, I will. Thank you.'

I press end.

'I think we got a little time to get to know each other,' I say, back in my own voice. My London voice. My mum's voice. 'Before the Feds come rescue you from the big-up scary Black man, let me tell you something. Pretty soon, when they come round to stop me smashing up your nice

246

boat, they going to find what you been up to. They're going to find all this.'

I kick one of them packages hard at a porthole but the glass don't break. This boat is built hench for transatlantic. It ain't no clinker-built thing. It's got to make it round the Caribbean Sea, up the Orinoco to Venezuela and back again with all this powder.

Lights and sirens come on the marina. Police park up by the Harbourmaster's office. I ain't got much time and I want him to know so I tell him, 'Someone once told me, when life keeps sending you shit, you got to duck and send it back. This is me sending back your shit. Look at yourself. You're old. You're fat. And pretty soon ...'

I look out the window. I'm impressed; they've sent four vans for me in, like, three minutes. You don't get that when some Younger gets stabbed.

'Yeah, pretty soon, you're going down.'

Soon as the police come up the gangway I drop the windlass like a good boy. Number One Fed kicks it into the corner the way they do in movies. I'm glad of that. I always wanted to be in a film and this is just about as near as it gets. Number Two ties up my wrists with plastic, same kind Laura uses in her garden when them roses start getting hyped and take up more room than they supposed to. Number Three sniffs the powder and puts on his gloves and Number Four starts tidying the packages and radios his crew for more bags.

Number Five goes, just like on TV: 'I'm arresting you on suspicion of aggravated criminal damage and the possession of an offensive weapon, with intent to endanger life. You do not have to say anything. But, it may harm your defence if you do

247

not mention when questioned something which you later rely on in court. Anything you do say may be given in evidence.'

Even though I know what I'm doing, I'm glad Zoe ain't here to see this bit. I'm glad she'll be back at *Zuma Jay* with Zigs, and when she's rung her fam like I told her, the grown-ups can take over.

I get gripsed up and dragged out and I keep looking at Chapman, right up till I can't look at him no more. I don't mean to resist arrest like the policeman says I am, but I pull them officers back with me because I got one last thing I need to say.

'London calls you home, don't it?' I go, but Chapman ain't listening. I laugh because of the look on his face when more of his packages go out to the vans. Man's going to be down thousands. 'Oi, Chapman,' I say. 'I get it. London calls me too. I came back for my mum though. She's going to be well pissed off when she finds out I've gone and got myself arrested. She's only just got out and we're going to be together. But it's worth it, Chapman. *You're* worth it.'

I smile at the policemen when they go by me. They're going to take a statement from the victim probably. A coot swims under the gangway and checks out a fifty spot on the water. Them notes make it look like autumn. He thinks it'll make a nice nest for his chicks, and off he goes.

'Don't forget to check them bilges,' I say. 'Man, my fingerprints is all over them bilges! And I think I dropped some drugs in his bedroom. You might need to get your working dogs. Dogs'll find it. Dogs is good at that.'

Ain't been so much people on Limehouse Basin watching film shit like this go down since Tom Cruise was filming

248

Mission Impossible. Waiters come out the pub. Boat peoples stand on their decks. Harbourmaster is chatting to Chapman and the boss lady Fed, and he points my way. I know what they think they see and I smile. There's even a man staring down at me at the top of a church tower and I think, Don't jump! I'm joking. He ain't going to jump because he's made of wood. He's a statue to tell old-time merchant ships they're home. Andrew said he's called Steering Christ. Mama Folu would like that.

As well, the Thames is proper rushing and I don't know how them East India merchant ships docked in London when the river was this high. It ain't easy to change course in a current; little mistakes bring big trouble. They didn't have no outboards like modern-time RIBs, no three-litre four-strokes guiding them in. Ain't no joke turning a hull low down in the river, on account of all that opium and sugar and cotton and tobacco they was delivering.

And don't forget Black men like me, crammed in them bulkheads. Their wrists was shackled and all.

Chapter 17

'Donald Leroy Samson, you've been arrested on suspicion of aggravated criminal damage of a luxury-class motorised yacht, belonging to Lawrence Chapman, at Limehouse Basin Marina, and the possession of an offensive weapon with intent –'

Man needs educating, so I tell him.

'Oh, my days! It ain't offensive. It's a windlass key. It opens lock gates.'

'– with intent to endanger life. Do you understand the charges?' I nod. He reads all them rights I got: medical, phone call, toilet, food. 'Please confirm your date of birth is the tenth of September 2004?' I nod. 'You're fifteen. We need to contact an appropriate adult. Who can we call?'

'Ghostbusters.'

I got to smile a bit. Fed Man frowns.

'Olu,' I say. I fix up my face because I weren't raised to take the piss. 'Olufemi Adeola.'

He pushes paper my way. Says: 'Write that for me, please. Is he over eighteen?' I nod. 'Relationship to you?'

'Brother. Foster brother.'

'Your address?' I can't tell him. Not yet. 'It's a simple question,' he goes. 'Where's home?'

'I ain't got no home.'

'According to our records, you were arrested for the theft of a moped and arson in 2016. Your address then was in Hackney. Has it changed?' I hear the man but I ain't saying nothing. He types, saying, 'Refuses to give address,' under his breath. 'Empty your pockets, please.'

I lie down *Zuma Jay*'s hatch keys, the vintage Nokia and my afro comb on the custody desk. Fed Man picks up the tennis ball.

'Odd choice of key ring,' he goes.

'It stops your boat keys sinking. In the canal.'

I smile at him and he looks at me for time, like he's thinking am I for real.

'ID?' I give him my Hertfordshire library card, with the Gruffalo thing on one side, and my Oyster, from 2016. Same brown skin, different hair. Me, younger. When I *was* a Younger. 'Any cash?'

I touch the letters – HUC – one last time before he tiefs my bronze coin.

'What's this?' he says, turning it round, and I think he likes me, even allowing the whole million-dollar boat thing. 'You been robbing a museum?'

I ain't saying nothing till I see the duty solicitor.

He puts me in Cell 12. Last time I was on this mattress, it was Cell 36 in Clapton. Not this mattress, but same blue plastic for trashing stuff what ain't mine. This time though, it ain't exactly same-same.

'Do you have any questions?'

I'm about to say no but I change my mind. I want to know.

'Yes,' I say. 'Did I sink him? Did he go down?'

Police Lady prints my fingers and asks if I want a drink because I came in between mealtimes and you can ask for a drink between mealtimes, as long as you don't take the piss. I ask if she got any lime juice because this is Limehouse. She says she ain't heard that one before.

'You're the boat boy, aren't you?' she goes.

I nod, because if you can strip a marine engine, cut a dead gull out your stern gear and re-enamel the Rose and Castle paint job on a narrowbeam, then yes, that's going to make you a boat boy.

'You're not what I expected.' Police Lady winks at me. She got a nice smile. 'I'll see if I can find you some juice.'

When I stop and think about it, I was always going to be a boat boy. Anytime I went near water I got this feeling in me like I could swim though I couldn't. Back in the day, when I was still little and in primary school, they took us down the pool and I didn't think swimming was something you had to learn. I know mum done the forms and I was supposed to go in the baby pool with the kids what can't swim, but I felt pulled by some invisible force. So I skipped the line, ran in the deep end and jumped in laughing my head off.

Don't worry though. I ain't died of drowning or nothing.

I was lucky the lifeguard man weren't on his phone. That man was taking note. One second I'm under, lying on the bottom, blue everywhere and for a little time I think it's beautiful. Next, he's in the water, creps and all, getting me out like Superman and I'm on the tiles on my side coughing and spluttering and thinking, Why did I even do that? I never went in no big pool after that, not one more deep than my shoulders is high. I just watch like a mug, like when I went Bognor and couldn't do them slides.

After that, boats just make sense.

Laura gave me this book called *Why Sailors Can't Swim and Other Marvellous Maritime Curiosities*. It's probably my best book of all time because it's got everything any man ever knowed or said or thought about boats. Anyway, like the name of the book says, most sailors in the world can't swim. Tell me something what I don't know.

Why would they? They got a boat, innit.

Them custody officers is taking a break. The cell doors go quiet and nobody's yelling about how much it ain't fair. They must've let the man go what was getting checked in same time as me. Or maybe he's gone down like a baby what can't cry no more, the way they sniff and hiccup and try a bit more crying before they sleep, like Kasim's baby sister done back in the day.

Makes me smile when I think what Ghislaine was like. Even if she was playing up, a little time with Kasim and she soon got happy and shut her eyes. Nearly nobody couldn't do that, except for Mrs Z, and I know because I sleeped round their yard for time and I seen it happen.

'Don't cry baby, baby, my baby,' he went. And just like that, she was okay because Ghislaine never liked no one but him to watch her when her mum was working nights cleaning the Homerton Hospital. It was him what made her smile, telling her about his best goals and doing one million keepie-uppies in the kitchen. She clapped her fat little hands when he done his high-low-over-the-toe, and after his back-of-the-neck skill she was all like, 'Where the ball, Fubby?' and her face dropped so Kasim laughed and *pop*, the ball flied over his head and on his knee for one million more knee-ups. Man, she did squeal. And that ball never dropped.

'Fubby, again!' she'd go because that's what she thinked his name was, on account of his mum going on at him about football this and football that. Like, 'Get that fichu football out the kitchen!' rah, rah, rah.

It was like Ghislaine was the only one who saw what Kasim was going to be. She couldn't even talk much or put food in her own mouth right, but it was like she could see into the future.

A bit of it, anyways. The good bit.

I wish I could press a button and switch my brains off but nobody sleeps on these rank mattresses. Cells is full of drinkers what spill their guts. You can smell it, even though they been over the plastic with bleach. I ain't sleeping, only dreaming with my eyes shut on account of waiting for Olu and thinking about them things I never knowed before. And I don't mean Chapman's nice boat. I don't even care about that no more. Let them come for me. They can do what they like.

Kasim keeps coming in my brain. He always did have the plan and the skills and I wish he'd been there to see that boat get mashed. He'd have laughed his head off.

If they let me, I swear down I'm going to do a speech about Kasim in assembly or church or madrassa or the

Hackney Gazette even. I got a thousand words to say about him. First up, I'll start with them plenty times Kasim got my back with a couple of bags of Beef McCoy's and my favourite Rubicon lychee juice.

'Left over, is all, D. Don't sweat it,' he'd go and I knowed he knowed I ain't ate breakfast. So I'd go, 'Okay, blood. If you don't want it,' like I was the one doing him a favour.

And I'd tell about the time when I lost my pound in tutor time and we was all looking for it. I started to cry and Teacher Man tells us, 'Sit down lads, it's only a pound,' and goes on about not bringing cash to school. 'Get your mums and dads to top up your ParentPay online,' Sir says, like that's something grown-ups can do like clicking their fingers. And when Tommy looks at me because I was going to switch, Kasim ducks under the table and goes, 'Found it, blood!' And later, down the chicken shop, K said he didn't feel like it and his mum was cooking anyway. So I knowed that was his pound all along. He dropped it out his pocket on purpose.

Just like that. For me. Because that's what he was like.

And I could say about how he started getting skills and the time when he got his first ball when we was seven. We clocked this nice Sondico Match ball on this old lady's boat down the canal. We knowed it weren't never hers; she was too old for playing. And maybe we was going to take it and leg it, but Boat Lady saw us and asked us was it ours and of course we said we kicked it on her boat by accident so can we have it back, please. Boat Lady went, 'That's funny, I fished it out the canal back in Camden. Must have floated two miles to get here.' And she did a little smile like we was bare funny and dashed it at us anyway. Said we ought to look after it better this time.

Next day, K went by her boat with these nice big flowers he found growing in the park to say thanks, but she was gone.

As well, it weren't only people he was nice to. I could tell them about how me and Kasim played *Animal Rescue* down the Regent's. One winter there was ice on the water and them birds needed eats so bad he gave them his multipack chocolate bourbons. He didn't care it cost 99p and he was going to sell them at break. Also, there was this time we found a mashed-up nest what needing fixing, hanging off the back of some houseboat. Something had to be done to help them yellow chicks and Kasim had the tools to do it even though it took bare planning to get enough string and elastic bands out of Teacher Lady's drawer.

So tell me now: exactly how many roadmans do you know like that?

But I ain't going to think about Kasim no more. I got to think about mum. I got to focus on the soon things, not what's been and done.

Even so, I wish he'd been there to see that nice boat go down.

Some mans don't give up, no matter what. Take that man switching in Cell 11 or Cell 13. I can't tell for sure, on account the way Custody plays sound around like them rugby balls in Hertfordshire what ain't even balls. You run one way, the way your brain tells you to go, and *pop*, you got to change up. Anyways, I'm going to say it's probably Cell 13. Mum says that's lucky for some and the man in there better get lucky soon because he ain't giving up yelling all kinds of shit. Being locked up makes you do that, no matter if it's Custody or prison, even in a place like Limehouse where they treat you nice.

Zoe says her house is like a prison because her parents make the au pair turn off the attic bedrooms' Wi-Fi at 8 p.m. so there ain't nothing to do but homework. Her place ain't like prison at all but I get what she means. It's that feeling when London is squeezing you like some monster boa and you got to get out. I seen all them miles of bricks and roofs what go on forever and then some. There are times when the city tightens so hard, you got to take a breath and relax. I seen what's outside and it's mostly fields, and I know what's inside and it's mostly streets, so if you don't got a Plan B like me and mum do, like I want *Zuma Jay* to be for us, then you got to try to keep going with where you is. Laura calls it being mindful. You got to take a deep breath on your inhaler and try again.

Limehouse Custody Man unlocks my door and says my appropriate adult is on her way so things'll get moving soon as she arrives.

'Olufemi ain't a female,' I say. 'He's my foster brother.'

Custody man looks at me like I'm tripping. 'Well, let me check that and get back to you. Oh, before I forget,' he says. 'You're down to see the Duty Solicitor, Mr Thompson. Scrub up.'

I ask Custody Man nice-nice, 'Can I have my phone back then, please?' I want to see if mum called.

He goes, 'Sure, sure,' and asks me if I want to have his keys and all, so I can take myself off for a nice little walk. I tell him my windlass is all the keys I need. It already opened up donkey locks just getting me here.

'And anyway,' I say, 'that phone's a 2006 Nokia, you get me? Old-school. Ain't like I can play *Fortnite* or nothing on it.'

'It's evidence.'

'Ah, give over, sir man. Your CPS crew don't seriously think I mashed up that yacht with a vintage Nokia?'

He laughs. I tell him I know they built them phones like bricks, but ain't it obvious? Only a windlass can do that level of damage.

'Safe,' I say. 'I ain't missing nothing. It's only got *Ghost House* and *Snake II*. Piece of shit, anyways.'

Now next door starts up yelling and cussing. I want to tell him, 'Chill, fam!' because they got it covered here and ain't nobody going to get no-place by banging. You got to be nice and sit down and time will go by because time ain't got nothing else to do. You got to wait it out. And when they get all the facts and enough time goes by, that door's going to open.

I swear down, it will.

I hope no criminal's going to lay his manky hands on *Zuma Jay*; Limehouse endz ain't exactly the safest in London and city canals is the worst. That's why me and Zoe done all our night mooring on the offside bank where it's like you're in a castle, water stopping the enemy. Enfield crew can look at us all they like, but there's no way they going to get their creps wet.

When Olu comes and they give me back Andrew's keys, I'm going to show him round *Zuma Jay* and maybe take him for a ride if we got time before I get mum. I'm going to ask him for some dollars and all. Marine diesel costs half what people put in their cars and I don't need much, maybe a gallon. Enough to get me and mum clear of London.

It's what she always wanted and I'm going to make it happen. I know that because one time, when I was little and we got told we had to move, mum said, 'This is it; we're done and gone and out of here. We don't need to wait around.'

So she got the suitcase packed and I waited downstairs in the hallway. I knowed we weren't coming back when she dropped the room key in next door's wheelie bin and slammed the front door. It had one of them locks what locks by itself so there was no going back, not even for stuff in the kitchen.

We sat in a park a bit. Mum downed a whole pack of Cheese Puffs, stuffing them in till her lips went orange.

'You want some?' she said when there weren't nearly no more left and tipped the crumbs in her mouth, smiling at me like she's on top of the world and ain't never coming down from some high-up place in the trees with the birds, and anyways, a long way from me by her side.

'You see, Don,' she went, opening her mini-marshmallows, 'We don't need to be here. We could be anywhere and that's the truth of it.'

Funny what peoples give to the food bank but nice too. Shows they're thinking about the kids and they got our back. Mum stuck maybe fifteen or even twenty in her gob and went, 'Go on, Don. Ask me!' but she didn't get past 'Ask me,' before she started laughing and all them marshmallows shot out down the path and she held her belly like she couldn't take it no more. I weren't laughing, so she chucked them at my head till I couldn't not laugh.

'Open your mouth,' she went. 'Head back – catch it, babes!'

It ain't easy because they're bare little and they don't weigh much neither but I tried it. Stuff always taste more nice when you got to catch it first.

'Okay,' I went. 'What are you saying?'

'I'm saying me and you could go anywhere. We don't need to be here.'

'Where's anywhere?'

'I don't know. Spain, maybe? Bognor. You went Bognor, ain't it? I always liked the seaside. Why don't me and you get us a flat on the beach so we can watch the sailboats? Seaside's a good place for a dog. We could get a Lilo!'

'What's a Lilo when it's at home?'

'You blow it up, Don. You fill it with air and float away. I had a Lilo back in the day. Pink one side, blue the other. And a bucket and spade, I had them and all. *Oh, I do like to be beside the seaside!* Your grandaddy used to sing that to me in Southend when I was little, before he got sick and couldn't keep me no more. He loved the sea. But let me tell you something: Bognor ain't Southend, Don. Southend makes your feet go grey when the tide's out and it don't matter how much you wash them, clay don't come off for days. And it's so shallow you can walk and walk and walk and the water never goes over your knee. Makes it safe for babies, you know, for playing, but you can't swim there.'

'Can you swim then, mum?'

'No. But that's not the point, is it, Don? The point is, you can't even if you could. So there's another reason we ain't going Southend.'

261

Mum told me Southend smells of dog shit on a hot day and it ain't got no proper sea like Bognor, only the River Thames. The land what you see on the other side is only Kent so it's technically still London and don't count. Her hands was twitching now, foot drumming against the bench. 'Bognor's sea goes all the way to France and the Isle of Wight,' she said. 'I went there and all when I was little. There's a ferry what takes you there and you can get a cup of tea on the way.'

She was still smiling but bits of sweat come up on her face, little stabs of pain in her eyes. I always know when she's hurting before she does; her face goes white, lips pull in tight.

'And we could go France and all. Time we got us some swimming lessons and a Lilo, eh, Don?' She kicks our suitcase. 'Come on, babes. Time we got going.'

'We going France first or Isle of Wight?'

'You choose, babes. Anywhere you like. Anywhere but here.'

'We going right now?'

'Tomorrow, babes. Things need planning. Got to see your Uncle Marcus first.'

She heard me breathe out too loud because she stopped walking and dropped the suitcase. She knows I don't like Marcus and he ain't no real uncle neither. Better sleeping on the streets than round his yard.

'What about Mrs Z?' I said.

'Last time, babes. Promise. Please? Get your old mum sorted so I can see straight and tomorrow, I promise, it'll be plain sailing out of here.'

'On a Lilo?'

'Why the bloody hell not? Don't let nobody ever say you can't do nothing!'

Mr Thompson the Duty Solicitor comes in for chats.

'Can you tell me who's supposed to be looking after you?' he goes, because they're still waiting on my appropriate adult. 'It's unclear to me who has parental responsibility. Where is your mother?'

I don't say nothing. I can tell he's vex with me but he's acting bare nice. He knows how to do that breathing thing you do, so you don't go dropping nobody.

'I'm going to advise a guilty plea,' he says and I interrupt.

'No problem. I ain't saying I never done it. I did it. Take me there right now and I'll do it again.'

'Well, I don't think a re-enactment is quite necessary, Mr Samson. You've made the right decision. Now we can do something about the tariff. By tariff, we mean the length of the …'

'I know what tariff means.'

He looks over the top of his glasses, a twist on his lips. 'I see.'

'Sentence, innit.'

He sighs and looks at his watch like he got someplace to be. 'Under the right circumstances, with the right judge, a custodial sentence might even be suspended. Your last offence was at thirteen, I believe?' He goes in his bag for more paper with my life all over it. 'Let me see. Ah, yes. Theft and arson of a motorbike.'

'Oh my days! Moped, man. It was only 50ccs.'

'And criminal damage. Tell me about your mother.'

I think of them crows they got in Hertfordshire what cough like they been smoking roll-ups and fly round looking for dead things, like a rabbit what got itself mashed up on the road. Mum's got the same cough and also she knows where to look, like the coffee shop what chucks out five-quid cakes for free round the back of Chapel Market, stacked up in black bags by the toilet she don't let me use on account of needles. So it don't matter if I get jacked at school for my chocolate croissant. Mum can get more.

And she knows Oxford Street when they change up the windows and dash them clothes under the streetlights, a bit cut up because they got to fix up the mannequins but they still go for a couple of quid.

And them nice ladies at Jerkz what says to mum, 'There you go, Jade, put some meat on your bones, girl,' and we get close-up-time pilau and fry dumpling for no money.

And Kingsland fruit and veg market when they pack up. So nobody can't say we don't get our five a day. Got to be rinsed, is all.

Except when I get out of here, I ain't going to let mum be like that no more. I'm calling time on hustling because when I'm sixteen, trust me, that ain't at all how it's going to be. I know what I got to do to make it right for her.

'Donald,' Mr Thompson goes. 'Please stay focused.'

'Sir, man, what did you eat when you was a kid?'

'That's irrelevant here.' He looks at his phone and gets up. 'If you'll excuse me,' he says and goes.

People think custody's all about good cop, bad cop. But it ain't like that.

Some man's yelling, 'All I want is a bleeding fag!' but they don't allow none of that till you go on remand or get sentenced and it proper merks people off because they seen it different on TV.

To be fair though, Custody Man brings me nice eats. If they did a blindfold test with Hillingford school canteen, Limehouse would win hands down, which ain't right when you think about it. They got some next-level nefarious mans in here for all kinds of serious shit and they go, 'Pasta Arrabiata or gluten-free curry, sir?' And it don't cost no money.

It ain't right, but it's what they do.

Now, there's kids in Hillingford what know exactly what Arrabiata is and maybe their mums can even make it, but then again they don't know the difference between a Wing Deal and a Pound Special. Zoe could tell me about the knives round my plate in the restaurant Laura took us to, but she don't know what a Younger's hand means low round the back of his belt.

And till I went Hillingford I never even knowed people did skiing when they was supposed to be in school. Them kids have got to be on 80 per cent attendance after all their holidaying, but their grown-ups don't even try lying. Teachers can see they ain't been sick when they come back stripy: pink noses, burnt-up lips, eye-sockets and chins white. Zoe says her dad saves money that way. Even with the penalty it's more cheaper to go skiing in termtime, on account of the extra half-term holiday prices. They just pay the fine and go play in the snow.

I know Maths but I still don't get how paying a fine makes them rich people richer. When mum gets fined, our lights go out.

Mr Thompson comes back saying they're going to check my phone history and he don't like surprises. He wants everything, straight up from the start.

'I need your affiliations,' he says. 'Past and present.'

'Okay,' I go. 'I'd say my mum.'

'I'm sorry,' he goes, 'I meant –'

'I know what you meant. Affiliation. Synonyms: loyalty, bond and all that.' He nods, makes his fingers into a triangle. He's listening. 'You're asking me about my colours, ain't you? You're asking me who I belong to.'

He picks up his pen to write down what I say. 'Yes,' he goes. 'The prosecution will use gang history. So?'

'So, my mum.' He frowns. I feel sorry for him. I don't think he done GCSE Latin like us top sets in Hillingford. 'You see, me and mum got ourselves affiliated when I was born.'

He lets a deep breath out slow.

'*Filius*,' I explain. 'Latin, innit.'

Mr Thompson looks at me, mouth open like he's dumb, which most likely he is. I was dumb once, but Laura taught me street don't cut it for life and there ain't no Gs in ghetto. Not long after I moved to hers, she put a stack of books on my bed and a note: *To Donny, Time to wake up, buddy!* I shifted them books to the window and shut the curtains. Weeks later, they're still sitting there, waiting for me. Post-it note goes, *Read me.*

Edward Said. Alice Walker. Patrick Chamoiseau. Aimé Césaire.

Names from a million miles away. Some of them is even from France.

First time I take a look I'm thinking, These people, man, they got too much words. They should chill out a bit. Try writing a tweet. But then I pick one up and each time I make myself go for longer and soon I wake up like a bucket of ice water just dashed me. I bet my pound Mr Thompson ain't read none of them books, but I did. And I start up reading Laura's newspaper what gets delivered and all. I even try a bit of her *Cambridge Law Journal*, but that book is extra dry. I'm going to leave that one till I done A-levels.

Them books make the pieces fit, and me and Laura start getting bare stuff to talk about. We watch clips of the rapper Akala getting interviewed and big-man Lammy speaking truth in the House of Commons and long films and all; old-time French ones, like this one called *La Haine* where these feds get mashed up in some Paris manor and they're playing NWA out the top flats, except they don't say – excuse my language – 'F the police!' like it is in the original. They go 'Nique la police!' and that makes me think of Kasim. I wished he could've seen that film. He'd get exactly what them French mans was saying and not even have to read the subtitles.

One time, Laura read me a next-level beef what Frederick Douglass done, mashing up his slave owner so he don't never get disrespected again. Frederick gripses him so hard the man's neck starts bleeding and after he mashed him, he tells Mr White Man: 'If you expect to succeed in whipping me, you got to succeed in killing me.' I don't never forget that. That's like saying you better know yourself; if you're coming for me, you better be sure of your capabilities. I copied down some of the lines I liked most from *Narrative of the Life of Frederick Douglass, an American Slave*. One goes, *My long-crushed*

267

spirit rose, cowardice departed, bold defiance took its place, which is the exact same thing as saying, 'Don't mess with me, blood, because I don't belong to you no more.'

That's kind of what I wanted to say to Chapman.

After all my reading, when Laura's lawyer friends come round for tagliatelle and red wine, they can't know who I am or even who I ever was. I'm like some ninja chameleon. Laura smiles when I talk their way about Black lives mattering and what shit the wasteman Prime Minister is chatting and what the government should do about mums like my mum and boys like me and endz like mine.

In no time, it don't even sound wrong in my mouth, like I'm taking charge of all the words and I know what they mean and what they can do. My whole brain changes and all, so I can't help but think in big-up words and long sentences. Soon, my English teacher started saying I got to think about taking English next year for A-levels, and History says the same, so does Maths and Science and all. Laura says I should study Law, like David Lammy, and I think she's right.

As well, if I went and did that, I'll make sure I go head-to head with Mr Thompson one day. I bet my pound Mr T don't know what *intersectionality* means. I bet he can't even say it. Man's so hyped on white privilege, he can't see out his own arse.

I guess it ain't his fault though. It's just a lottery where peoples get born.

Custody Officer comes in smiling, saying my appropriate adult's here. Finally, I think. Olu took his time. I start wishing they allowed me my comb because after hours in this dump my 'fro ain't looking too good. But it ain't Olu what comes in the interview room. It's Laura.

Duty Solicitor pushes back his chair and goes to shake her hand like he already knows she's a proper lawyer. He gets mugged off though.

'Thank you, Mr Thompson. Would you mind? I'm here to take Donny,' she goes.

Custody Officer nods. That's his way of giving her back-up and Mr Thompson knows when he's beat. He stuffs my papers in his bag and they get all bent-up and twisted. He should be more careful with my life.

'And Mr Thompson,' Laura says, 'stop advising Black teenagers to plead guilty. It's disproportionate.'

When he's gone, my Custody Officer goes, 'So, Mr Thompson told you to plead guilty to this case, did he?' He's smiling like he knows something I don't.

'You say case, Sergeant, but there is no case,' Laura goes. 'You're not to plead guilty or not guilty. There is *no case*.'

'But I smashed up Chapman's yacht,' I argue. Fair's fair. 'I ain't saying I ain't done it because I did. And I'd do it again.'

'I believe you,' she says, a little smile on her lips. 'When a property has been criminally damaged, the owner has the right to seek redress in law. But Donny, Chapman doesn't own a yacht. At least not any more. He owns precisely zero. His assets have been frozen under an Unexplained Wealth Order. Let's go, shall we?'

Custody Officer opens the door for me. When I go by, he taps my shoulder and leans close to me. 'Well done, Donny,' he whispers so nobody don't hear. 'You got the scumbag.'

He slams the windlass on the desk and says, 'You'll want this back, I suppose, to open those locks.'

'I told you it was a key. It weren't never offensive.'

'Anything can be an offensive weapon in the wrong hands,' he goes.

'I doubt it,' I say. 'Like an offensive KitKat?' and I know I'm giving cheek so I tell him, 'Thanks, and – no disrespect, sir man – but I hope I don't see this place again.'

Chapter 18

Laura says we can't be long because she's got the car parked up on a meter. Mama Folu's outside and all. She's bare happy, telling me how tall I got and gripsing me up so much I got to comb my 'fro again.

'Mrs Adeola telephoned Children's Services as soon as the police called her,' Laura says and I get it.

Adeola. It makes sense. It weren't never Olu's number in the contacts.

'You're infuriating, Donny,' Laura says. 'It's only a forty-five-minute drive here. I would have brought you. You only had to ask. Whatever possessed you to take a boat and run away for three days? And why didn't you at least call?'

It don't take much time to walk from Limehouse police station back to the Regent's. Zoe's with Ziggy and her dad on the towpath by *Zuma Jay*. Zigs jumps up to lick my face and her dad shakes my hand and says, 'Thank you for my daughter.'

Them grown-ups start up chatting. Zoe pulls my hand so we're on our ones.

'I'm sorry,' she goes. 'I'm really sorry.'

'It's okay,' I say. 'I understand.'

'All those drugs, I promise I never knew that kind of thing was real. Donny, you got arrested for me and –'

'It's okay.'

'But Donny, it's not and I am so, so sorry.'

'It's cool.'

'Are you okay?'

'I guess. You?'

'Grounded forever, probably. But the summer holidays start tomorrow. We're flying down to the South of France for six weeks. I've asked dad if you can come and he says yes.'

I shake my head. 'That's nice, Zoe, but I don't know what's going to happen with me and mum. I'm going to go get her now. We got to work out where we going to live. I've got to get a job. Listen, I'm sorry you ain't got to do no modelling.'

'It's all right.' She smiles and lifts my chin. 'Hey, I meant it, you know, when I said going on this trip was the most fun ever. I wouldn't change that. You'll message me, won't you?'

Black man's jogging up the towpath. I tug Zoe's hand. 'That's Olu,' I say. 'That's my foster brother. He's come. He said he would. I knew he would!'

'Mama!' Olu goes.

'You should be in lectures,' Mama Folu says. 'What are you doing here?'

'Queen Mary's only round the corner, and I was in the library anyway. I don't have lectures now. I want to see Donny.'

'Using your mobile phone in the library?' Mama Folu goes and she looks at Laura. 'I am surprised they permit that,' she stops, 'at the School of Engineering and Materials Science.'

'Nice to see you again, Donny,' Olu says. 'It's been time.'

Don't cry now, I think, but Olu puts his hand on my shoulder and I can't stop crying on him, and all kinds of shit I ain't planned on saying come out my mouth.

'They don't tell you nothing when you're little,' I say. 'Or they think they've told you but they ain't. And you fill in the bits you don't know with what you hope's going on. And I thought it was your digits you gave me, in the contacts, but –'

'Nah, bruv, not me,' Olu says. 'Sometimes you got to say "this is too much". Sometimes you got to let the grown-ups take charge. My mama knows what she's doing. There ain't nobody like she.'

I want to ask about Michael. I want to know.

'I was there with Prince that night,' I say. 'Bruv, there's so much they ain't said about what happened to Michael.'

'Easy,' he goes. 'I'm carrying it too. I know it ain't all right but it's going to be all right, you get me? I'm going to go through it with you, so you know. You ain't a kid no more. I'm going to hook up with you soon and we can say it all.'

I'm still crying so I don't know why I say, 'School of Engineering? Ain't you a bit grown for school?'

'It's a uni, you chief. It's called the School of Engineering, but it's part of Queen Mary College, University of London.'

'Your father was –'

'I know. My father was an engineer. I heard that somewhere before.' He looks at his mum. 'Listen up, I got to go. Got exams coming up. Safe?'

I nod. Our fists touch.

273

He goes to Mama Folu and kisses her head. She swipes him like he's some kid acting up and he smiles at her and shines his smile on us and all. And like a king, he waves and heads back down the towpath and I think we ain't never going to see a better-looking man our whole life.

'Donny,' Laura says, 'I've left the car on a meter. We'll leave Andrew's boat here. Make sure it's locked and bring Ziggy. If we leave now, we'll avoid the traffic.'

I tell her I ain't having that. 'Where is she?' I go. 'I've come for mum. Tell me where she is! I want to see her now!'

'Donny, please. We can talk in the car.'

I ain't going nowhere without mum so I drop where I am on the stones. Bike Lady rings her bell. Coots start up their hooting.

'Okay.' Laura waits for a man walking his dog to go by. 'I spoke to her probation officer. Donny, I'm sorry. I'm afraid that when she left Downview, your mum wasn't able to stay off the drugs. She overdosed again last night, but she's come through safe and sound. They've put her on a residential rehabilitation programme in Camden. This time, it may work. She wants you to stay with me, at least until your exams. It's not something I usually do, but I've said she's welcome to stay with us, when she's ready. You can show her the canal, can't you? She can watch you play rugby.'

'Why don't she say it to my face?'

'She's …'

'Ashamed.'

'*No.*' Laura goes down on her knees in front of me and takes hold of my shoulders. 'Proud. Very proud,' she goes with a little shake. 'Donny, she loves you so much.'

274

'She was supposed to see me.' I turn *Zuma Jay*'s keys slow through my fingers. 'I was supposed to take care of her.'

I wipe my wet face on my sleeve. Laura gives me that look I seen before, time. And now I know all them things what I planned for me and mum ain't going to happen.

Here's what ain't going to happen:

I check *Zuma Jay*'s mooring is tight and lay the windlass down so I can hold mum's hand because she ain't never been on no narrowboat before.

'Time to embark, mum,' I say and she goes, 'Hark at you!'

So it's me and mum on our ones and we don't care. We're like them birds in the air what don't reap or sow. We get our eats anyways because I got a line and the canal got trout so it don't mean shit if the Universal Credit takes bare long. As well, we got *Zuma Jay* and she's got a network what's two thousand miles long. I show mum the chart of how it can be. 'Stay on the Regent's till Grand Union,' I say, 'and we'll see places we ain't never seen.'

Mum says we got to take back what ain't ours. I don't like it but I know she's right. This is Andrew's boat and when he comes out of hospital all fixed, he's going to need it back.

I start up the engine and tell her it only starts that good because I stripped it down and serviced it myself. I untie them mooring knots and show her what deck officers do in the Merchant Navy. We got bare time so I can show her all the donkey kind of knots I know: bowline, clover, reef, hitch, sheet bend. I can say, 'Look: this is this and that is that.'

As well, I can tell her them things they said about her was proper lies.

'You know when we picked up that Snake and Ladder from the Salvation Army shop in Dalston,' I say, 'and it was only 10p?'

'Ain't it funny what you remember!'

'And I got to eighty-six and you said, "Roll a four and you've won the game," because there was a ladder on ninety what goes up to one hundred, and if you land there, you ain't got to go the long way round past all them snakes. You just win and it's over. So I rolled and I got a –'

'Four, Don. I remember. You got a four.'

'And you went to me, "That's it, Don, you got luck for life now," and you said, "Even if it don't look much like luck, even if bad luck seems more closer, it's only because it's hiding the better luck you going to find round the corner." You was right, mum.'

That's the nice thing about canals. Me and mum got time; twenty-nine locks of time. Because time's what they jacked from us and the onliest thing we need. Time so we can talk about all them things what matter, and all them things what ain't nothing at all.

Note on the Text
and Glossary

Some of the words and expressions in this book are from Multicultural London English (MLE). This glossary will help explain these to readers unfamiliar with them. MLE is a language spoken throughout London by people of all ethnicities. Based on Cockney and influenced by Caribbean creole and American slang, it also contains many loanwords from African and South Asian languages. Evolving faster than Standard English, it is often poetic, musical and inclusive of newcomers to the capital.

Allow it! *(exclamation; pronounced 'low it!)* – Please, stop. Also a playful form of 'give over!'
Angsting *(verb)* – Worrying

Bait *(adjective)* – Dreadful, bad, disgusting
Bare *(adjective)* – Very, really, extremely
Batty/Battyman *(noun)* – Homophobic insults used to control boys by using fear and threat of violence/rejection
Beef *(noun)* – Argument, fight

Blaze *(noun/verb)* – Smoke drugs

Blood *(noun)* – Brother, relative, friend

Bounce *(verb)* – To leave

Chatting *(verb)* – Speaking nonsense/rubbish. An abbreviation of 'chatting shit'

County line *(noun)* – National distribution network for illegal drugs using children and vulnerable people. 'Line' refers to the mobile phones used to take drug orders

Creps *(noun)* – Trainers/sneakers

Crew *(noun)* – Gang, or music collective

Cutlass *(noun)* – Machete, long-blade knife

Digits *(noun)* – Telephone number

Donkey *(adjective)* – Lots, many, loads; comes from *donkey's years* (i.e. a long time). 'Donkey' is also used as a simile: 'like a donkey', meaning in a care-free or clown-like way.

Drop *(verb)* – To knock down in a fight

Endz *(noun)* – An area, home streets, postcode

Feds *(noun)* – Police (taken from the US)

Fresh *(adjective)* – Used as an insult for naivety. A compliment when directed at clothes

'Fro *(noun)* – Afro hairstyle, unplaited or unstraightened hair

Gas *(noun/verb)* – Nonsense, rubbish

Girldem *(noun)* – A group of female friends

Greens/Gs/Dollars *(noun)* – Money

Head *(noun)* – Nautical term for a boat toilet
Hench *(adjective)* – Muscular, strong, powerful
Henchman *(noun)* – Member of a gang
Hyping *(verb)* – Arguing or fighting

Is it! *(expression)* – Equivalent to 'wow!' *Not* a question

Jack *(verb/noun)* – To steal (from *hijack*). As a noun, it means 'nothing' (from *jack shit*)

Lekkie meter *(noun)* – Electricity meter. A meter is 'fed' with coins or a token topped up at a corner shop. Unlike a monthly account, when the meter runs out there can be no lighting, heating or cooking. Living in poverty means families must choose whether to 'heat or eat'
Lime *(verb)* – To relax, hang out with friends/family

Mandem/Mans *(noun)* – A group of men, plural of man.
Mash/Drop/Waste *(verb)* – Wreck, ruin, beat up, destroy
Merk/Merky *(verb/adjective)* – To be annoyed or insulted. As an adjective, risky, sinister or dangerous
Money-up *(noun)* – A gambling game, involving throwing pound coins up a wall. The winner predicts which face will show when they settle

Nutmeg *(verb)* – The most humiliating move in football when a football is kicked between an opponent's legs, often leading to a rough pile on, or jeering at the victim

Offie *(noun)* – Off-licence / small corner shop (sells sweets, drinks, newspapers and cigarettes)

OKR soldiers / crew *(abbreviation)* – An Old Kent Road gang

Older *(noun)* – Senior member of a gang, often aged between 17 and 24

One-time *(adverb)* – Simultaneously, at the same time

On my ones *(adjective)* – On my own, alone

Packing *(verb)* – Carrying a concealed weapon

Ped *(noun)* – Moped

Piece *(noun)* – Gun

Raw *(adjective)* – Used to describe a serious or life-threatening situation

Roadman *(noun)* – Minor drug dealer

Screw-face *(verb)* – An intimidating expression displaying contempt and / or violent intent

Shank *(noun / verb)* – A knife and the verb 'to stab'

Shape-up *(noun)* – A close-shaved haircut

Sick *(adjective)* – Brilliant

Smoked *(verb)* – Killed

Spit *(verb)* – in rap, to improvise rhymes

Spot *(noun)* – Five spot = £5 note. Ten spot = £10 note

Stripses / Suck teeth / Kiss teeth *(verb)* – A sounded intake of air through teeth indicating disapproval

Switch *(verb)* – The moment when someone loses their temper and becomes violent

Tax *(verb)* – Rob, steal, take

Topboy *(noun)* – Senior member of a gang

Tripping *(verb)* – Wishful thinking, naivety (also stupidity)

Wasteman *(noun)* – Insult, meaning a stupid person

Yard *(noun)* – Back garden or communal areas of a housing estate. Also used as a synonym for a home such as a flat, even where there is no garden

Younger *(noun)* – Junior member of a gang, sometimes as young as 8

Organisations offering advice and support:

BARNARDO'S
Like Donny, an estimated 310,000 children have a parent in prison in England and Wales, and 10,000 prison visits are made by children every year. Barnardo's supports children and young people who have a parent in prison. barnardos.org.uk

CHILDLINE
ChildLine is a counselling service for children and young people. If you are feeling scared or out of control, or just want to talk to someone, you can contact ChildLine.
Helpline: 0800 11 11. www.childline.org.uk

CRIMESTOPPERS
If you have witnessed or know about a crime, call anonymously on 0800 555 111 or fill in an online form https://crimestoppers-uk.org

GANGSLINE
Helps and supports young men and women involved in gang culture. www.gangsline.com

HOWARD LEAGUE FOR PENAL REFORM
The Howard League campaigns for less crime, safer communities and fewer people in prison. It also supports young people with experience of the criminal justice system to secure legal rights. https://howardleague.org/

KNIFE CRIMES.ORG

A charity offering information and support after murder and manslaughter.

Helpline: 0845 872 3440 knifecrimes.org

YOUR CHOICE YOUR FUTURE

Your Choice Your Future helps young people shape their future, from practical life skills to money management and writing CVs. https://yourchoiceyourfuture.wordpress.com

VICTIM SUPPORT

A national charity that helps people affected by crime, providing free and confidential support, whether or not you report the crime.

Helpline: 08 08 16 89 111. www.victimsupport.org.uk

Further reading - poetry and fiction:

Sarah Crossan and Brian Conaghan WE COME APART
Caleb Femi POOR
Patrice Lawrence ORANGEBOY
Stephen Kelman PIGEON ENGLISH
Jason Reynolds LONG WAY DOWN
Nikesh Shukla RUN, RIOT and THE BOXER
Angie Thomas THE HATE U GIVE
Alex Wheatle BRIXTON ROCK and the CRONGTON Series

Acknowledgements

Firstly, thank you to my publisher, Rosemarie Hudson, for championing this story, Joan Deitch, for your expert editorial guidance, and the rest of the HopeRoad team: Charles Phillips, Jessica Spivey and Victoria Gilder. Thanks also to James Nunn and Olivia Anthony for the wonderful cover that perfectly captures the spirit of the book.

Thank you to the inspirational team at The Good Literary Agency: my agent Abi Fellows, Nikesh Shukla, Julia Kingsford, Arzu Tahsin and Salma Begum.

Thank you to my first readers, Kiara Sterne-Rodgers, Theresa Gooda, Emma Middleton, Naomi Valencia and Daniel Sheehan, for your generosity and insight.

I am very grateful to the judges of the *Mslexia* Children's Novel Competition 2018 and the Lucy Cavendish Fiction Prize 2019 for shortlisting *29 Locks*.

Thank you to Nadia Mahabir for sharing the richness of London-Caribbean food and culture with me.

Thank you to the young people I had the privilege of teaching at Highbury Grove School between 2002 and

2017, for trusting me with your stories and teaching me MLE.

Special thanks goes to my former student Daniel Sheehan. Your story is an inspiration.

Thank you, Naima Farah, for being Mahad's mum. My heart goes out to you for your unbearable loss. In a recent conversation, you told me you will love him forever, and I promised to record that here in black and white.

I first taught Mahad when he was ten years old, during a primary school secondment. His sense of fun and optimism was contagious and his smile lit up my classroom. He was loved by his family, friends and teachers. At just eighteen, he was tragically stabbed to death in London.

He will never be forgotten.

Thank you to my former colleagues in Islington, in particular Bob, Gloria, Gurpartap, Rav, Ruth and Simba, who helped me early in my career to understand the difficulties our students faced. Thank you to the educators, mentors, youth workers, grass-roots charities and food bank supporters who make such a difference to young people whom successive governments have failed.

I want to thank my uncle and aunt, Richard and Jane, for the bluebells, and my loving parents, David and Susan, for your unswerving confidence in me.

Lastly, thank you to my three beautiful children, Elsie, Ben and Sophie, and my wonderful wife, Miriam, without whose loving encouragement and razor-sharp editorial talent *29 Locks* would simply not exist. I love you all so very much.

Book Group/Teacher's Notes

Discussion (for 14-18 year olds)

1. Donny and Zoe are from very different backgrounds. Donny grew up in a city and has experienced poverty and crime. Zoe is from a wealthy family in a rural area and has experienced expensive restaurants and luxury holidays abroad.
   a. What do you think makes them become best friends?
   b. What do they have in common?
   c. Do you have friends from very different backgrounds?
   d. What do people gain from making friends with people from different backgrounds?
   e. Why is diversity important in society?
   f. How can we connect with those from different backgrounds in spite of our differences?
   g. How can our differences make us consider social inequality?

2. Donny and Zoe both experience 'grooming', where adults try to lure young people into abusive and exploitative relationships. Donny is groomed to join a drugs gang and Zoe is groomed online by men posing as a modelling agency in order to sexually abuse girls.
   a. What tactics do the adults use to gain Donny and Zoe's trust?
   b. If this was happening to someone you know, what advice would you give?
   c. How can we raise awareness about this issue among young people in schools?

3. Like Donny, over 300,000 children have a parent in prison and over 80,000 children are 'looked-after' (living

with foster parents or in children's residential homes.) These children sometimes do less well in school and are more likely to grow up in poverty. They are also more likely to have behavioural difficulties, sometimes get into trouble and often have complex emotional needs.

   a. What do you think could be done to help children affected by poverty and the problems Donny experiences?
   b. Talk about the scene in Donny's school when he truants. What could his teachers have done differently?
   c. What could your school do better to help children like Donny?
   d. What can the government do to further support disadvantaged children?
4. Is Olu a good or a bad character, or somewhere in between?
5. Which character is your favourite in the novel and which character do you most identify with? Can you explain why?
6. Donny's experience of life is affected by his ethnicity and being a teenage boy. People make assumptions that he might be dangerous, which he uses to his advantage in the final scene.

   a. Have you ever experienced being treated differently because of your appearance, age, sexuality, religion, disability, gender or ethnicity? How did it make you feel?
   b. What can we do to make sure that racism and prejudice are challenged?
7. Some young people who live in areas with high levels of crime choose to carry knives.

a. What motivates them to carry a weapon?

b. What are the consequences of carrying a weapon?

c. What are some of the ways we could combat knife crime in society?

8. Donny experiences pressure to join a drugs gang in Peckham and later in Hackney.

a. What are the pressures on young people to join a gang?

b. If you knew someone who was affected in this way, how would you advise them?

c. What could schools do better to help young people like Donny who are vulnerable to becoming involved in gangs?

d. What measures could the government put in place to support young people who are involved in gangs or who are in danger of getting involved with one?

9. If you could walk into any scene in the novel, which would it be? What would you say or do?

10. The Scottish poet Tom Leonard writes in his poem, *This is the Six O'Clock News,* "thirza right/ way ti spell/ ana right way/ to tok it. this/ is me tokn yir/ right way a/ spellin. this/ is ma trooth." Donny tells his 'truth' in MLE (Multicultural London English). Read the Note on the Text and Glossary on page 277 and try the following tasks:

a. In what other contexts have you heard the language Donny uses?

b. What is your attitude to MLE and has it changed since reading *29 Locks?*

c. Are non-Standard English speakers discriminated against? Discuss the potential damage caused by stereotyping British regional accents and dialects.

d. By the end of the novel, Donny learns how to 'code-switch' between Standard English and MLE and uses this skill to his advantage. Why is it important to become proficient in both Standard English and your regional accent and dialect?

e. Try writing a short story or poem in your accent and dialect, spelling words phonetically and using your natural vocabulary and syntax.

Creative Writing Prompts

1. Imagine two friends your age have an hour on a canal boat. Describe what happens:
   a. What wildlife and nature do they see?
   b. What is the weather like?
   c. What snacks have they brought on board?
   d. Do they feel confident or nervous about boats and water?
   e. Make your characters tell each other a secret or something special about their lives during the voyage.

2. At the end of the novel, Zoe invites Donny to join her family on holiday, but he declines. Imagine that he changes his mind and joins her. Write a single day from that holiday from Zoe's diary. They might talk about the things that have happened in the story and about their hopes for the future.

3. Write a letter to Donny from a minor character in the novel, at a time much later in their life. What would they

say has happened in their life since they knew Donny? Choose from:

a. Sebastian (from primary school)

b. Little Hassan (from the PGL trip)

c. Bossman (from Peckham)

d. Top Boy (the London Fields Boys)

4. 'The current funds and support to tackle poverty and knife crime among young people in society are insufficient'. To what extent do you agree? Write an article to explain your point of view.

Further Action

If some of the real-life issues in the novel have made you feel angry or upset, such as knife crime, social inequality and poverty, there are many things you can do to help make changes:

1. Find the name of your Member of Parliament (www. theyworkforyou.com) and write to them about the issue you feel strongly about.

2. Run a fundraising event for a foodbank or youth scheme. Ask your family to consider donating to a foodbank, if they can afford it. This can be done either by leaving food in supermarket collection baskets or by donating to a charity such as The Trussell Trust.

3. Write a speech or give a presentation to your tutor group or in a school assembly about the issues you care about.

4. Write a letter to your headteacher and school governors to ask what your school is doing to help looked-after

students, those living in poverty and those with a parent in prison.

The author, Nicola Garrard, loves to talk about her novel in schools, libraries and book groups, and runs creative-writing workshops. Get in touch with her at: nicola-garrard.co.uk

Nicola Garrard has taught English in secondary schools for twenty-three years, including fifteen at an inner-city London comprehensive. *29 Locks* is her debut novel, and it was shortlisted for both the Lucy Cavendish Fiction Prize and *Mslexia* Children's Novel Competition. Her poetry has been published in *Mslexia* magazine and the *IRON Book of Tree Poetry,* and she writes a blog for the *Writers' & Artists' Yearbook*. Nicola's favourite things about being a teacher are not found in classrooms but on school trips to wild places: capsizing canoes in icy lakes and getting lost in the mountains. Young people, she says, always find the way home.

Nicola lives in Sussex with her family and a Jack Russell terrier called Little Bear.

Twitter: @nmgarrard
Website: nicola-garrard.co.uk

CPSIA information can be obtained
at www.ICGtesting.com
Printed in the USA
LVHW052048100921
697564LV00003B/207